The Shadowlink

Two Sides of Hexel

By

Stefanie Schatzman

COPYRIGHT

The Shadowlink Two Sides of Hexel

Library of Congress Cataloging-in-Publication Data
Registration Number
TXu 2-382-668

Name: Schatzman, Stefanie author.
Title: The Shadowlink Two Sides of Hexel
Description: Florida: Stefanie Schatzman, (2023)
Series: The Shadowlink
Identifiers: ISBN: 9781960353023 (Paperback)
ISBN: 9781960353030 (Kindle)

Butterfly design by Sarah Schatzman
Daft Governor design by Thomas Gentry

Dedication

This book is dedicated to my two number-one fans –
Amanda and Ryan

Table of Contents

Chapter 1
A Ton of Peppermints

Exhausted, Natalie felt her will to continue crumble. She was beyond tired. Yet, Lorcan, a three-foot-tall Ruiri gnome, demanded that she keep her elemental powers flowing into the three-headed tree stump. Natalie obeyed because of the sheer panic in his voice and because she knew her powers were the only thing keeping the shield up. If she failed, the shield would vanish. Within seconds, the outside presence would enter the old homestead and come for them.

"Focus, Natalie," Lorcan commanded as he squeezed her hands until her fingers smashed together.

"Natalie, you can do it!" Lorcan demanded of her. She didn't answer, but her dazed expression told a different story. After two hours at full throttle, she was done.

Slumped forward in a sitting position, her long black hair stuck to her clammy face. Her hands ached as she struggled to concentrate on continuing the flow of elemental power. Even in pain, she drifted in and out of consciousness. Minutes dragged by, and from somewhere deep in her mind, she heard Lorcan ask her about opening a portal.

A portal? Natalie frowned. *Are we talking about the hidden mirror in my mother's closet or something else? I don't know anymore.* Her mind plunged into darkness. In the darkness, she stood before the floor-to-ceiling Mirror of Durin, watching a gray mist cover it. A shadow formed. Wait, it wasn't forming. Unformed and misty, it reached for her. As it did, an arrow pierced her back. She screamed.

Natalie's eyes snapped open to Lorcan sitting across from her. Alarmed at his crazed expression, she shouted, "Lorcan!" and repositioned herself so her hands covered his hands. She tightened her grip and focused on her remaining elemental power; she blasted it into Lorcan. Pulling her hands away, she watched in horror as his back arched and his eyes went wide before he collapsed forward. She began to shake. That had been so close.

The full lunar eclipse was over. With it went the danger, but not the toll it had taken on them. Lorcan slumped forward, unconscious. Natalie, exhausted, could not rest from the throbbing back wound and the blood streaming down her back.

Taking a deep breath to steady herself, she glanced around the room. *Where's the person who shot me with an arrow?* Strangely, she saw no evidence that someone else had been in the house with them. She shook her head in confusion. *It doesn't make sense. There has to be someone else.* She could still feel the arrow jammed in her back.

Unless...No! She fought hard to block the thought, but it was already there. *Darn it.* There was no way to avoid it. *Did Lorcan conjure the arrow?* She didn't see how. She faced him when he became possessed. *It couldn't be him. He is my mentor, not my enemy.* She shook her head again, trying to make sense of the situation. Whatever it was, she refused to believe that even possessed Lorcan would betray her. *There has to be another answer.*

Bracing herself with her right hand on the old hardwood floor, her left hand searched around the back wound and then around the floor. She came up with nothing except bloody fingers. After studying her fingers for a few seconds, she wiped them on the front of her black shirt. Puzzled and exhausted, she wasn't aware of using her shirt to clean her left hand.

"That's so odd," she muttered. How could there not be an arrow? She wanted answers, but she would need to solve that mystery later. What little energy and focus she had needed to be on Lorcan.

Alarmed at what she saw, Natalie hesitated to touch Lorcan. She leaned close and looked for signs of movement. None. She leaned closer to check on his breathing. He was barely breathing. Flinching in pain as she straightened up, she tried to figure out what to do. Nothing came to mind except to make him more comfortable.

Taking a deep breath to calm her nerves, she put her left hand on his cold forehead and her right hand on his back. She placed Lorcan flat on the floor. He was still and cold to the touch. She searched for a pulse; it was slow and faint. She studied his face and determined he was no longer possessed, but she wondered at what cost.

She had hit him hard with her remaining elemental energy. Would there be permanent damage because of her erratic control and powers? Untrained, she did not know what was too much or too little. She had instinctively reacted to the evil inhabiting Lorcan that was coming for her.

Exhausted by everything that had happened, Natalie groaned in frustration as Coal flew in and started circling the room. She wanted peace, but no, an agitated crow circled and turned its head so that its eyes were always on her. All that fluttering overwhelmed her. She ignored Coal and focused on Lorcan. Coal squawked, dropped lower, and made shorter circles above her head.

Annoyed, Natalie looked up, intending to yell at Coal to find someplace else to release his anxiety. As she focused on Coal, she panicked. Blood dripped from him. Did something go after him, too? Natalie's heart raced. She held her left hand up for Coal to land on her, but he continued to fly in circles above them.

"Coal," Natalie implored, "come to me!"

He ignored her request and continued his endless flights around her. Lacking the energy to get up, she resigned herself to observing him as he made continuous loops above her. Over and over, he circled her, but she couldn't see any injuries. Coal slowed and glided lower over her. She spotted blood on his beak.

"You're not injured," she said in a relieved tone. "You're the arrow!" Coal squawked and returned to flying higher around the room.

Realizing he was the one who had roused her out of the blackness, Natalie relaxed. "Thank you, Coal!"

Now, knowing Coal's role, her recollection of the events changed. Before she could rehash what had happened, loud, continuous gurgling sounds erupted from the three-headed tree stump. Gagging, she tried to tell herself it couldn't be what Lorcan had hinted would occur when it was over. Unfortunately, she couldn't deny what was happening. She fought hard to block a visual from forming in her head.

As the gurgling sounds continued, images of the three-headed tree stump with three wide open mouths gulping and devouring the reverse-flowing slime consumed her thoughts. She visualized the slime flowing down into the earth's bowels and filling vast underground seas with stinky, slimy goo. *It's so gross. I can't believe this slime is good magic protecting the homestead and us. Seriously, this is wrong on so many levels.* Nonetheless, she knew it was true. Somehow, she needed to find the strength to move; otherwise, she was going to barf right there.

Slowly and painfully getting up, Natalie stood on unsteady legs, trying to determine if she had the strength to move Lorcan. There really wasn't an option. She would not leave him, and she could not stay there. She took a deep breath and released it before reaching down and picking him up. Concentrating on Lorcan, she ignored Coal as he continued to circle.

"You know, you would be much easier to manage if you were in your cat form."

She tried to move Lorcan away from the front windows. Exhausted, in pain, and sickened by the continual gurgling noises, she struggled to carry Lorcan. His long, white braid dragged on the ground. The golden trinkets and crystals tied to chains on his belt clanked against the floor. She couldn't help it.

Her goal of the couch in the feather collection room seemed miles away. Deep in her heart, she knew she would not make it. All she could do was try. With that in mind, any distance away from those grotesque sounds would be worthwhile.

Wearily stumbling along while repositioning Lorcan in her arms, Natalie was halfway through the Room of Mirrors when the front door flung open. She stopped and turned her head to see who had burst into the homestead. Sighing in relief, she saw Draon. She repositioned Lorcan in her arms, watching Draon's eyes follow the blood trail to where she stood.

Natalie turned her focus back on Lorcan. She shouldn't have stopped, as he seemed to have grown heavier; she could no longer handle his weight in her shaking arms. In horror, she watched as if Lorcan slid from her arms in slow motion. She couldn't stop it. Draon ran over and caught him before he hit the floor.

"The feather collection room has a couch," Natalie mumbled. With nothing left but sheer determination, she forced herself to move in that direction.

"I know the way."

Draon carried Lorcan towards that room.

Still moving at a slow pace, she neared the feather collection door when Draon rushed out of the room.

"To the potion room." Draon grasped her arm to guide her.

"Draon, I don't have the energy." She pulled away and continued moving into the room towards a chair near Lorcan. Dropping down, she made sure not to lean against the back of the chair and mess up the blaring colors in the gaudy floral pattern.

Unaware that Draon had headed for the potion room, Natalie slumped forward in the chair. With her elbows on her knees and her hands over her eyes, she was oblivious to her surroundings. She didn't hear Draon return. She wasn't aware of him lifting the back of her shirt and dumping globs of ice-cold, mud-colored potion on the wound. A stream of potion ran down her back and onto the chair.

She didn't budge for over an hour. Lost in a dreamless sleep, she heard someone call her name. As minutes ticked by, she heard her name called again—this time loud.

She tried to clear the cobwebs from her mind. Opening her eyes, she looked up and studied Draon's face. Then, glancing around the room, she spotted Lorcan on the couch. She sighed. "Is it over?"

"Yes, please tell me what happened."

Natalie continued sitting, but she stretched her back and her arms, hoping to become more awake. "It tried to find a weak link. Close to the end, I was blacking out even though we were still connected. We were talking about a mirror when Lorcan asked me a question about a portal. It didn't make sense to me."

She didn't see Draon's shocked expression as she stopped talking and stared past him. Her eyes locked in on a spot below the mantle, and she stayed that way for several minutes. Lost in her thoughts, she shut everything out.

"Natalie," Draon said, trying to get her attention.

She didn't hear him. She stayed fixated on that spot. Then, shaking her head, trying to wake up, she continued her report as if she had never stopped.

"Losing consciousness again, I visualized mist spreading across the mirror and a form appearing in the mist. I thought it was you. Then, it became obvious that the outside mist was reaching for me. As I struggled to become alert, Coal helped by smashing his beak into my back. That pain woke me. Lorcan's wild eyes made it clear something sinister possessed him."

Natalie took a deep breath, shuddered, and stopped talking. She lowered her head and stared at the floor. *I failed Lorcan. I don't want to talk anymore.*

"Natalie, finish the story."

She couldn't bring herself to look at Draon. *This is my fault. I wasn't strong enough to protect Lorcan and the homestead during the full eclipse. I miserably failed, and it cost Lorcan. He should mentor someone else. I don't deserve any of this.* She slumped in defeat as tears rolled down her cheeks.

"Natalie, no one could have been prepared for what happened to you and Lorcan. Please finish the story."

She wiped her eyes and whispered, "I felt pure evil and directed my energy into Lorcan. It was awful. He's unconscious because of me. First, it's my fault for letting the evil in, and second, it's my fault for not having enough control over my powers to save Lorcan. What I had left is what he received."

"You did what you had to do."

"Is Lorcan going to be okay?"

"He will be fine. It is not just your energy bolt that puts him in this condition. He was possessed. You could have been possessed. Lorcan has chosen to shut down. When he has the answers he needs, he will wake up."

She let out a long sigh of relief. Lorcan would get better when he had the answers to whatever had frightened him into this state. *Still, I failed him.*

"Do you think it would be better if Lorcan mentored someone else?"

"I do not understand the question," Draon said, looking puzzled.

"I failed him. I'm not good with people or my powers." Natalie was on the verge of tears.

"Nonsense. Neither of you had any idea what you would encounter. Truthfully, I blame myself for not realizing the danger. I should have sent Samoon."

She shook her head; she understood. Her slumped shoulders and teary eyes showed she believed she had let Lorcan down. She avoided looking at Draon.

"Look at me because I want you to hear and understand what I am saying to you. You are exhausted and underestimating yourself. You did something that more experienced mages might not have been able to do. Stop worrying. You are where you belong."

"Thank you, but I feel responsible for Lorcan's situation. Did the others encounter what we did, and were they successful?"

"It seems to have directed its energy on you and Lorcan. The others are fine."

Changing his focus, Draon took his crow-feathered cloak off. He turned and faced Natalie. "Many things have magical powers. My cloak is one of those things. By placing it over Lorcan, it will expedite his ability to get the answers he needs."

"Thank you."

She watched Draon place his crow-feathered cloak over Lorcan. She relaxed, feeling his compassion and concern as he took his time to gently tuck his cloak around him. She placed her elbows on her knees, her hands under her chin, and dropped her gaze to the floor.

She thought *his cherished cloak might be one of those things with magical powers, but it isn't always about magic. It's about how you treat and protect the people you love.*

"Come back, Lorcan," Natalie whispered.

Unaware that Draon had sat down in a chair opposite her and watched her, her thoughts moved to the glowing green eyes of the scarecrows. *That's what started the two hours of hell that ended with Lorcan being possessed, but it could have been worse if my instinct hadn't taken over when I blasted Lorcan. Maybe that silly card game he has us practice every day to increase our instincts has paid off. I'm not sure, but it did pay off having Coal with us.*

In silence, Natalie and Draon sat lost in their own thoughts for almost an hour. As the clock clicked into the third hour, she became more attuned to her surroundings and occasionally caught Draon observing them for signs of improvement. She saw that Lorcan was still unresponsive, but she grew restless. Undesirable sounds were stirring up earlier visions.

Draon noticed Natalie frowning and squirming in her chair. "Anything I can do for you?"

Her mood changed. Always sensitive to sound, she had one desperate wish. "Can you please stop or speed up that grotesque tree stump activity!? It is soooo disgusting! I'd rather see worms oozing out of the mouths and eyes than hear that and know what it's doing."

She gave Draon no time to speak as she continued to whine about the tree stump. "That is so overwhelmingly gross! I had zero energy, but another minute sitting there, I would have been barfing my guts out. Even sitting in here, I can hear it. It's not as loud, but it's disgusting, which means barfing is still an option."

"Seriously, Natalie, that is a little dramatic," Draon replied, rolling his eyes at her vivid description. Obviously, she had recovered.

"Nope. True statement. There's a possibility it might become a reality."

"I am unsure who created the end result, but it is an easy fix."

Draon stepped out of the room. Within a few minutes, he returned. This time, he returned with Coal sitting on his right hand. Coal flew over to Natalie and rested on her right shoulder.

"It is done," Draon said as he sat down.

"Thank you! I can't believe I'm saying this, but I bet the scarecrows thank you, too!"

She turned to face Coal. "I owe you big time! Next time I'm at the Barracks, I'm buying you a week's supply of treats from the Mystical Pets Treat Store."

Coal made one happy loop around the room before settling on her shoulder.

"I don't know if I will ever get used to having Coal on my shoulder. Somehow, I feel like one of the bad pirates in one of those old pirate movies." Natalie laughed as Draon raised an eyebrow at the comment but said nothing.

She stood up and moved in front of Lorcan. "Get well, my little buddy."

She smiled. *If he heard that as Jericho, I would deal with a full claws-out swat. I don't care; I want Lorcan back.*

Changing her focus, she needed to see her father.

"Now that my mind isn't totally focused on Lorcan and that tree stump activity, I need to check on my father and let the pixies and fairies out."

"I would like to meet your father."

"Of course, but he doesn't like magic. Fair warning. My dad is 100% mageless. I don't talk magic, and I don't do magic around my father."

"I am not interested in your father for his views on magic. I want to meet the man who married Nessa."

"Sure. That makes sense. Lorcan briefly told me about your close relationship with my mother. They're in the basement waiting for the all-clear message."

Walking the short distance to the stairs, Natalie was thankful Draon wasn't wearing the huge crow-feathered cloak. Even though his eyes were large and black, without it, he could fit in with the mageless. Being tall wasn't a factor either, as he seemed the same height as her father.

Thinking about Draon's appearance, Natalie remembered her back wound, the trail of blood, and the potion soaking her clothes. She stopped and glanced down at her shirt and pants. *Ew.* She turned and looked at Draon.

"Walking behind you, I was already thinking you cannot walk into the room with blood all over your clothes," Draon said as the emerald tip of his ring began to glow. He said a short spell.

"Thanks! My dad would have freaked out and probably forbidden me from ever going into the homestead again."

"I am sure you would have been able to calm him down."

"Ah, no. We're talking about my dad and magic in the same sentence."

"We would have worked something out."

"Well, to be safe, can you say a spell that cleans up the blood on the floor and chair? My father doesn't need to see blood as he's leaving."

Natalie opened the basement door and headed down the stairs.

"Your father cannot hide from your world forever," Draon said before he muttered a spell that cleaned up the front rooms.

"Tell him that."

Natalie opened the door to the secured room.

She grinned at the surprised look on her father's face. She watched as he glanced at the chair beside him, and his eyes grew wider. Natalie stood at the door, but she also sat on the chair next to him.

"Sunshine Lily, you can stop pretending you're me." Natalie laughed.

Just as Natalie figured, her father pretended nothing unusual had happened. He stood up.

"Obviously, it turned out all right. I'll get my briefcase and head for work."

"Okay, Dad, we'll walk you out."

"We'll?" Karl asked, and then he noticed Draon standing behind her.

She watched her dad study Draon, and Draon did the same to Karl. It was awkward for a few minutes until Karl smiled. "Draon, it is nice to meet you."

Natalie's eyes widened at her father's comment. Both she and Draon were shocked.

Karl explained. "Nessa frequently talked about you. She shared so many stories about her time with you. Believe me, Nessa felt so loved and cherished that she often called you Dad. She wanted us to meet, but I wasn't ready. I'm glad we're finally meeting."

Karl stepped around Natalie and held out his right hand.

As the two shook hands, Natalie noticed Draon struggling to contain his composure. Wanting to help him, she brought Draon back to reality. "Does this mean I can call you grandpa?"

"Not if you want to survive your training!"

She laughed. Draon didn't look like grandpa material, but she could see the dad material. He acted much like her father. Another general. *Mmm, I wonder if Mom was attracted to my dad because he and Draon have similar qualities?*

Pleased at how well the meeting turned out, Natalie felt much better. Now, she turned her focus on her dad's comments. It was a gigantic surprise that her father knew her mother's childhood and was open to her stories. She was interested to hear them. When Lorcan recovered, she would spend more time with her dad. Maybe when Draon wasn't being so serious, he would share some stories with her, too.

Relief flooded her that Draon had handled the grotesque sounds and slime from the three-headed tree stump before they entered the basement and opened the secured room. Now, with her father upstairs and leaving through the front door, he had no clue what had been happening not that long ago.

Stepping onto the walkway, Karl turned to Natalie. "Do you need anything?"

"A ton of mints...peppermint!" Natalie blurted out.

Natalie's father glanced at Draon standing behind her, and then he focused on his daughter. "Natalie, aren't you being a little dramatic? Why would you need a ton of peppermints?"

She couldn't see it, but she knew Draon had a smirk on his face.

"Dad, I'm not being dramatic! If you saw and heard what happened here, you would buy me the entire stock of peppermint, wintergreen, spearmint, red mint, white mint…you name it! Some mouthwash by the gallon would be good, too!"

"Natalie, stop! Seriously! I'll buy you a bag of mints. That's it."

Karl looked over Natalie's head to Draon. "All I can say is good luck, Draon, on training my daughter!"

"Ha! Ha!" Natalie said in annoyance.

They stood there until her father entered the path to the house. Draon held the door open as she stepped back inside. He moved ahead and turned to face her.

"After we check on Lorcan, we need to address a serious potential problem."

She didn't answer him, but she surmised it had to do with the third sign. Both of them were almost possessed. *Why were we the only ones attacked? What did it want? I hope Draon has the answer.*

Still hoping she hadn't hurt Lorcan, they walked into the feather collection room to check on him. He hadn't moved. He looked like he was sleeping. After observing him for a few minutes, Draon motioned for her to follow him out of the room.

"He is probably going to be out for another day. In the meantime, we can help him with what is troubling him."

"Whatever helps Lorcan, I'm willing to do it."

"I want you to fully understand what will happen. The fairies and pixies can look after Lorcan while we return downstairs to the protected room. I do not want anyone to overhear our conversation. You go first while I speak to them about caring for Lorcan."

Natalie only waited a few minutes for Draon. She watched as he closed the door, focused on his ring, and whispered a few words she couldn't hear. She gave Draon a puzzled look. Even though she had said nothing, Draon understood the look.

"It is another layer of protection."

Natalie nodded. She understood, but she was concerned they needed extra layers of protection. The thought brought images of ears against the walls, eyes staring through cracks, and evil beings listening from the ground beneath the room. Those thoughts alarmed her. She shook her head to clear her mind and focused on Draon as he sat in a chair opposite her.

"Natalie, you have already seen the Mirror of Durin. In fact, I recall it was activated some weeks back."

"Yes, it was me. Mom came to me in my dreams. I thought the answer was in her private room. While the room is beautiful, there really isn't anything magical except for the mirror. It's hidden in a closet that has no light source. Actually, it's not hidden, as it's the only thing in the closet. Anyway, it had a strange pull on me, so I went over to it. After a few minutes, I started touching some of the markings. That alerted you to me being at the mirror."

"That is correct. I have an identical mirror in Stormfield."

"Well, you know the end of that story, too. I saw your shape forming in the mist, and I tripped all over myself, trying to get out of there."

"Yes," Draon smiled, "you did not last as long as your mother did. She was much younger and stared at me for several minutes before running out of there. The mirror was how I met your mother and communicated with her for some time. Do you understand what the mirror does?"

"I think so. It connects to your mirror where we can see each other while talking…face time."

"That is the most basic feature. The mirror is a portal to Stormfield."

Draon waited for her to make the connection to what Lorcan had asked her.

After a few minutes of thinking it over, Natalie asked, "Was Lorcan asking me, or was he being directed?"

"Knowing Lorcan, he would not have mentioned it if he had felt threatened. However, he may have already been under the influence. Fortunately, you were unaware it was a portal, so you did not understand the question."

"How does it operate as a portal?"

"There is a sequence on the runes that opens both Mirrors of Durin. This would allow you to step through the mirror and enter Stormfield."

"Wow!" Natalie was stunned to discover that she had a magic gateway in her house. At any time, she could walk through the mirror into a whole new world of magic and magical creatures and beings.

She struggled to process this incredible news when she blurted out, "Draon, I don't know the sequence. Even being possessed, I couldn't have opened the portal."

Draon sat still for a moment before he answered Natalie. "Maybe. It is a complicated sequence, but I think it is natural for you to open the portal. Your mother was young when I gave her the instructions. I thought it was the one time she paid attention and listened without doing things her way. However, now I am not so sure. Just as you did, she opened the communication by feeling the order of the runes."

"Don't you need to accept my sequence to open the portal on your side?"

While shaking his head no, Draon replied, "The mirrors were once one. Even though they are now two, they operate as one. I doubt there is a spell powerful enough to

16

require approval before the portal opens. It is not a good thing, but it is what it is."

She sat for a few minutes, trying to visualize how a mirror could split, with each part being identical. She didn't see how that was possible. "What was the original purpose of the mirror, and why did it split?"

"We need to address the current issue, so that is a story for another time."

"Okay, I guess there isn't a choice." Natalie changed the subject. "Did my mother spend a lot of time in Stormfield?"

"Yes, she spent much of her teenage years there."

"That is so cool." She wondered how many different types of magical creatures were in Stormfield. Flying would be normal there. Spells and all things magical would be normal. She would meet Samoon. Another world.

"Natalie," Draon interrupted her visions of Stormfield, "your mother did not tell you about this because she wanted you to have a normal childhood until high school started. Nessa was so excited that the time was near for her to share this world with you. Unfortunately, that did not happen, and you had to discover it with the help of Lorcan or, if we are being honest, Jericho."

"True," Natalie said, smiling at the big entrance that cat made into her life.

"Natalie, we need to get back on track," Draon said seriously, focusing back on the Mirror of Durin. "You are the rightful owner of the Mirror of Durin. It only responds to you. That means you are the key to the portal, even without knowing it, and you may have opened it and brought more than yourself to Stormfield. Do you understand how serious that would be to our world?"

Suddenly, she fully understood the severe consequences of having the Mirror of Durin in her home.

She also understood why Lorcan remained locked in his mind. He knew what he could possibly have done.

Now aware of the grave situation, Natalie asked Draon, "Can you take the mirror to Stormfield?"

"I can," Draon said, slightly nodding yes, "but that means you can't enter Stormfield."

"I understand that, but the first priority is your safety and the safety of your world."

Draon got up and walked over to Natalie. For a moment, she saw warmth in his eyes before he turned serious. "Thank you. I was hoping you would see that it is the only choice at the moment."

"You can still get to us, right?" She had grown fond of Draon. She knew much of it was because he reminded her of her father, but also because he had a good heart. He wasn't good at showing it…just like her father.

"Nothing changes on my side."

"Then that is what needs to happen. However, promise me that one day I will get to visit Stormfield. It would be wonderful to see where my mother spent her teenage years."

"It is a promise. However, the Mirror of Durin has to remain a secret. Even after it is returned to you, you can tell no one about the mirror."

Chapter 2

You're an Oaf!

Natalie stormed into the school and headed to the front office. She didn't want to be at school. She wanted to be with Lorcan when he woke up, but her father made that impossible. No amount of pleading changed his mind. She had already missed Wednesday. He had written an excuse for her absence with the understanding that she would be at school on Thursday and Friday. Attendance and good grades were mandatory, or she would face the wrath of an irate father. As far as she was concerned, an angry father was more powerful than a boatload of magic.

"All students go directly to your homeroom." The announcement continually blasted over the PA system.

Natalie pivoted and angrily headed in that direction. She didn't care that she bumped and smashed into other students along the way. A few called her out. *Let them yell at me. Nothing they say compares to my anger with Dad's unreasonable demand that I be in school instead of with Lorcan.*

Furious, she didn't question why there was an unscheduled homeroom today. She didn't care. This wasn't where she wanted to be, and it showed as she yanked the door open, stormed through, and slammed it shut. The teacher jumped at the loud bang and looked at her in surprise. Ignoring him, Natalie stomped over to her seat and slammed her bookbag to the floor as she sat down.

She was ready to explode. She should be with Lorcan. *It's not right! Why be here when school is boring?* The way she was feeling, it was a good thing no one spoke to her in homeroom. She didn't want any part of them or school today. She closed her eyes and wished Sunshine Lily would show up, take on her appearance, and sit in her place.

Visions of the clueless fairy dealing with an overwhelming number of teenagers lightened her mood. She could see Sunshine Lily panicking and coating the entire school in colorful fairy dust. There was no telling what would happen to the teenagers who annoyed the fairy. Lorcan had told her about the demon candles with fairies and pixies reaping revenge on him. One image after another popped into her head of her least favorite classmates, developing purple eyes, pig noses, green warts, and pink fur. It was too much. Natalie snickered.

Reality hit when she thought of Draon. Her father's anger was scary enough, but Draon's anger was something she never wanted to experience. *Scratch that idea.* The fairies needed to be restricted inside the old homestead. She got that, but what if there was some way for them to notify her when Lorcan woke up?

While mulling over that idea, the boy beside her poked her on the shoulder. Startled, she glanced over and saw the smirking student holding colorful flyers to be distributed along their row. He obviously heard her snicker for no good reason. Annoyed with his attitude, Natalie grabbed the flyers from him. She wanted to give him head-to-toe pink fur. *Jerk!*

After taking a flyer and passing the others down the row, she looked down at her flyer. She stared at the man in the large photo at the top of the paper. "It can't be," she exclaimed as the flyer fell from her hands, but she knew it was true.

Clutching her mother's pendant by the outside of her shirt, Natalie recalled the day she saw him in the front office. The man had oozed so much negative energy that her crystal had burned her before turning black. It had warned her of the dangerous man. Now, she had a name for the leather-faced, cold-eyed man, Charles Arthur Denton.

It definitely wasn't a good sign. Come to think about it, yesterday was the third sign. They had been told the third sign was the last sign before something bad happened. As if yesterday wasn't bad enough, today there's a flyer announcing the new Janus Club controlled by him. Nothing good could come out of this club.

"Drop something," the smirker stated as he held her flyer out to her. Natalie turned towards him and stared long and hard. She was so tempted to use her powers and deal with that arrogant attitude. If only she could trust her powers to do something small, but she always ended up with full-blown disasters. While struggling with all her willpower not to do something she would regret, he laughed and muttered, "Daffy." She snatched the flyer from his hand and turned away. *Double jerk!*

Fuming, she decided she needed to concentrate on something besides the jerk sitting next to her. Otherwise, she would lose control. Taking a deep breath and slowly releasing it, she read what Charles Arthur Denton and the Janus Club had to offer. It seemed they had the world to provide. The flyer invited all students to join the club. Learn a skill or several skills. Earn extra credits. Earn money. Connect. Travel. The goals were endless. Reaping success and money depended on the effort of the person taking part in the program.

As Natalie read the flyer, a loud mixture of excited voices started bouncing off the walls. Cringing, she placed the palms of her hands over her ears to dampen the bombarding noise. It helped, but she felt out of place as the other students eagerly discussed the club and its benefits while she sat alone with her ears blocked. She wanted to sink down in her chair. Disappear was even better because she wanted no part of this questionable club.

Couldn't they see this club was too good to be true, especially considering who was behind it? His large photo and his name in bold letters fully displayed on the flyer meant the club was about him. Full of himself, Natalie was sure that at some point, there would be a high price to pay. Whatever they were going to earn, she was sure he was going to get more. Disheartened, she sat watching them act like they had won the lotto.

While watching them, she had an uncomfortable feeling that she was being watched. She turned her attention to the teacher. He stared at her. Removing her hands from her ears, she silently mouthed that she had a headache. He nodded that he understood before turning his attention to his laptop. She grimaced. *Sure, he understands. It's payback for me slamming the door so hard that he jumped in his chair.*

Flustered with the noise and the club, Natalie took the flyer and folded it into the tiniest possible square before stuffing it into the bottom of her bookbag. While she focused on that, the room became quiet. Looking up, she noticed a tall, blonde-haired boy in a letterman jacket standing before the teacher. Wow, she thought as she looked at the athletic and academic award patches covering the back of his jacket.

Soft giggling and appreciative muttering spread through the room, growing louder. She glanced around and noticed girls watching him. Whispering and giggling were constant. The boy next to her made a snide remark she didn't catch. She smiled, thinking the smirker was jealous.

The blonde-haired boy turned around and faced the class. His charming smile and twinkling, mischievous blue eyes hooked the class. He had their undivided attention.

"Hi, my name is Victor Mountebank. I'm here to promote the new Janus Club that's being backed by the legendary Charles Denton. Mr. Denton believes we are the future. He wants every single one of us to be wildly successful. To ensure we have the tools to reach that goal, he has spent a fortune of his own money developing this club for our benefit."

Victor held the flyer up. "The flyer you received lists many of the club's features. However, there are other incredible opportunities waiting for you to discover at future meetings. The first meeting will be right after school next Wednesday and each Wednesday thereafter. Each meeting will last approximately two hours. We'll meet in the auditorium, as we expect most students will want to take advantage of what the club offers."

Pausing, he held his right hand up to show off a beautiful silver ring with a large blue gemstone. He twisted and turned his hand so light radiated off the gemstone. Its beauty captured their attention. Tousled hair, blue-eyed Victor smiled in his devious, charming way as the ring's allure had mutters of excitement.

"This," Victor said, smiling and pointing to the ring, "is what you receive when you join the club. It's yours to keep, even if you quit the club at the end of the school year."

Excited oohs and aahs sounded throughout the class. To cement their interest, Victor walked over to each student so they could get a closer look at the beautiful ring.

As Victor approached Natalie, she became uncomfortable. The crystal in her pants pocket burned her leg. Her mother's pendant vibrated. The Variegated Orb Weaver bracelet flashed on and off. She pulled her sleeve over the flashing bracelet and dropped her hand down into her lap. She didn't look up at Victor but focused on the ring.

The beautiful ring didn't look evil. Was it the ring, or was it Victor? Maybe it was both. She looked away. Victor and his cologne lingered at her desk. Natalie thought, *Elf,* and smirked at some ideas on how to deal with Victor to the point that he would no longer smell that great or look much like eye candy.

"You're wasting your time with that one," the student beside Natalie said to Victor. "She's a little daft."

Natalie blushed bright red. She turned and glared at the jerk next to her. As he laughed, her embarrassment erupted into fury. A wind started to swirl around them. Her powers were taking over; she knew she was losing control. In a few minutes, the room would be destroyed, and everyone would know her secret.

At the moment, she didn't care if the entire room imploded. It would wipe the smirk off the jerk's face. It'd be worth it. Then she thought of Draon. She couldn't bear disappointing him. Sighing, she closed her eyes and blocked out the long, rumbling laugh of the jerk beside her. She blocked out Victor. She focused on an image of Draon.

Natalie didn't see Victor roll his eyes in agreement as she focused on Draon. With her eyes closed and calming her breathing, she noticed the bracelet had stopped flashing, and the crystal had stopped burning. Good, with Victor moving on to other students clamoring to get a closer look at the ring, she might have a chance at getting herself under control.

Focus on Draon, but what about being stuck at school and sitting next to a jerk? She told herself he wasn't important; Draon was the one who mattered. Victor was halfway across the room, and Natalie still wavered from a manageable level to a dangerous level.

Just when she thought she would lose the battle, pink fur popped into her mind. She changed her focus to visualizing the jerk next to her in head-to-toe pink fur. She added green warts, purple eyes, and monkey lips. She calmed down as she continued building his new look in her mind.

The bell rang. She grabbed her backpack and jumped up. The jerk next to her muttered "daffy" one last time. As she looked over in anger, her expression changed to one of surprise. He had a very prominent pink mustache. Biting her lip, she lowered her head and bolted from the room. She pushed her way through the crowded hallway. Once seated in science, she burst out laughing.

Wherever Natalie went in school, there were enormous posters advertising the new club and the starting date next Wednesday. Normally, none of the other clubs or programs received this much promotion. Obviously, Mr. Denton not only had big bucks, but he had clout. He also had a ton of negative energy. Oddly, she had felt a smaller version of that negative energy with Victor. While Victor hadn't destroyed the crystal in her pocket, it was no longer crystal clear.

Other than the wall-to-wall Janus Club posters throughout the entire school, nothing else happened. *Good.* All Natalie wanted to do was see Lorcan. Elated to be home, she dropped her bookbag at the garage door. She jogged through the long path from the house to the old homestead and hoped that Lorcan would be the one who greeted her at the door.

Stepping under the jasmine vine-covered arbor, she opened the rusty metal gate. Usually creaking when opened, it made little sound. Uninterested in her, the ragged scarecrows stared straight ahead. Likewise, the bizarre three-headed tree stump seemed invisible to her. The entire atmosphere seemed surreal. It was not a good sign.

Opening the door to the old homestead, she slumped in disappointment as the fairies and pixies greeted her. "No change?" Natalie asked as they fluttered around her.

High-pitched chatter erupted. Too many voices at once at that level made it impossible to understand a single word.

"Thanks for the update," Natalie said, although she was clueless about Lorcan's condition.

The pixies and fairies flew to their bedrooms as she headed for the feather collection room. Pushing a gaudy-colored chair over to the matching couch, she sat down and pulled Lorcan's right hand out from under Draon's cloak. She gasped at his ice-cold hand. Not knowing what to do, she placed his hand between her hands and tried rubbing some warmth into it. She studied his pale face and wondered if he would recover.

"Draon took the mirror, so that isn't an issue anymore. You can wake up now. Come on, Lorcan…don't you have the answers you need?" She sat back and watched him. He didn't move; she only heard his shallow breathing.

"Maybe, while you're unconscious, I'll have this furniture reupholstered. The garish, eye-straining colors almost require me to wear sunglasses in here." She couldn't understand how he found the outrageous colors attractive. Then, again, all she had to do was look at his colorful, mismatched outfits. It appeared the gaudier and rougher on the eyes, the more attractive it was to him. Sadly, she saw no change in Lorcan when she threatened pleasant colors.

She softly ran her fingers down Lorcan's rough cheek. His cheek felt cold. Concerned, she placed the back of her left hand on his forehead. It was cold. With the room warm and the heavy crow-feathered cloak tucked around him, he should be roasting. She needed him to wake up.

"If I can't change the outrageous colors on your furniture, maybe I can trim your hair? Would you like short hair for a change?"

26

She pulled Lorcan's long white braid out from under the cloak. All the mentors had the same long, white braid. Why, she didn't know, but maybe it was a status symbol of being a Ruiri gnome. Whatever it meant, Lorcan didn't respond to her idea of cutting his hair.

She decided on a different approach. "I can't believe Draon trusts you with his crow-feathered cloak. If he could have seen you with your mouth stuffed full of vulture feathers, he would have known you are obsessed with feathers. In fact, just look around this room. It's floor-to-ceiling shelving that holds endless containers full of feathers. I don't see how Draon missed that when he was in here yesterday."

Natalie sighed. He gave no sign that he heard anything she said; she tried another angle. "You know what is absolutely astounding, Lorcan? Well, even after my energy maxed out yesterday, I now feel fully charged. Should I test it on you?"

Amazingly, she watched Lorcan slip his right hand back under the cloak. Ecstatic, she knew he could hear her.

"Lorcan, I wanted to be with you today, but you know how my dad is regarding school. I tried, but there wasn't a choice. I suppose it's a good thing because we received flyers today about a new club. It's called the Janus Club. A representative came to homeroom this morning, and when he stood near me, all three of the warning systems went off. The crystal burned my leg, Mom's pendant vibrated, and the Variegated Orb Weaver bracelet glittered."

Natalie paused and looked for signs that he had heard her. Nothing. She continued. "Darn, Lorcan, I hope you can hear this, as the whole thing is surreal and backed by a guy named Charles Denton. It's the same person who destroyed my first crystal. He appears to have an endless source of funds for this club. When you get accepted into the club, you

27

receive this gorgeous silver ring. It looks like it has a blue gemstone...possibly a blue diamond. I couldn't tell if the guy in homeroom this morning, talking about the program, was evil. It could be him or the ring or both, but it seems this Janus Club is the source of evil. Sadly, all the kids in my homeroom class want to join. Probably most of the students feel the same way. It's not a good sign."

Natalie finished as Lorcan shifted under the cloak. He grew restless. Sitting back, she watched and waited. Lorcan grew more restless, but he failed to come out of his self-induced coma.

More time passed as she watched the internal struggle. His face flushed from the effort. Beads of sweat poured down his face as he tossed and turned in his struggle to wake up. She felt helpless watching him continually fail. It went on for almost an hour. Then he went still. She checked his pulse. It was up, and he was warm.

Was he trapped? Her heart rate picked up at the claustrophobic feeling of being trapped within his body. What could she do? She wouldn't let him stay this way, but how could she help him wake up? She wasn't about to use her energy on him again. Maybe, if she could make him angry, he would come out of it.

"Lorcan, why are you slacking off!? You think I don't know the truth, but I do. You were hardly giving anything in the way of energy. I carried the bulk of the load. How dare you let me drain myself while you were contributing so little to protect this place!"

Natalie checked him for signs that he might wake up. She didn't see any physical signs, but she picked up a strange vibe in the air. She decided to make her rant more personal.

"I did my part, but you let me down. We weren't equals. How can I trust you when you were obviously using me? Just like at school, am I merely a useful tool? Were you laughing at me behind my back, too, as you took the easy street and drained me?"

As the vibration grew stronger, she leaned in and inspected Lorcan. His eyes were moving back and forth under his eyelids. With the rest of his body still, it disturbed her to watch. For several minutes, Natalie watched as his eyes went from rapid movement to going still. He remained imprisoned in his own mind; she had failed to reach him.

They were back at square one, except she thought Lorcan's toes used to be under the cloak. Now she could see his colorful socks peeking out. Not wanting to believe this could be a bad sign, she decided to try again to wake Lorcan. Making it personal didn't work. This time, she would insult him.

"Lorcan, I should be the one taking a long break. I was the one who did all the heavy lifting. You had your nap while I was doing everything I could to save us and the old homestead. Do you deserve this lengthy nap? You do not! You are not Rip Van Winkle! You are Lorcan, my mentor. Now, wake up and start doing your job because I'm tired of carrying your load! Slacker! Make yourself useful!"

Natalie watched in horror as Lorcan's feet stretched over the end of the couch. His socks ripped apart and dropped to the floor. His head grew in size, as did his arms and hands, which were now out from under the cloak. Alarmed, she stood up and backed several feet away from the couch. She questioned if she should continue, but she decided he needed this verbal abuse to wake up. He couldn't do it alone; she would do it for him. She hoped her powers would aid her if she needed to protect herself.

Taking a deep breath to steady her nerves, Natalie continued insulting Lorcan. "Oh, that's it. I was careful not to get blood on this chair, but you seem to be quite comfortable putting too much weight on the couch. The

29

springs are going to pop. You're becoming an oaf. Do you hear me, Lorcan? You're not a gnome or a black cat. You're an oaf!"

Before she could say another word, Lorcan sat up. All nine feet of him sat on what looked like a smashed toy couch. Between his weight and size, he had shattered it. The look on his face told her he would also be looking to shatter her.

Natalie bolted for the door, flung it open, ran through, and slammed it behind her. She heard the giant smash through the door right behind her with the crow-feathered cloak wrapped around his waist. She ran into the Room of Mirrors as the fairies and pixies headed in that direction.

She looked around for something she could use to stop the giant. The room only had mirrors...lots of mirrors, each reflecting the approaching angry giant.

"What do I do!?" Natalie cried out as the pixies and fairies flew to her, swooped her up, and moved her to the stairs.

The fuming giant lumbered in that direction. He focused on Natalie. She backed up the steps as the pixies and fairies swarmed and blasted him with fairy dust. She watched him swing his arms out at the fairies, but the thick, multi-colored fairy dust made it impossible for him to see.

Natalie moved up the staircase and watched the fairies bring in their primary weapon. Hundreds of spiders of assorted sizes dropped from the ceiling onto the giant. They latched onto his hair, face, arms, legs, and the cloak. It took a few minutes for the angry giant to realize he had layers of spiders sticking to him. Each minute, more spiders dropped on him. He screamed, sounding like a glass-shattering soprano diva.

In his panicked state, the pixies and fairies continued to circle him and bring up more and more spiders from the dark crevices underneath the house. Opening his mouth to let out another piercing, high-pitched scream, a humongous spider fell into his gaping mouth. Half swallowing it, he repeatedly gagged and tried to spit it out. Legs hung from his mouth. Grabbing the legs, he yanked the rest of the spider out. Terror seized him. Flailing, he dropped the crow-feathered cloak to the floor. He didn't even notice as he frantically tried to brush the spiders off. It wasn't working. Saturated in spiders, he panicked and headed straight for the front door.

Without pausing, the giant smashed through the door and crashed into Draon, who stepped onto the porch. Draon, thrown to the side, fell hard on the porch as wooden shards from the shattered door flew into the air. Unaware, the giant slammed his full weight down on the steps in his frantic attempt to escape the endless spiders.

Feet-hitting the dirt, the giant transformed into Jericho. A very irate black cat still covered in roving spiders. Jericho wildly shook to shake the spiders off his fur. Then, swirling around, he angrily pounced up what little was left of the steps. Draon, now standing, had his wand extended out and his ring lit. In no mood for whatever this was, Draon blocked Jericho's entry into the house. They stood stiffly, facing one another for some time until Jericho regained his composure.

Draon waited until Jericho had his temper under control before putting his wand away. Leaving his ring activated, he opened the broken door and stepped aside. Jericho entered the old homestead and transformed into a naked Lorcan. Shocked, Draon focused on his ring and uttered a spell that put colorful, mismatched clothes on

Lorcan. He didn't acknowledge the clothes. It didn't change his mood or course.

Natalie heard the stomping of Lorcan's feet as he approached the staircase. Afraid, she took several steps up the stairs as the pixies and fairies fluttered around her and blocked Lorcan from getting close to her. Reaching the base of the staircase, he angrily stared up at her. Draon limped into position behind Lorcan.

Wide-eyed and nervous, Natalie wasn't sure what to say to him. Should she apologize for all the mean things she said, should she try to explain herself, or should she wait until Lorcan spoke to her? She mulled over what to do when Draon took his focus off Lorcan and focused on her.

Natalie knew that look. Draon, she could read. It was obvious he was resigned to the fact that there had been another catastrophic Natalie event.

He proved her point by remarking, "I am not sure I want to hear about this latest disaster."

She nervously stated, "I tried to wake Lorcan because, as hard as he tried, he couldn't wake up."

"So, what did you do?" Draon asked as he looked around the room for his cloak. Spotting what appeared to be his cloak in a heap of colorful fairy dust, he hobbled over, picked it up, and started checking it over.

Watching Draon check his cloak for damage, Natalie said, "I insulted Lorcan until it made him angry."

"Not that long ago, I mentioned you do not want a Ruiri to go livid."

She looked down at Lorcan. "Nothing I said to him was working. I watched him struggle to wake up, but he seemed unable to come out of it without some motivation. It scared me. Even so, I had no idea he would get that angry. You also never explained that a three-foot gnome changes into a nine-foot giant. Who would ever think that was possible?"

Draon limped back to Natalie and Lorcan. "You could have waited for me to return."

"I didn't know when you were going to return."

"Natalie, what am I holding in my hand?" Draon said as he focused on his crow-feathered cloak.

Draon made a point to slowly look around the room at all the fairy dust lingering in the air and covering everything. Numerous fairy-dusted spiders of assorted sizes scurried around, looking for ways to escape back to their underground cavern.

Natalie cringed. She hadn't thought of Draon returning for his cloak. Now it seemed obvious. It's a little too late for her to worry about it, as the damage was done.

"I'm sorry for getting you upset, Lorcan. Seeing you locked in your mind, I panicked and kept trying different things to get you to wake up."

"At the time, I thought you meant the insults. I took each one personally, as I suppose was your whole point," Lorcan said, relaxing.

"It frightened me seeing you struggling and failing. At least, with all my methods to help you wake up, I didn't follow through on giving you a haircut." Natalie smiled.

Lorcan checked his braid and turned to Draon. "Being possessed must have influenced my ability to wake up because, in the last couple of hours, I was wide awake inside the coma. I couldn't break out of it. It frightened me that I might be trapped in there. As you know, I've been livid many times without having a problem reverting to a gnome. This time I couldn't do it. I wasn't sure what else I could do. Then Natalie started insulting me. Being her mentor and protector, I took each insult to heart. We Ruiri gnomes don't have any control when we become livid. I have no memory of coming out of the coma as a giant. However, it worked, and here we stand."

Natalie relaxed as Draon looked from Lorcan to her and back to Lorcan.

"What?" Natalie asked.

"Somehow, you made it work. Somehow, we survived another one of your calamities."

"It was a team effort. All that matters is that Lorcan is back," Natalie said as she looked from Draon to the pixies and fairies and Lorcan. She would sleep well tonight.

Chapter 3

Haze in the Air

Looking forward to their first class since the third sign, Pru, Madison, and Skylar were the first to show up at Natalie's old homestead. Lorcan opened the door and impatiently waved them into the Room of Mirrors. A few minutes later, Joel and Connor knocked on the door. Lorcan greeted them with the same irritated mood.

"NATALIE, GET DOWN HERE!" Lorcan bellowed from the bottom of the stairs.

Even behind the closed door and happily chattering fairies, Natalie jumped at hearing Lorcan's angry voice yelling her name. She dropped the basket of assorted candies on the floor and headed for the staircase. Taking two steps at a time, she reached the bottom step in record time. She gave Lorcan a questioning look, but he turned and stomped his way towards the kitchen at the back of the house.

"I don't see any fairy dust on you," Pru remarked as Natalie approached the group.

She pushed Lorcan's abrupt behavior to the back of her mind when she heard the words fairy dust. She laughed, knowing how easy it was to offend or annoy the fairies and pixies.

"Not this time. I have a bribe system with the flying tantrums. If I give them something from the outside world, they are much better behaved. They also give me solitude in the gem room. This time, it's nothing special. It's just a bunch of various kinds of candy. I hope sugar doesn't have a strange reaction on them."

"Wow, that's what it takes to get some peace and quiet?" Connor asked, surprised.

"That's what it takes. They stay inside, so they're fascinated with anything from the outside. Make a deal with them that one room is off-limits. For that deal, once a week, bring them something from the outside world. Start out with a kaleidoscope. Kaleidoscopes fascinate them. Also, it's easy for them to mass produce anything, so you only need to bring one unless it's something to eat."

"Awesome. That'll be the first project I complete when I return home," Connor replied with relief.

Lorcan returned to the group and snapped, "Shouldn't you be heading to class?"

All of them looked at him in surprise. He could be curt, but they had never seen this behavior before.

"Are you okay?" Natalie asked, alarmed at his attitude.

Without answering, Lorcan turned around and stormed off. His wide, flat feet made loud thumping sounds as he deliberately stomped on the old wooden floor all the way to the back of the house. While the other mages awkwardly stood there feeling like intruders, Natalie hoped this was a temporary grouchy mood.

She recalled him telling her that becoming livid took an enormous amount of energy. He would need time to recover. Yesterday, he was in a better frame of mind. Today, he had a short fuse. She didn't see any signs that indicated he was on the road to recovery.

Lorcan's foul mood dampened the group. They trudged in silence to the basement door. Gathered before the door, they smelled bug spray. It wafted in the air, overwhelming them. No one volunteered to open the door.

"Is there something you want to tell us, Natalie?" Pru asked.

Natalie shuddered at the visual and exclaimed, "Spiders! Lots of spiders."

"What exactly does that mean?" Pru questioned, not sure she wanted to know the answer.

"There's not enough time to tell the full story. Well, at least not up here with a chance of Lorcan returning. Just know that thousands of spiders of various sizes dwell in the crevices and caverns beneath these old homesteads. Believe me, until the other day, I had no idea what lurked beneath this place. Then, the fairies got the bright idea of bringing hundreds of spiders up for a visit. Nightmare material. Hence, the smell of bug spray, or more precisely, bug bombs."

"That is so gross," Skylar exclaimed. "We're bug-bombing our old homestead when we get home!"

"Definitely," Madison agreed.

"Good idea. However, even if I bug-bombed this place every day, I know I'd never be able to sleep in here again." Natalie cringed as an image of the howling giant coated in spiders popped into her mind.

"Why would the flying dudettes want a spider invasion?" Connor asked.

"I'll explain after class."

As she ended the conversation, Joel, who had listened with amused interest as the others discussed spiders, looked at the group. Natalie stared back from their tight line at the door. He laughed while pointing at her and each of the other mages.

"It's just dead spiders. Get a grip."

Joel stepped to the front of the line. He grabbed the doorknob and turned it slowly before swinging the door wide open. The door hit the wall with a bang. The girls jumped and screamed. Connor glared at him in annoyance. Joel couldn't resist; he tilted his head back and roared with laughter.

"Not funny," Pru scolded.

"It's a good thing you're the size of a linebacker," Madison hissed.

"Because we're very tempted to shove you through the doorway and slam the door shut!" Skylar yelled.

The rest all shook their heads in agreement.

Nerves shot; they stood crammed together, facing the dark basement. The unpleasant, lingering smell hung heavy in the air, causing them to take short breaths through their mouths. Joel leaned in, reached up, and pulled on the long, hanging chain. A mellow light flickered on, exposing a gray floating haze. They couldn't see the bottom steps.

"Can we drive over to the bookstore instead of using the basement?" Madison asked. "I really don't like spiders."

"Not possible with Lorcan's current mood. Besides, I put so many bug bombs down there that I doubt any spiders survived. We just need to deal with the smell," Natalie stated as she stepped in front of Joel.

Holding onto the worn wooden railing, she placed her left foot and then her right foot on the first wooden step. It creaked under her weight. She paused before stepping down to the next step. It creaked. She stopped and waited for the others to follow her.

Joel turned to Madison and stated with confidence, "No more tricks. I'll stay in front; you stay close behind me. I have no fear of spiders or roaches. Zilch. Nada. Zippo."

"Okay," Madison said, standing close to him.

They moved as a close group down the creaking steps. Halfway down, they froze. Now visible in the floating haze was an endless sea of dead spiders coating the entire basement floor. Mounds of spiders. Some of the larger spiders had twitching legs. A few specks of red flickered on and off.

Focused on the horror before them, they didn't see the humongous dead spider barely hanging onto a broken web on the overhead beam. It dangled there before one leg detached from the web. Another leg broke away, and then others, until only one leg remained on the web. It snapped from the spider's weight. Silently falling through the air, it plopped on Joel's shoulder.

Puzzled by what had just happened, Joel glanced at his shoulder. A scream of pure terror erupted from him and started endlessly echoing off the basement walls. Over and over, his scream bounced off the walls and throughout the room. Terrified, the other mages backed away in the dusty chamber of endless screams. Joel ignored them and the screams as he frantically tried to brush the spider off.

Sticky ooze had it stuck to his shirt. Sweating and breathing heavily, Joel pulled at the body until it came off of his shirt. It stuck to his hand. Wildly flinging his hand around high in the air, he repeatedly screamed, "GET OFF!" without success. "GET OFF!" began to echo throughout the basement, along with his fading first scream. Frantic, Joel grabbed it with his other hand, and it released. With a flick of his wrist, the spider sailed through the air.

The mages screamed and ducked as the spider flew up and backward. It landed with a thump in Skylar's hair. Erupting in ear-piercing screams, she reached up and felt the sticky thing stuck to her hair. With trembling fingers, Skylar worked to pull the slimy body out. In her hand, she slammed it on the step. Over and over, she stomped and twisted on it until nothing remained.

They raced for the top of the staircase. Lorcan opened the door as they reached the top step.

"What are you doing?" Lorcan demanded, ignoring all the screams bouncing off the basement walls.

"Spiders, lots of spiders!" Joel breathlessly exclaimed.

39

"Deal with it," Lorcan commanded as he slammed the door shut.

"Lorcan," Natalie yelled, "you can't leave us down here! It's too scary, and there are too many dead spiders!"

In an annoyed tone, Lorcan yelled through the door. "I see six mages in a non-life-threatening situation. Either get a backbone or use your powers to solve this trivial problem."

Joel pounded on the door, but it didn't do any good. He turned around and looked at the scared group.

Natalie looked up at Joel and said in all seriousness, "Can you torch this place?"

Joel looked like it was worth considering.

"Settle down," Pru demanded, trying to sound calm. "We can't connect to our powers except for Natalie. Surely, Lorcan knows this. I hesitate to ask because I don't think this is a good place to use unpredictable powers. However, this is a dire situation. Natalie, can you do something?"

"Unfortunately, I can't do anything about the creepy echoing, but I can do something with the spiders. Sometimes, I connect; other times, emotion allows me to tap into my powers. Fair warning, this will be under distress, so it will probably be a typhoon when a light rain would have fixed our situation."

"Don't care…make it happen!" Joel demanded. "We need to get out of here, pronto!"

"Whatever I do, I'm thinking of collecting a pile of these dead spiders and sticking them on Lorcan's bed. He hates spiders, yet he has us down here dealing with this endless spider cemetery. Not happy."

Natalie took a deep breath to calm her nerves and then ambled to the last step of the staircase. Madison and Pru stayed near the door as the others descended the stairs. Joel stood closest to Natalie, with Skylar close behind him. Connor stood behind Skylar.

Natalie squinted, trying to get a better look through the gray haze without having to step onto the floor. Spider-laden, misty shapes of stored antiques, unwanted furniture, and anything that might have a future use rested along the southern wall. She found it nearly impossible to identify the fuzzy items stacked all over the floor and on top of each other, but she stayed focused.

"Is this going to take long?" Joel asked.

"Nope, I've found what I need."

Sure of her plan, she closed her eyes. Wind began to swirl around the stored furniture, filling the air with a heavier layer of spider dust. The wind moved in and out and around objects until it located a large wooden trunk. Swirling around the trunk, the wind slid it into the center of the room. The lid shot up. As it did, the wind turned into a small wind funnel. Spinning around the room, it sucked up the spiders as it made a path. Half of the spiders got sucked into the funnel, and the other half sprayed out onto the mages.

Bombarded with spider limbs and debris, the others screamed, "NATALIE!" and raced up the stairs.

Skylar didn't turn and get away fast enough. Natalie reached out and grabbed her arm. Skylar slumped at the same time Natalie received a jolt of energy. Combined with her energy, it overloaded her.

A cyclone full of flashing lightning appeared and began tearing through the basement, destroying everything in its path. Shards flew through the air. Like a wild man, Joel pounded on the door.

"LORCAN!" Joel screamed, "WE'RE IN DANGER! GET US OUT OF HERE!"

"DUCK!" Natalie yelled as she turned her focus on the door. Her hands went straight out; energy burst from them. The door blew apart. A shocked Lorcan stood on the other side of the door.

Joel pushed Lorcan aside as they bolted out of the basement. They rushed for the front door. Lorcan regained his footing and stood at the shattered door. Hearing the sounds of destruction while peering down the stairs, he panicked at the weakening cyclone wreaking havoc in the basement. Muttering a quick spell, the cyclone and echoing screams ended.

Lorcan turned and commanded, "STOP!"

No longer concerned with anything except escaping, the mages continued for the front door. Joel grabbed the doorknob and yanked on the locked door. They turned around, looking for another way out. At that moment, Lorcan walked into the room and approached the spider dust-coated mages.

"What's the matter with you!? Can't you do something as easy as clearing a path?" Lorcan yelled, focusing on Natalie.

She started to say something, but seven pixies and fairies, hearing Lorcan's loud, angry voice, entered the room. Natalie tried to shoo them away, but it was too late. They saw the mages and burst into hysterical laughter. While some doubled over in laughter, a couple of fairies flew away.

"Go away!" Lorcan yelled. He turned his focus back to Natalie.

"Why couldn't you do something as simple as clear a path?" Lorcan fumed at her.

She didn't even bother to answer when she saw the two fairies return. They held small devices in their hands. Click. Click. Click. Some pictures were individual shots, and some were group photos of the distraught mages.

"Knock it off!" Lorcan hollered at them.

They ignored him. The mages turned their focus on the bubbly fairies. Constantly turning towards the fairies as they flew around them, the fairies kept taking pictures. Lorcan pulled his wand from his pocket. They were finished. Giggling, the fairies and pixies retreated upstairs.

With them gone, Lorcan turned his focus back on the mages and again demanded an answer. "Third time asking, Natalie. Why did this turn into a colossal mess?"

"I don't know what happened. One minute, there was a trunk open to collect the spiders from a small wind funnel, and the next minute, there was a full-blown cyclone."

"Just so you know, the trunk trick wasn't really working," Connor said while trying to use the bottom of his T-shirt to wipe spider dust off his face.

"As you can see, we were all being sprayed with flying spider parts. We were already heading for the door when the cyclone appeared." Madison shuddered, recalling that thing heading in their direction.

"Natalie?" Lorcan crossed his arms and waited for her answer.

"I don't know. The rest were leaving me. I grabbed hold of Skylar so I wouldn't be the only one down there. When I did, I felt a jolt, and that's when the cyclone appeared."

Lorcan, wide-eyed, deeply inhaled as his face drained of color. He dropped his rigid stance and turned to Skylar. She looked tired and exhausted.

"Skylar," Lorcan began, but dreaded the most likely answer, "did you say yes?"

Skylar said nothing, but she nodded yes. Lorcan looked back at Natalie. Something wasn't right.

Puzzled, Natalie looked over at her. "Skylar, I didn't ask you anything. I didn't want to be alone."

Skylar glanced at Natalie before looking away. "It wasn't a direct question. Just a feeling. I said yes."

Natalie's eyes widened in surprise as she looked back at Lorcan, who studied her. *Oh, great. I have obviously crossed a line. Does it ever end?*

"Tell Skylar thank you."

"What? Why?"

"Just do it now!" Lorcan demanded.

"Skylar, thank you." Natalie flatly stated it, wondering why she had to thank her. She only did it so Lorcan wouldn't become angrier.

"There won't be class today," Lorcan stated as he turned his focus to the other mages. "I'll see if the teacher will have class tomorrow. Your mentor will let you know. Now go home."

Lorcan didn't need to say it a second time. They all wanted out. Turning around, they bolted for the front door.

After they left, Natalie stood there, bewildered and afraid. "Lorcan, I swear I didn't ask to use her power. I didn't even know that was possible, especially after we drank that rancid potion. Everyone's going to be afraid of me. I'm even scaring myself."

"I don't know what's happening or why," Lorcan said, trying to make some sense of it. "Your mother was powerful. In fact, she was one of the most powerful Shadowlinks I've ever known, but your powers surpass hers. I don't understand it." He started pacing the room, appearing as if he were trying to make sense of the latest event. She watched him go back and forth.

He stopped pacing and looked at her. "Natalie, your powers are amazing. Don't take it as a curse."

Natalie wasn't so sure. She felt like a redlined locomotive with no way to stop. How could that be good, especially if she were angry or in distress? It happened too often.

"Lorcan, you say that, but it's going to make the others avoid me. I'm too different."

"Every person is unique. Every person struggles with something. Even people that you think have everything going for them have something dark or painful in their history. No one has a perfect life."

"I can do a lot of damage, Lorcan. That's a much bigger issue than someone who had a crummy childhood."

"Is it?" Lorcan said, taking her hand and leading her to the feather collection room. Lorcan sat on one gaudy chair and motioned for Natalie to sit on the other gaudy chair. Covered in spider remains, she continued to stand.

"Sit!" He waited until she settled and faced him.

"That's better. With magic, the chairs are safe from permanent damage."

Lorcan scratched his head and looked puzzled for a moment. "Where was I?"

"You were talking about no one has a perfect life." Natalie pushed her bangs to the side, scratched her forehead, and then her neck.

"That's right. We don't know what someone has gone through or is going through. Some people are good at hiding the hurt, but that history lingers in the heart forever. We don't judge, and we don't make assumptions. A loyal friend is there for you as you are for that friend."

"It isn't that simple, Lorcan."

"Yes, it is that simple."

"So, you think the others are going to be there for me when I have one of my disasters? I mean, the disasters seem to be quite frequent." Natalie flashed back to Thursday when she almost lost her cool in homeroom. Message to self, work on a defusing technique before I reach the boiling stage.

"This is only temporary. You aren't in control of your powers, but you'll get there. It's too bad your training didn't start earlier. Your mother wanted you to have a normal childhood, but if she had known how powerful you are, she would have started your training long ago."

"Would I have had a mentor like my mother had when she was young?" She pushed her sleeves back and started scratching her arms.

"No. Your mother didn't have a mentor unless you count Kothar, which isn't saying much. With his whiny, negative attitude, he failed at being a Ruiri, so Draon gave him the job of facilitator of the inventory at the Stormfield fortress. Draon had your mother assist Kothar, but she did her best to ignore him. I guess if anyone guided your mother, it was Draon. I wasn't there, but I know your mother frequently tested Draon's patience. She would seem mild compared to you."

"Thanks, Lorcan," Natalie said in a sarcastic tone.

"The truth, always the truth."

Ignoring the last comment, she said, "Well, it sounds like waiting was the right thing to do. I seem to have people regularly comment that I'm dramatic. My father even calls me a drama queen. Drama and anger are a terrible combination. I'm sure if I were angry at an early age, I would have shown it and not care who knew that I had powers." She scratched the top of her head.

"Isn't that the truth!" Lorcan exclaimed.

She gave him a look that indicated he wasn't supposed to agree with that statement.

"Lorcan, after the elf meltdown, I mentioned to Draon that I used to be calm. I don't understand what has made me so angry. I wasn't like this prior to my powers. Even if I was upset before, I could control myself. Now I get so angry that I almost don't care if someone knows I have powers. The only thing that keeps me in check when I'm angry in the mageless world is thinking of you and Draon. Hopefully, that keeps working until I have better control of myself." Natalie reached her left hand to her back and scratched.

"I know what you're saying, but I don't have an answer as to why your powers have you struggling with anger. With you, nothing is simple."

"I'm sorry."

"You don't need to apologize for something we don't understand," Lorcan said, feeling tired. He sighed.

"You okay, Lorcan?"

"Still tired. Today's disaster didn't help," Lorcan grumbled. With his right elbow resting on the arm of the chair, he placed his hand on his cheek. Leaning on it, he tried to relax.

Natalie watched him. At least he wasn't grumpy like earlier in the day. She tried to sit back and wait for him to focus on their conversation, but she struggled with every part of her body itching.

"In my wildest nightmare, I couldn't have dreamed up the volume of dead spiders down in the basement," Lorcan said, shifting uncomfortably in his chair.

"Maybe the enchantments attached to the old homestead bring those kinds of nightmares."

"Maybe."

"You're lucky, Lorcan. If we had been down there much longer, you were going to get a boatload of spiders on your bed."

"A frightening thought." He shuddered.

"Not as frightening as actually being down there in it." She was back to scratching her arms.

"True. Since I didn't check it out before your group headed to the Barracks, I didn't know what was down there.

I thought your group overreacted. It had to be a harrowing experience for Skylar to do what she did."

"And Joel...didn't you hear him scream?"

"Like a girl. The basement spirits seemed to mock him with the repeating echoes," Lorcan recalled, trying to lighten up the conversation.

"How about like a Ruiri that goes livid? You sounded like a heavyweight soprano without the echoing part." She scratched the top of her left hand and then switched to scratching the top of her right hand.

"I'll let you in on a secret," Lorcan paused and leaned towards Natalie. "All Ruiri gnomes that go livid are deathly afraid of spiders."

"Seriously?"

"Yes. The fairies and pixies know it and use it against us," Lorcan said, slowly getting up. "Focusing back on the original situation, I'm going to talk with Draon about what happened and see if he wants the class to take place tomorrow."

Natalie lifted her hair up and scratched the back of her neck before returning to scratching her arms. Her long fingernails were full of spider dust. She glanced at the disgusting, dirty nails, but she couldn't stop scratching. With each passing minute, it got worse. Lorcan didn't seem to notice or appear interested in using a spell to make it disappear. She couldn't take it any longer and stood up.

"Go home and get a nice long shower. I'll let you and the others know if training is tomorrow."

"Gladly, the spider dust is like a horrible itching potion. I desperately need relief." She aggressively scratched her face and neck.

"It is a key ingredient in itching potions."

"Good to know," Natalie said as she headed towards the front door. Lorcan followed.

At the door with her hand on the doorknob, she half turned and said, "I hope those in the Barracks don't find out about this latest disaster. It seems most of the Barracks' leaders already think I'm a train wreck waiting to happen over and over."

"With good reason," Lorcan laughed.

Before she could respond, he turned and left the room.

"I hope there isn't class tomorrow," Natalie muttered as she stepped outside. She wanted today to be no news or old news.

Chapter 4

Angus Thornton

Lorcan's golden trinkets clinked together against his leg as he bounced confidently down the basement stairs. The mages hesitated at the top of the staircase and nervously glanced around for traces of lingering spider debris. A new ceiling light brightly lit the area, showing no evidence of spiders, cyclones, or destroyed furniture. Even the smell of bug bombs was gone.

Feeling safe, they made their way down the narrow steps and caught up to Lorcan. Now and then, giggles and snickers erupted as they watched Lorcan sashay across the basement. Things were looking up. Even so, if the bookstore had been open on Sunday, the mages would have entered the Barracks through the bookstore's front door.

"As you are now witnessing, everything is back to normal…thanks to me," Lorcan announced. Puffed up, he waited for them to show their appreciation.

Instead, glancing at one another in amazement, they stood there thinking he was the one who turned it into a disaster because he wouldn't let them escape. An awkward silence filled the room.

"It took several spells to clean up the spider mess. I cast more spells to repair the damage. That doesn't count the spells needed to get rid of the smell and…"

Connor interrupted Lorcan. "Outstanding job, Lorcan! It's perfect! Wow! Thanks, dude!"

"Thank you!" Joel exclaimed as he reached his right hand out for Lorcan to shake.

"It looks like yesterday never happened," Pru said with a wide grin.

"It's amazing how you've cleaned this place up. We need to learn those spells," Madison said, without smiling, but raising her hands up and giving two thumbs up.

"No spiders, thanks to you, Lorcan," Skylar said, drawing an imaginary heart over her heart and pointing at Lorcan.

Natalie smirked and stayed quiet as the others broke out, "Three cheers for Lorcan!"

"Okay, okay," Lorcan yelled over the cheer. "We made special arrangements for you to have class today, so you need to get there on time. Now get going!"

Lorcan trotted off and left them standing at what appeared to be a solid wall, except that a door blended into the wall. Only accessible by mages and magical creatures, Joel pushed the door open. They entered a railway tunnel eerily lit by large sconces holding red dragon fire crystals. Mystic flickering red light danced before the cart, waiting for them to board. It was a tight squeeze, but all six loaded into the cart. Clicking along the railroad tracks, they rumbled towards the bookstore.

"That was fun," Joel chuckled.

"Seriously, he created most of the mess by keeping us locked down there. He forgot that part," Madison complained.

"True, but it couldn't have been easy to clean up," Pru countered. "It was a simple way to show Lorcan our appreciation."

"I guess," Madison said, sounding like she didn't want to talk about anything that had to do with yesterday.

The mages sat still, lost in their own thoughts, until they were close to the bookstore. At that point, Natalie asked, "Did I ever mention that I once saw a hunchbacked person changing out the dragon fire crystals?"

"No," Madison said, "wouldn't the crystals burn?"

"They'll burn us. However, Lorcan told me that's their job, and they're immune to the crystals. When I used deformity to describe the person, Lorcan told me it was because the person committed a hideous crime. The punishment was to become hideous."

"That sounds awful," Pru said, "like there's no way to redeem yourself."

"It must have been pure evil to get that punishment," Joel countered.

"Do you think it was a mage gone bad?" Connor asked, considering for the first time that there could be dire consequences for evil mages.

"Maybe it was one of those rotten elves that tried to steal our powers," Skylar said.

"I don't know. All I know is it surprised Lorcan that I saw one. He didn't want to talk about it, so we don't know if this person did something long ago or if you can get the curse now."

"How do they get into the tunnel system?" Skylar asked.

"Not sure. He seemed to appear and then disappear when I spotted him."

"We need to get more information from our mentors. Actually, we need to ask if there is anything else we should know about this tunnel system. Yesterday's spiders were enough of a surprise. We don't need any more surprises. We don't want any more surprises." Pru was adamant she was done with surprises.

"I'm with you," Joel agreed as they landed at the bookstore's secret entrance.

Climbing the narrow stairs, they entered the brightly lit bookstore and made their way to the back of the store. They didn't waste any time moving through the aisle to reach the last bookcase of red books. Joel faced a small wall at the end of the room as the others gathered around him.

He raised his hand and placed it on a black rectangle painted on the white wall. Instantly, the wall opened into a doorway. Stepping through, they ambled down the familiar path of the old, narrow stone tunnel. As they headed towards the Barracks, they talked about the dank and decaying smells that lingered on the cobblestone path. Connor mentioned it prepared them for the smell of Hexel when they entered the Crossroads Barracks. They all laughed, but it was true. Hexel smelled like a decaying corpse.

Familiar with them, a disinterested Hexel didn't even bother to float over to inspect them. It didn't matter. She stayed near enough that they held their breaths. Natalie smiled and waved as Connor dragged her with him until they were clear of Hexel. Then, they took in deep breaths of fresh air. The gulps of fresh air ritual had them laughing as they headed to the classroom at the rear of the Fire elemental building.

The laughter ended when they spotted a tall man sternly standing outside the classroom door. With perfect posture, salt and pepper short hair, and keenly observing gray eyes, he stared at each mage as each one passed by him. No one questioned why Mr. Xanders was absent. No one said a word. They settled into their chairs. The door closed. The teacher walked in front of the desk and stood looking over the mages.

Their eyes widened as they viewed the large photos displayed on the blackboard behind the teacher. They squirmed in their seats as they glanced at one another.

Connor silently mouthed to Joel, "Is this for real?"

If the teacher had been Mr. Xanders, there would have been a commotion, but he wasn't there. It was a stiff, unfriendly, no-nonsense-looking teacher. Even so, they

53

glanced at the large group photo at the top, then each mage sought their own photo, and then the photos of the other mages. Irritated at what she saw, Natalie couldn't wait to get home and have a firm talk with those fairy traitors.

The arrogant teacher turned around and looked at the pictures taped to the blackboard. Connor took that moment to frown and hiss "demon fairies" to Joel. Joel ignored him. Connor turned back to face the front as the teacher turned around with a superior expression plastered on his face. For several long minutes, he remained quiet while boring holes into each student.

"Mr. Xanders expected you yesterday. From the photos displayed behind me, I would say yesterday wasn't a good day for any of you. Would someone care to explain what happened yesterday?"

The teacher's baritone voice surprised Natalie. She studied him and wondered why he needed to ask the question. She felt he already had the answer. A "tsk" escaped her lips as she rolled her eyes. He turned his focus on her.

"Oh, crap," Natalie muttered while staring up into his unsmiling eyes.

"I imagine you're Natalie."

"Yes, sir."

"Are you the reason for yesterday's disaster?" The teacher folded his arms across his chest and waited for the answer.

"Not entirely."

"What part didn't you have at yesterday's event?" The teacher continued to stare at Natalie.

His unrelenting stare left her feeling uncomfortable. She tried to stare back, but she blinked several times even though her focus was elsewhere. Well, she sort of focused on him, but she also thought about the fairies. *How could they do that to us?*

That was the million-dollar question because it was impossible without help. Restriction to the old homestead isolated them. *What then?* Lorcan flashed into her mind. *Would he do that? Is he okay with making us the butt of jokes and conversations in the Barracks yesterday and today?* Natalie's shoulders tightened in anger as fury lit her eyes.

"Natalie!" the teacher's voice boomed in the classroom. All eyes turned from him to her.

"What?" Natalie said, and then she remembered he had asked her a question.

"It was all me," Natalie snapped.

She had better things to do than play his superiority game. Still staring at him, she angrily thought *this class better not be about yesterday.*

"Just as I thought," the teacher replied.

He turned his attention to the entire class as Natalie's temper flared. She didn't comment, but the sudden wind swirling around her showed her displeasure. She fumed at his arrogant behavior towards her.

"My name is Angus Thornton. I'm the Master Wizard here at the Barracks," he announced, sounding impressed with his position.

Still annoyed, Natalie looked at him and thought, *if you're the Master Wizard, then Draon is the Archimage Wizard. You, sir, are woefully beneath Draon. And, if we are giving ourselves titles, well then, I'm the Master Disaster. That definitely fits me.* Then Joel flashed into her mind. *He would be the Master Donut Chomper.* She bit her lip not to laugh at the perfect title. Any time he had extra money, he spent it on a Flaky Kuchen donut. *Connor would be…she* felt all eyes were on her. She looked up. *Now what?*

"Natalie, what did I just say?"

"You're Angus Thornton, the Barracks' master wizard."

"After that?"

"I don't know."

"What was so important that it had your attention instead of paying attention in class?" Angus Thornton asked in a cool tone.

No way would she tell him the truth. She was sure he wouldn't find the Master Donut Chomper funny. She sighed. "It had to do with the fairies betraying us."

"Stay focused on today's class."

"Yes, sir."

"As I was saying, the last time you had training was before the third sign. That has come and gone. As rumor has it, the only ones affected were Natalie and Lorcan. Is that true?"

He focused on each mage before Pru answered. "It's true. We had the winds with the eclipse. We saw our magical protections react, but nothing was trying to break the enchantments. After talking it over with the others, the only ones attacked were Natalie and Lorcan."

"Natalie, tell me what happened," Angus Thornton said as he stepped around the desk and sat down. Even when he sat down, he intimidated her.

Natalie didn't like him, nor did she trust him. She didn't know why he wanted her to report the events, as she was sure he had heard the entire story many times. It was a significant event that led to a major crisis. There would have been meetings that included Draon, Lorcan, and all the other mentors. Why did he need her side of the event unless he was trying to make her look stupid? Was he trying to trip up Draon or Lorcan? They knew the real reason, and all of them were keeping the secret.

Locking her eyes with his, Natalie explained what had happened that day. "It managed to find a weak link and possess Lorcan. I was drifting in and out of consciousness, which might have given it a way to reach us. Luckily, my bird saw we were in trouble. Coal jammed his beak into my back to wake me up. I saw Lorcan possessed. I zapped him with my remaining energy; that blast defeated the enemy. That's all I know."

Natalie felt uncomfortable as the master wizard studied her face the whole time she reported what had happened that day. Even after she finished her report, he continued to observe her. She stared at his forehead to give the impression of focusing on him while maintaining a calm exterior.

"So, you were the weak link? You don't need to answer that question. The answer is obvious," Angus Thornton said in a smug tone.

Surprised at the rude comment, Natalie turned towards Pru and rolled her eyes in his direction. Her body language indicated she couldn't believe this guy's behavior. Pru shook her head and whispered, "No," while the others leaned in to assure her they were with her. Feeling better, she turned her attention back to the teacher.

"Natalie, do you have something the others might not have that attracted the attack on you?"

She decided to put her thinking look on by resting her right elbow on the desk and placing her right index finger on her chin. She lifted her head up while raising her eyes to the left. She pretended to give the question serious consideration. Several minutes passed as she mulled over the question. She heard Connor snicker, but she pretended not to hear him. When she sensed it was about to lead to the teacher yelling at her, she answered the question.

"For each sign, it has attacked me. It could be because I am the Shadowlink."

Natalie had stayed innocent-looking while she emphasized the word 'the' to rub it in that she was a

57

Shadowlink. She smiled as she rested both of her hands on the desk. She wondered why he was so interested in her describing what happened at the old homestead. He had the answers from Lorcan and Draon.

"Anything else come to mind?" Angus Thornton asked her.

She shook her head no, watched him consider if she was being honest, and then he accepted her answer.

"A Shadowlink is rare, so it makes sense it would go after you. If you think of anything else, let me know." Natalie nodded yes, but she thought *a full-blown blizzard would occur in Florida before that ever happens*.

He turned his attention back to the class. "The third sign has passed, meaning we should start seeing more strange happenings. Of interest is the newly formed Janus Club, which officially starts this Wednesday at your school. We have researched the sponsor of the club and know this is where trouble will reign. Unfortunately, because of the unknown, you cannot join the club."

He paused as the mages looked surprised at that comment. It was apparent that none of them had considered joining the club.

"Avoiding the club isn't an option. We need to deal with it without becoming part of it. To achieve that, we can take actions that could disrupt the club. Over the next few weeks, we're going to enhance your magical abilities with unique skills and tools. Since you're in the school, you have access before the meetings. We'll use these skills to help stop it from becoming successful."

Connor raised his hand as Angus Thornton got up from his chair.

"Connor?"

"Do you have any idea what we're fighting?"

"Not a clue," Angus Thornton said as he opened the door to the big closet at the back wall. The mages got a whiff of something that would not be pleasant. They looked at each other with raised eyebrows as the master wizard brought a large, covered basket to the group.

"In magic," Connor groaned, "why does everything have to smell like Hexel?"

"Seriously," Natalie replied, "you have no idea of smell until you have the three-headed tree stump activated, and it's spewing stinky, slimy goo. I thought it was bad with the regurgitated stuff flowing out, but when the three heads started gulping the slime back down, well, that was almost a barf fest."

Pru, sitting next to Natalie, placed her hand over her mouth. "Enough!"

Joel and Connor burst out laughing, but Pru, Madison, and Skylar sat horrified. Angus Thornton ignored them as he pulled the cover off the basket. Everyone stilled as they stared at the strange animal. It looked like an oversized, plump rat, except it had a pouch, a short, fluffy tail, and long purplish gray fur.

"What is that?" Skylar exclaimed.

"His name is Odi; he's an Odious Rattus." He started scratching its head. It hummed.

"Wh-what are w-we sup-supposed to d-do with it?" Pru stammered, pushing herself further back in her chair.

"In magic, you can ask to borrow the energy of any creature except humans, elves, and gnomes. It's not recommended to borrow the energy of your familiar. While the borrowed energy will magnify your powers, it renders the creature defenseless, so only use it in dire situations."

Angus Thornton placed the basket on his desk and picked Odi up. He continued to pet Odi as he turned him around. Natalie smiled as she noticed Pru relaxing, relieved to see that the strange animal was friendly.

"Not all creatures will lend you their energy. That's their right. Odi is here today because he comes from the magical realm and is more willing to lend you his energy. With that said, we will not wear him down by each of you practicing on him. That would be too much for him. You will find him and a few other Odious Rattus in the building that houses the library. You can train on your own time. Today is only a demonstration."

The master wizard stopped petting the rat. It stopped humming and opened its eyes. The mages stared at the large purple eyes that took in each mage. Its brilliant white teeth were long like rat teeth.

"Why does it have to stink?" Connor complained. "If it didn't smell so horribly foul, it would be fairly cute with its little pouch and fluffy tail."

"The smell is its defense. Most predators aren't going to eat something that smells this rancid."

"Most predators would prefer to be in a different county."

"Connor, since you find the rat so repugnant, you'll be the one to provide the demonstration." Angus Thornton motioned for Connor to come up and stand near him as he placed the rat on the floor.

Connor hesitated and continued sitting in his chair.

"Connor, now."

Reluctantly, he got up and stood near the master wizard.

"What you need to do is extend your arm out and have your hand open and over the rat. The closer, the better. Speak in a soft voice so only Odi can hear your request to borrow his energy. You can make it as simple as asking to borrow his energy. He needs to trust you. Thank Odi. You don't need to be over him to return the energy, but you need to be over him to borrow the energy. Try it."

Connor extended his right arm and held his hand over the rat. He whispered, "Can I borrow your energy?" Not feeling anything, Connor looked up at the teacher for direction.

"You need to be sincere, Connor. The frown on your face says you don't really want to do this."

"If I borrow his energy, do I end up smelling like him?"

As the others laughed, Angus Thornton snapped, "No, you won't. Energy is invisible and has no form. You aren't borrowing his body. Now concentrate."

Connor took a deep breath, slowly let it out, and tried to change his frame of mind. He looked over at Pru for support. She gave him an encouraging smile. Focusing back on Odi, Connor again asked to borrow Odi's energy.

"How do I know when it has happened?" Connor asked.

"You'll feel it. It hasn't happened. That's why all of you need to practice on your own at the…"

Connor interrupted the master wizard. "Natalie has it down. She took Skylar's energy yesterday."

Natalie's eyes went wide as she looked at Connor in disbelief. *Why did he blurt that out?* Angus Thornton turned to Natalie.

"Explain yourself!" the master wizard demanded of her as he gave Connor a look that told him to sit down.

"I can't explain what I don't know. I didn't ask Skylar. It just happened."

The master wizard walked up to her and stared down at her. "You're meddling where you shouldn't go."

"Draon and Lorcan know what happened. I wasn't looking to borrow anyone's powers. I didn't even know it was possible."

"I'll be speaking with Draon and Lorcan."

"Fine, I have nothing to hide about yesterday," Natalie fumed.

"I hope that is true," Angus Thornton said as he stepped back to Odi and picked him up.

Natalie glared at the teacher as he focused on Odi. She tried to calm down as his attention on Odi meant he wouldn't look for reasons to aggravate her. Suddenly, he turned his back on the mages.

Smirking, Natalie told herself that was his better side. Pulling her phone out, she looked at the time and saw class dismissal wasn't soon enough. As she put her phone away, she questioned his motives for turning away from them.

She jumped as Odi began to chatter. The animal sounded distressed, yet Angus Thornton still hadn't turned around. She glanced at Pru and then leaned out to look at the others. His anxious chatter upset her.

"Is Odi okay?" Connor asked.

When Angus Thornton didn't answer, Natalie stood up to check on Odi. Lightheaded, she collapsed and fell back into her chair. She rubbed her forehead with one hand, trying to clear the strange feeling, and grabbed Pru's arm with the other hand.

"Are you okay?" Pru asked, seeing the look of confusion and discomfort on Natalie's face. She shook her head no.

Folding her arms on her desk, she rested her head on them, but she couldn't get comfortable with the distraught chatter. Her eyes remained open as she watched Connor get up to check on Odi. Angus Thornton motioned him to back off. Even with nausea and weakness, she knew Angus

Thornton had something to do with Odi's behavior and her illness.

"Is Odi all right?" Connor asked, several feet away from Angus Thornton.

"Yes" was the short answer, but Odi continued to chatter.

Natalie watched as Connor tried to lean forward and get a look at Odi. To Natalie and Connor's surprise, Angus Thornton turned around and gave Connor a look that told him to get back in his seat. Then he focused on Natalie.

"Sit up. Take a nap on your own time."

"Excuse me, but Natalie," Pru began, but the master wizard interrupted her.

"Natalie, you need to stand up and show us how it's done."

He walked over to her and placed a chattering Odi by her chair. Feeling better, she sat up, but she didn't stand up. She looked at Angus Thornton like he had lost his mind.

"No."

"Are you afraid you can't do it and you'll embarrass yourself in front of your classmates?"

She continued to look at him as if he had lost his marbles. "No."

"What is it?"

"There are a couple of reasons. First, Odi is panicking right now; he needs to feel safe. He will not give me any energy when he is this distraught. Second, even if he could, it would be a power overload. I don't need more power. Yesterday proved that point…and regular times prove it gets out of hand. Being the master wizard, I'm sure you've heard some of the stories."

Before Angus Thornton could respond to Natalie, she turned her attention to Connor. "Connor, would you help Odi feel safe?"

Natalie watched as the teacher's eyes narrowed at her. "No need, Connor."

Angus Thornton picked up Odi, and as he petted him, Odi became quiet. Getting the basket, he pushed the blanket aside and placed Odi inside. Within seconds, the rat buried himself under the blanket.

Smiling at the other mages and then focusing on Connor, Angus Thornton calmly said, "Connor, you have the physical part down. You just need to work on being sincere and getting the animal to trust you. I'm sure you'll master it in no time. When you're done using the energy, a simple thank you will restore the energy to the rightful owner."

He looked at each mage before continuing his instruction. "When you advance in experience, there is energy in water, trees, rocks, and many other things. Animals have a higher level of energy. Avoid graveyards." Angus Thornton looked directly at Natalie. "People are off limits."

She stayed perfectly still and didn't look up. She pretended she didn't hear him, but she gave him the nickname of Master Annoying Twaddler. Glancing up, she smirked, thinking about using his initials in that way. She saw him frown. She was sure he would needle her some more, but Pru asked, "Would someone really ask for energy from a grave?"

The master wizard shifted his attention from Natalie to Pru. "There are all types of mages out there. There are also dire situations requiring an immediate response. Graveyards carry the unknown. Dealing with the unknown is not what you want to be doing."

Natalie watched Odi push the blanket off and place his paws on the edge of the basket. She felt sorry for the distressed animal as he looked at Angus Thornton and squeaked.

"Does he need to go to the bathroom?" Connor asked, concerned with the rapid, high-pitched squeaks.

"What?" Angus Thornton looked at Connor and realized it was a sincere question. "No, Odi and his kind are sensitive to emotions…especially negative emotions. Today exhausted him."

Leaving the basket on the desk and covering Odi to quiet him, the master wizard took one last look at the photos on the blackboard and then one last look at each mage.

"Grave times are approaching for the mageless. Is it coming in waves like the Four Horsemen or all at once? We don't know. For now, we have no details on the sinister plot put in place. It will be up to this group to discover the plan and stop it. Master your elements; excel at magic. Our faith is in you to bring down the Janus Club. Class dismissed."

He didn't need to say class dismissed a second time. Natalie jumped up and headed straight for the door. She had fairies to see.

Chapter 5

She Has a Temper

While the mages were at the Barracks, Draon met with Lorcan. Sitting at the small wooden kitchen table, Lorcan reported yesterday's events. Draon sat listening until he mentioned Natalie had taken Skylar's powers.

Stunned, Draon questioned what he had heard. "Did you say Natalie took Skylar's powers?"

Lorcan repeatedly shook his head yes before leaning forward and providing more details. "Natalie thought she had things under control, but the mages were getting coated with flying spider debris. They took off for the top of the stairs. Skylar didn't move quickly enough. Natalie grabbed her. As she held on, Skylar's powers transferred to her. Natalie said she didn't ask Skylar for her powers. She said she didn't want to be alone down there. Skylar said she felt permission was being asked; she said yes."

Thunderstruck, Draon put his elbows on the table and then placed his thumbs into his cheeks and his fingers over his eyebrows. He leaned into his hands. He desperately needed time to think to figure out how this latest mishap was even possible. He kept asking himself that question as he mulled it over and over. At first, he had no answers. Then, somewhere deep in a corner of his mind, the answer came to him. Draon gasped.

"Draon?"

Draon did not answer. He stayed leaning against his hands. What an unforeseeable mess; they could only blame themselves. He was sure of it. Why had they not thought about potential future consequences? He knew the answer. Nessa had been terrified. That had alarmed him. Something needed to happen immediately, but it didn't have to remain for all these years. They had...Lorcan interrupted Draon's thoughts with another "Draon??"

Straightening up, Draon said, "I honestly do not know where to begin with Natalie. She needs to learn to control her powers and her emotions. We also need to know how advanced she is in magic. The oracular stone only told us that her powers are beyond what it can read."

As Draon paused, Lorcan interjected. "Both of us have been questioning her abilities since the first disaster. It's amazing what we've seen, but it's also scary. We can appreciate that the powers are within a good person."

Draon sighed. "That is true. It is the attacks on her character or her friends that result in the disasters. Regardless of the reason, this latest event should not have happened. She is too inexperienced. Even with Skylar giving her permission, Natalie should not have been able to access the power. Yet, it seems like it was a natural event for her."

Draon paused in frustration and then changed the subject. "How many centuries old am I?"

Lorcan shook his head, indicating that he didn't know. His expression told Draon that he didn't understand the reason for asking him that question.

"My hair is black today, but with Natalie, I feel gray will pop in there any minute."

"That sounds like a joke, but anyone training or mentoring Natalie would see the reality of that comment," Lorcan said, noting his hair was already white, so he was safe.

"Prolonged training or mentoring might lead to baldness," Draon frowned at the visual.

"Well, Ruiries don't go bald. Then again, none of us have ever mentored someone like Natalie,' Lorcan said as he grabbed onto his prized long, snow-white braid.

"There is always a first," Draon said.

"Crows don't go gray or bald. You're safe."

"You know I am 100% human," Draon said. "What may happen is instead of submerging once a month in the Alchemy River, I may need to drink it daily."

Lorcan laughed. "I may need to join you."

Draon went quiet and studied Lorcan. He wanted to confess the decision he and Nessa had made long ago. Now that he remembered what they did, it weighed on him. Nervous, he sat there. He knew he could trust Lorcan, but he had never told anyone a secret.

"Lorcan."

Lorcan saw Draon's expression and became serious. "What's bothering you, Draon?"

"I have a confession to make, but it must stay between us."

"You have my word." Lorcan sat up straighter and waited.

"You have heard some of my stories about the difficulty of dealing with Nessa growing up. She was headstrong and determined to do everything her way. She rarely, if ever, listened to instructions. The one thing she did was keep magic within Stormfield. Growing up, no one outside of Stormfield knew she was a mage. Her mother did not even know. It was ironic since her mother was a Shadowlink, but she was unaware of her mage ancestry."

Lorcan nodded in agreement. "Yes. Nessa had mentioned her strained relationship with her mother. She considered you her family and Stormfield her true home."

Surprised, Draon looked down and hoped he could stop tears from gushing down his face. Nessa's passing still hurt him, as if it had happened yesterday. He told himself she was gone and not coming back. Get control. Breathing deeply and slowly releasing it, he fought to regain his composure.

Draon could see that Lorcan was mad for upsetting him. Before he could say it was all right, Lorcan jumped up and headed over to the refrigerator. Yanking the door open, he moved to the side so Draon could see there were six pitchers of fairy punch. Draon's mouth watered, not because of tasty fairy punch, but because of his experience with sour fairy punch.

"Do we dare?"

"Yes," Draon said, "they may surprise us."

"Okay, you pick the punch. We have two oranges, one red, one purple, one yellow, and one mud color."

"Mud color is out," Draon laughed, feeling better. "I say orange."

"Orange it is," Lorcan said as he pulled the pitcher out, took two glasses from the cabinet, and filled both glasses.

"Thanks." Draon took a tall glass from Lorcan's hand.

"Don't thank me yet. Fairy punch is always a toss-up between scrumptiously delicious and horrifically devastating. We may dash for the kitchen sink."

"True, but the color looks promising," Draon said, raising his glass to take a sip. A sugary smell floated up to his nose. Taking the tiniest of sips, he looked up, satisfied. "That is the best fairy punch I have ever tasted."

"It is extraordinarily good," Lorcan said as he licked his lips. "Now, if you're ready, please continue." Lorcan settled and took another sip of the punch.

Draon put his glass down and continued his story.

"Nessa kept the secret of Stormfield and magic from everyone except her husband. With Karl, she shared everything. He was all right with it as long as it was only stories. He did not want to see magic. Magic was forbidden unless Nessa visited Stormfield. Nessa kept her promise, even though she had a room in their house that was off-limits to everyone else. The only magical items she kept in there were her graduation picture and the Mirror of Durin. All was fine until Natalie was born. This is when it got difficult."

Draon paused, but only for a moment. It was time to confess.

"At first, Nessa thought she imagined things, but as she saw more and more unusual happenings, her fear became a reality. Nessa asked me to evaluate Natalie, which I did in Stormfield. Natalie was not even a toddler, and yet she had powers. She was too young to understand she differed from most people. She did not understand the rules or how to control her powers. Nessa feared Karl could not handle it. With me present, Nessa received Natalie's permission and did a binding spell. The death of Nessa broke the spell. Like a floodgate opening, all those restricted powers unleashed in a fury."

"Wow, Draon, I'm stunned. Give me a few minutes to process what you said." Lorcan leaned forward, his eyes wide with shock.

Draon nodded. While waiting, he sipped the fairy punch. More time passed. Draon got up and brought the pitcher to the table. After filling both glasses, he could see that Lorcan was ready to talk.

"Whew, Draon. Never in my lifetime would I have considered a binding spell…that spell is rare. Yet, I knew something wasn't right because Natalie remarked about her anger and powers coming simultaneously."

"I do not know if we did the right thing," Draon said in a troubled voice.

He looked across the table at Lorcan for reassurance that they had made the best decision for Natalie.

Without hesitation, Lorcan reassured him. "You did the right thing. Karl wouldn't have been able to handle it. There was no way to know if Natalie would have been able to control her powers out in public. I think it would have been impossible. That left the only option of raising her in Stormfield. You don't know what that would have done to Karl and Nessa's marriage. Natalie grew up where she needed to be raised."

"Thank you. I feel better not holding it inside and wondering if we did the right thing."

"Can I ask you a question?"

"Yes."

"Did you just remember today that Nessa put a binding spell on Natalie?"

"Yes. That day, long ago, was the last time I saw Natalie. Until recently, Nessa had not even mentioned her to me. So many years had gone by, and then Nessa died. My focus has been on the devastation of losing her. I failed to question why Natalie thought her powers were causing anger issues."

Draon headed over to the Barracks as Natalie and the other mages headed home. Angus Thornton had sent word that he would like to speak with him. Draon knew it would be about Natalie. He was sure that with Angus newly elected as master wizard, he could not resist acting superior. That would not go over well with Natalie or the other mages. He knew the other mages would handle it, but with Natalie, a disaster always lurked around the corner. Sighing, he figured he would find out soon enough.

Draon greeted Hexel and headed for the master wizard's office. Sunday, and everything was peaceful. Nothing was happening, and there were zero signs of destruction. Draon relaxed and continued his walk.

He recalled his surprise when he learned the Barracks existed. He did not know how it remained a secret from him until a few months ago. With his own apartment, he felt like he belonged. He smiled, thinking about living in this self-contained treasure without ever venturing outside the Barracks' walls. While it sounded inviting, he knew it would never happen. He belonged in Stormfield.

Upon reaching headquarters, Draon pulled open a lavishly ornate front door, leading into a vast, magnificent lobby. The floor and walls were black, gold-veined marble, and the ceiling was golden. A massive chandelier hung from the center of the room. Beautiful iridescent bluish-purple butterflies leisurely floated around the chandelier. Life-size white marble statues of past master wizards stood in groups of twos and threes in different areas of the immense lobby.

Each step Draon took echoed throughout the vast lobby. The butterflies slowed and appeared to be watching him. He had no problem with the butterflies.

Disturbing came to mind as he walked near statues positioned to appear as if they were speaking. He might have been able to manage it if the eyes of each statue were marble instead of a moving replica of the past wizard's eyes. With blue, green, or brown eyes peering out of the white marble statues, it was too bizarre for Draon.

Not taking any chances, Draon muttered a spell that caused all the statues to turn and face the north wall. He glanced around the room to see that it was done. Good. No more eerie statues watched him; still, he did not relax. He tried focusing on some ancient artifacts on display while he neared the elevator. He relaxed as the plain elevator headed for the master wizard's private offices on the top floor.

Angus Thornton waited for Draon outside his office. Draon walked over to him and froze. Something in the background caught his attention. He glanced past Angus and saw a white porcelain mannequin in a long white dress. A long sleeve draped down from her outstretched arm. Another statue, but this one was more ominous than the ones in the lobby. Draon avoided looking at the black prophecy stone eyes that peered in his direction. He returned his focus to Angus.

"Thank you for seeing me on such short notice," Angus said, motioning for Draon to join him in his study.

Draon let out a sigh of relief. The study didn't have statues. Instead, it had a couch and comfortable brown leather reclining chairs. Complementing the large, overstuffed furniture were walls of cherry wood, endless bookshelves on the east wall, ancient books of mage history, and soft twinkling from hundreds of crystals on the massive chandelier. The serene atmosphere provided a very relaxing environment. Draon could easily take a nap in here, except the topic was going to be Natalie. She never induced a sleeping mood. It was the exact opposite. He waited.

"Mr. Xanders agreed to teach today, but at the last minute, something came up, and he had to cancel. It worked out, as it was an excellent opportunity for me to meet each mage and put a name to a face. I will say one mage stood out from the others. Natalie. She's unique. Incredibly unique. I've never met another mage like her."

"Unique is an understatement."

"True. It seems inadequate to describe her," Angus said before continuing with what he really wanted to say.

"You know, I have the ability to read people and their powers. It's my expertise. Without bragging, I have successfully read over a hundred mages. All were successful except for one wizard. Today, I had the rare experience of another failure. I tried to read Natalie, but it was impossible to get a reading. Instead, I came away with a horrific headache."

"She is too powerful for you to read," Draon replied, watching Angus with his self-inflated ego.

"Hence the headache."

"I had the same reading issue when testing Natalie with the oracular stone, except sparks burst out and zapped all of us." Draon repositioned himself as he tried to relax, but he felt uncomfortable.

He did not like talking with Angus about Natalie. It had nothing to do with sharing secrets, so why did he feel like he was talking about her behind her back? Something was off. Suddenly, he realized why he was uncomfortable. Angus did not ask permission or tell Natalie he was reading her; he was deceitful about it.

"She has a temper," Angus announced. He began to tap a pencil on the top of his desk. Draon tried to block the annoying sound.

"She has acknowledged she struggles to control her temper, especially when she believes someone is attacking her character," Draon said, knowing Angus must have done some things to anger Natalie. The pencil tapping increased his annoyance with him.

"Do you know wind swirls around her when she's mad? She tried to control it today, but I could see it. It's what made me want to focus on her." The pencil tapping continued.

"Yes, it has its good and bad points. When she sees it, she knows she needs to calm down. The bad point is it draws attention to her." Draon wondered if Angus was annoying him on purpose with the pencil tapping.

"She seems easily sidetracked."

Draon frowned. He did not like the negative direction of this conversation. However, it no longer mattered. Whatever his motive, Angus could find someone else to play his game. He detested mind games. Game over.

74

"What is the reason I am here, Angus?" The tone was cool.

"Natalie. I want to get to know her better. Understand her powers. Understand why she is so powerful."

"I cannot help you there," Draon said, now his tone was cold.

"You can't, or you won't?" The pencil tapping stopped.

"Natalie is my student. My focus is on training her. I made that promise to her mother and intend to keep it. I will not be distracted from her training and what needs to happen to defeat the Janus Club." Draon sat forward in his chair. He was ready to leave.

"I probably didn't say what I meant in the best possible way. I apologize. I've never met someone as powerful as Natalie except for you. I want to get to know her better." Angus tried to sound sincere, but Draon did not believe it.

"Natalie will be here for her classes. Her focus will be on that training. Even though she has an apartment at the Barracks, she prefers being home. I am not sure there is time here for you to meet with her." Draon kept his tone cold.

His black eyes bored into Angus Thornton. Power. Control. Those things popped into Draon's mind. If he wanted, he could read Angus. He was also an expert, but would not do that to someone without their knowledge. He did not play games.

"I apologize again, Draon," Angus said, trying to regain solid footing with him.

"You should not have tried to read Natalie without her permission. I hope that is not the normal way you get readings on mages. Frankly, I do not understand why you needed to read a hundred mages. You are not a teacher or a mentor trying to understand how best to train your students.

In fact, from what you said earlier, it sounds like you tried to read me." Draon felt his irritation with Angus explode. Anger lit his eyes as he stared hard at Angus. A breeze started to swirl around him.

"I was curious about you," Angus said apologetically. "I knew you would never give me permission."

"That is not a valid excuse!" Draon shot back while silently fuming that Angus did not respect boundaries.

Right there, Draon decided Natalie needed to stay away from him. He would train her at the old homestead. Saturday classes at the Barracks with the other mages would be enough for now. He cooled down, thinking of Natalie and what her dramatic description of Angus would be. Draon stood up.

Angus stood up. "Draon, I know there isn't anything I can do now to make amends for some of my poor choices, but I hope you'll give me a chance. I also hope that there's a chance to work with Natalie. I can help her with controlling her emotions."

"I will let her know," Draon coolly responded.

Chapter 6

Exceptionally Ridiculous

Natalie burst through the open basement door and stomped to the staircase leading up to the fairies' and pixies' rooms. She wanted to scream at them to get down here, but she needed to keep her cool. Movement caught her attention. Looking to the right, she saw Lorcan sitting at the small kitchen table. She marched over and into the kitchen.

Standing over Lorcan, she tried to keep her temper in check and her tone even. "Did you have anything to do with the pictures on display at the Barracks today?"

Lorcan looked up from his book in surprise. "What?"

"The pictures of us saturated in spider dust and body parts. Did you have anything to do with those humongous pictures displayed in the classroom today?" Natalie felt her cheeks burn red. She told herself to hold it together as the wind whipped around her.

"Seriously, the pictures were in the Barracks?" Lorcan raised his eyebrows in surprise.

"No one could miss the enlarged pictures plastered all over the blackboard behind the teacher's desk. Do you think those are the only pictures? I bet not!"

"Wow! What did Mr. Xanders say about the pictures?"

"He wasn't there."

"He wasn't?"

"No. It sounds like you had nothing to do with it, so how did the fairies get those pictures to the Barracks?"

"Let's ask the fairies," Lorcan calmly replied, getting up from his chair and pretending he didn't see the wind swirling around Natalie.

He went first as they headed up the staircase. When they reached the fairies' room, they found the door locked. That had never happened before. Lorcan stared down at the lock and yelled, "*REPERIO!*" The lock clicked. He turned the knob and swung the door wide open.

Lorcan and Natalie peered into the quiet room. Usually bustling with chattering, babbling fairies, it was so quiet a pin could have dropped, and they would have heard it. As quiet as it was, they easily spotted each guilty fairy. Every bed had a small mound completely covered in many colorful blankets. Twelve little beds; twelve covered fairies.

"Sooty Boots Kalina, Rosie Poppertop, Stormy Iris, Lavender Moonflower, Cherrytoes Rose, and the rest of you, pay attention. I can pull the covers off, or you can come out here and talk with me now," Lorcan said.

Pulling back their bed covers, one after another, the fairies sat up and sheepishly looked at Lorcan. They avoided looking at Natalie.

On the other hand, Natalie glared at each of those traitors. *How could they do that to me?* She glanced around the room, expecting the pictures to be on their walls. There weren't any, but the lack of pictures didn't soften her mood.

"Which one of you would like to tell us what happened with the pictures?" Lorcan asked, glancing from one fairy to another.

All at once, the room filled with high-pitched gibberish chatter. Too loud, too shrill, and too much nonsense, Natalie stuck her fingers in her ears. Meanwhile, Lorcan listened to every word and nodded his head up and down in agreement.

Periwinkle Blue Star jumped up and started bouncing on her bed as she chattered about the pictures. Lacey Gilly Flower joined her. Soon, they were all jumping up and down on their beds.

"ENOUGH!" Lorcan yelled. They stopped. Wide-eyed, they stood still and watched him turn to Natalie.

"It seems they used the mentors' mirrors, which are strictly forbidden to them, to contact the fairies and pixies of the other mentors. They shared the pictures with them. Oxley saw the pictures. Having a sweet tooth, he stopped at the Flaky Kuchen on Saturday. He showed the pictures to Candace, the owner. She offered him two silver dollars' worth of pastries if she could keep them."

"Did you learn your lesson?" Natalie blurted out, furious with them. "If you hadn't broken the rules and used the mentors' mirrors, none of this would have happened. It's embarrassing what you did. Now we're going to be laughed at for weeks. I'm outraged with all of you!"

They stood dejectedly with their shoulders slumped and their heads down. Natalie turned and stormed out.

Yanking open the front door, she screamed in anger. Stomping down the old homestead's wooden steps into the front yard, she stood near the three-headed tree stump, raised her hands toward the sky, and shrieked again. A colorful beam shot from her hands and soared into the sky. Fireworks exploded, with booms echoing throughout the neighborhood. Having released her frustration, she walked back inside the homestead to wait for Lorcan.

She sat at the kitchen table until her throat, hoarse from screaming, begged for a drink. She opened the refrigerator to see if there were any drinks. Five pitchers of different-flavored fairy punch were on the top shelf. She saw a pitcher that held an orange punch in the sink. Seeing that as a good sign, she took the last orange pitcher from the refrigerator and filled a glass.

She sat at the kitchen table sipping the punch when Lorcan entered the room.

"They thought the mentors would be the only ones seeing the pictures," Lorcan said, grabbing a glass and filling it with punch.

"Well, that didn't happen, so it added to the outrageously crummy day." Natalie frowned, recalling Angus Thornton's rude behavior.

"Is that the reason for the fireworks?" Lorcan sat down.

"A good portion of it. I would have imploded if I didn't release my anger and frustration. Have you met Angus Thornton?"

"Yes, why?"

"Angus Thornton was our teacher today. He drips arrogance and drools insults. He's annoyingly annoying. I nicknamed him the Master Annoying Twaddler."

"Seriously, you didn't," Lorcan said, trying not to laugh.

"I did, but you're the only one who knows."

"He is very pompous. I think it's because he's only had that job or title for a few months, and it has gone to his head. Give him time; he may do better. However, he may not, so keep your guard up."

"Well, that's some wishy-washy advice," Natalie laughed, feeling better.

"True, I win whichever way it turns out," Lorcan agreed, glad Natalie was in a better mood.

"Since you have free time this afternoon, I want us to work on calming techniques today. It isn't good for you to get angry so often or to let people get under your skin."

"I would appreciate that, especially with what happened today."

"We could do it anywhere in the house because the fairies will hide for the rest of the day. They don't like to see you angry at them. However, we'll use your favorite room, the gem room."

"It is the most soothing room in the house…at least for me," Natalie said as they approached it.

Lorcan conjured up big, soft, and comfortable bean bag chairs in pale blue. They sank into them; it was cozy. She relaxed, settled, and yawned. Lorcan started the meditation lesson. She concentrated on her breathing and cleared her mind. Before she knew it, she was sound asleep.

Natalie's eyes fluttered open to sitting in a cool, dark room. Groggy, it took a few minutes for her to recall the bean bag chair meditation lesson in the gem room. Epic failure, as she didn't last five minutes before she fell asleep. It didn't matter because she felt great.

Natalie wanted to get up, but something sat on her. Reaching into her pocket, she pulled out her phone. She tapped for light and focused the light on her lap. Sunshine Lily, curled up with her tiny yellow blanket, soundly slept.

Natalie watched her sleep for several minutes. She couldn't stay mad at someone so cute. She gently brushed long blonde hair from her face.

With a wide yawn, Sunshine Lily stretched out as far as she could and then looked up. Natalie smiled. Sunshine Lily stretched again and then sat up. With a snap of her fingers, the lights came on. The sudden bright light had both of them shut their eyes.

"Whoa, Sunshine Lily, that is way too rough on the eyes," Natalie said while keeping her eyes closed.

Sunshine Lily giggled and placed a small picture in Natalie's hands. She opened her eyes, looked at the picture, and laughed.

"We look exceptionally ridiculous." Natalie stared at the group photo. Sunshine Lily nodded in agreement.

"However, while it's hilarious between us, it isn't funny outside of the old homestead. We laugh because it's funny. Those on the outside spread the picture around to laugh at us. There is an enormous difference. I know you didn't think it would be a disaster, but it did become one. Believe me, I know all about things turning into disasters. Lesson learned?"

Shaking her head yes, Sunshine Lily stood up, grabbed her blanket, and flew to the door. Natalie ungracefully got herself out of the bean bag chair. Yawning while stretching her arms behind her back, she finished waking up. She headed out to lock up the chickens, shower, and go to bed. Tomorrow was a school day. Besides classes, she would need to learn more about the Janus Club to figure out how to sabotage it.

Chapter 7

Wands Have Changed

"Science," Natalie muttered while doodling inside her notebook, "blah, blah, blah."

Mr. Parrish's booming voice filled the room as he stood before his desk and read what he considered the tenth excellent student paper on the Super Blue Blood Moon. Natalie wasn't sure how many ways you could say the same thing, but she figured the teacher had another eighteen excellent papers to read. That would be the entire class, minus her and Connor. She didn't do the extra credit because she stayed busy living the Super Blue Blood Moon experience.

"I won't read anymore, but a fantastic job for those who turned in the extra credit assignment," Mr. Parrish said as he beamed his approval.

Natalie released an enormous sigh of relief while the rest of the class moaned in disappointment. She knew they weren't paying attention; they wanted to stall the short lecture that preceded the homework assignment.

Gathering all the graded assignments from his desk, the teacher started walking around the classroom, distributing them to the students. When Mr. Parrish reached Natalie's desk, he stopped. Natalie looked up and then down. She could feel her bracelet flashing under her shirt sleeve. Puzzled, she looked around. She saw nothing that would make the bracelet flash.

"Not that you need the extra points, but it's unlike you not to turn in an extra credit assignment. What happened?"

"I blacked out," Natalie said, with a half-smile that disappeared when she saw the hand holding the papers had a Janus Club ring.

"Really!" the teacher exclaimed. Natalie stopped staring at the ring and looked up at the teacher. He appeared to think she was being sarcastic, so he stood there waiting for a more believable answer.

"Honestly, I wasn't feeling like myself that night, but I'm sure I'm not the only one who didn't turn in the extra credit assignment."

"If you're thinking of Connor, you would be wrong. He submitted a paper. It took a little effort to decipher Red Hot Mama as the lunar eclipse part of the assignment, but I'm getting better at decoding his work."

Natalie sat there, surprised and speechless. The teacher moved on, handing out completed assignments.

She turned and looked over at Connor. As usual, he was writing in his notebook. She watched him write, cross out, write some more, and draw lines, moving things around. Natalie smiled. That guy was oblivious to the world around him. Still, he managed to turn in the assignment.

Turning back, she glimpsed Lainey frowning at her graded assignment. She didn't understand why, as she knew Lainey had an A. It had to be something else. Could it be that erasing her memory of magic had her feelings off? What about Pru avoiding her so she wouldn't accidentally expose magic to her? Lainey had to be wondering why Pru didn't want her visiting anymore. They had been so close.

Mr. Parrish returned to the front of the class and started discussing their new assignment. Natalie opened her science book and went to the current chapter. She pretended to follow along with the teacher's lecture, but she couldn't focus. The despair on Lainey's face tore at her. Lainey lost her cherished aunt because of magic. *Is there anything I can do to help?*

Natalie hoped so, but focusing on Lainey's dilemma was impossible with the loud, never-ending monotone lecture. She couldn't concentrate. Frustration increased as she struggled to come up with options. She glared at the teacher. *Is he intentionally boring us to death? Why can't he do his normal method of giving the highlights, writing the homework assignment on the blackboard, and giving us time to start the assignment in class?* This new style annoyed her. *Seriously, we can figure it out as we always do. Please...Stop...Already.*

Mr. Parrish didn't stop. He hardly took time to catch his breath as he rambled on until a few minutes before the bell rang. Finally, it ended. There was a longed-for silence.

As everyone packed up, Mr. Parrish made a surprise announcement. "Teachers received an early invitation to join the Janus Club. I joined this morning."

He held up his hand, showing off his Janus Club ring before continuing. "I'm excited to announce that the Janus Club plans to construct a new building as a training and work center. Construction will begin once the school board and the county approve the plans. It should be ready for the next school year. Exciting times! I'm looking forward to seeing each of you at the Janus Club meeting on Wednesday after school."

Natalie felt uncomfortable. Something about his look and how he said it made it seem mandatory for them to join the club. What happens when he discovers someone didn't join? She didn't want to think about it. The bell rang. She jumped up and got out of there.

During lunch break, instead of sitting outside the auditorium reading, Natalie walked towards the doors to see if preparations were underway for the Wednesday Janus

Club meeting. She thought she would peek inside the building, but she didn't get anywhere near the place. Two athletic male students in letterman jackets stood outside the darkened double doors. Their stance made it obvious they were security. They coldly locked their eyes on her. Her heart hammered in her chest; she could feel sweat beading on her forehead. Trying to look calm, she strolled past them and headed towards the portables at the back of the school. They watched her until she turned.

In the next class, Natalie sat there wondering how they would sabotage the meeting. They couldn't get near the auditorium to place anything. To get inside, they would need to attend a meeting. She wouldn't do that, as going in might mean not getting out of there until she wore one of those rings. She puzzled over what they could do as Odi was useless at stopping the club, and they needed something that wasn't a disaster.

Natalie didn't pay attention in any of her classes. She focused on finding a way to stop the Janus Club from meeting on Wednesday. How could they do that if they hadn't learned any spells? She knew she was the only one who had tapped into her elemental powers, but she didn't have control. It was either a disaster or nothing. So annoying.

School ended in frustration. There were no answers. Natalie hopped on the school bus and completed all of her homework assignments before getting dropped off at the front of her subdivision. Leaving her bookbag at the back door, she headed for the old homestead. She hoped Lorcan would have some suggestions.

To her surprise, Draon waited to see her. "Draon, it's Monday. We don't have training until Tuesday."

"True, no training today. I would like to speak with you and Lorcan."

"Did something happen?"

"No. We will meet in the kitchen."

The tiny square table normally had two chairs, but adding a third made it crowded. Natalie sat rigidly. Uncomfortable sitting close to the others, she looked down instead of at Lorcan or Draon.

"Natalie, Angus Thornton instructed your class yesterday. What do you think of him?"

"How many ways can I say annoying and arrogant? If it's endless, that describes him." She pushed her chair back to a more comfortable distance from Lorcan and Draon.

Draon half-smiled. "He has offered to help train you in emotional control."

Natalie looked over at Draon and laughed. "I think the Master Annoying Twaddler needs to work on his own emotions."

"What!" Draon's eyebrows shot up at Natalie's comment. "What did you call Angus?"

"Master Annoying Twaddler," Natalie replied in all seriousness. "I put his initials to good use."

"That is disrespectful," Draon firmly stated, trying hard to keep a stern face and not laugh.

"Seriously," Natalie shot back, "to get respect, you give respect. Angus Thornton wasn't respectful at any point during our class. He not only behaved like a Grand Poobah, but something occurred in class that made me feel strange. I know he caused it, as that feeling disappeared when he turned around. In my book, he's earned his title and my intention of having nothing to do with him."

"I agree. You should avoid him for now. I have decided your elemental training classes will be here. Your Saturday class will still be at the Barracks."

"Fine by me, except I need to go to the Barracks. I promised Coal a week's worth of treats from the pet store."

"I will get the treats for him this afternoon so that you will have them for tomorrow."

"Thanks."

"Now that we have that decided, is there anything else to discuss?" Draon looked from Natalie to Lorcan.

"I have a few things. First thing, the auditorium has guards. We can't get in there to place anything that would disrupt the meeting. Not that we have learned anything useful so far to disrupt it. Odi was cute, but learning to take on extra powers isn't especially useful at the moment. The others haven't tapped into their powers, and the last thing I need to do is increase mine."

"Stop," Lorcan interjected before Natalie kept going. "Your lesson was on Odi?"

"Yes."

"Draon, did you know this? Was Chris going to instruct them on Odi, or was this something Angus dreamed up?"

"Not sure. Who provided the demonstration?"

"Connor, because he complained too much about the smell."

"He would," Lorcan groaned. "Connor always has a comment about Hexel. Little does he know Hexel has very keen hearing."

"Yikes, I wouldn't want to get on her bad side."

"None of us do," Draon said.

"By the way, Connor failed. Worse, he told the teacher I had already done it, so I could show them how it was done. I already felt picked on, and then Connor let that slip out."

"That kid doesn't have a filter. He says whatever pops into his mind," Lorcan complained, shaking his head.

Draon ignored Lorcan's comment even though he agreed with it. "Anything else?"

"Yes, one of my teachers said there's a new building in the works for the Janus Club. We must find a way to get into the meetings without joining the club."

"Not even the first meeting, and they're already planning on building a new place. Wow! They seem 100 percent sure it will be successful," Lorcan said in amazement.

"They are. I wonder if there would be a way to get Lainey into the club, working for us. She seems so unhappy. It's like she knows something has changed, but she doesn't know what. It's not fair to keep Pru away from her."

"I am not sure, Natalie," Draon said. "We do not know what this club is about and how much control it will have over anyone who joins."

"It has to be the ring."

"What do you mean?"

"Every person gets a ring. It's a keeper even if they drop out of the club at the end of the school year. Mr. Parrish had one on today. When he got close to me, my bracelet started glittering."

"We need to get our hands on one of the rings. Can you do it?" Lorcan asked.

"Without magic, I don't know. It's too bad we can't send Hexel in there. The club would be over before it even began," Natalie said.

"True, but the entire world would also know that magic is real," Lorcan said.

"Bummer." Natalie couldn't think of a way to get a Janus Club ring.

"Speaking of rings," Draon said as he dug into a pocket inside his cloak, "I have something for you."

Draon pulled out a silver ring with tiny gemstones on top of the barrel and handed it to Natalie.

"Is this what the elves made?" Natalie asked, admiring it.

"Yes. Since you are a Shadowlink, there is a crystal for each element on the top of the barrel. Green crystals are inside the barrel."

Natalie slipped it on her left hand. A perfect fit. She felt a connection to it.

"Lorcan will train you on how to use it. Never take it off."

"Wow, wands have changed a lot since the old days." Natalie held her hand up and studied the ring.

"They needed to change so they do not call attention to the mage," Draon said.

"There's going to be five of us in school with this unique ring, so isn't that going to call attention to the ring?"

"Someone in the Barracks has a connection with a big retailer. The rings are already in their stores. Of course, those rings are fake, but they give you cover," Lorcan said.

"Awesome. I hope the elves didn't curse my ring since I got them in trouble."

"They got themselves in trouble. Even so, they would not dare," Draon said, getting up. "I need to get back to Stormfield, but I will return for tomorrow's training."

"Wait up, I want to ask you something," Natalie said as Draon walked out of the kitchen. He slowed his pace.

Natalie caught up. "Do you think my not coming and going with the rest of the group will make me an outsider?"

"Why would you think that?"

"Because I won't be spending any time with them except for a few minutes as they come and go from the Barracks. I'll only be with them on Saturdays."

"Take the ride in the afternoon. Just do not go into the Barracks. Do not worry; it is only a matter of time before this resolves itself."

"Okay," Natalie said, hoping that was true. "By the way, do you want to know your nickname?"

The look on Draon's face was priceless. "I hesitate to know."

"Oh, don't be silly," Natalie said, which received another priceless expression from Draon. She laughed.

"Archimage wizard. There's no way Angus Thornton comes close to measuring up to you."

Caught off guard, Draon stood looking down at a smiling Natalie.

"It's a good thing." Natalie turned and headed back towards the kitchen.

She quietly entered the kitchen and stopped a short distance from Lorcan. She wasn't sure if she should interrupt him. Even at this distance, she could see the severe frown on his face. She moved closer and waited. He still didn't notice her, so she moved beside him, but he didn't look up.

"Excuse me, Lorcan. Can I ask you something?"

Lorcan looked surprised at seeing Natalie standing near him. "Of course."

"This is way off-topic, but when you were in the coma, and I was at school, I wanted a way to get word from you that you were awake. Since that time, there have been a few times when I would have liked a connection to you. Since you won't use a phone, is there any way for you to contact me without it being obvious?"

"Yes, there is a way for limited contact. You would know I tried to reach you, but that's all you would know. That might make you more concerned than providing you with peace."

"Can I reverse it if it ends up causing too much stress?"

"Yes, and no. It can deactivate, but it will remain."

Pulling out a piece of his long, white hair, he carefully wrapped it around his hand before handing it to Natalie.

She looked down in confusion. "What do I do with your hair?"

"Go to Daisy's Bodacious Nails. Ask for Daisy. She's the only one who can do the intricate artwork and spell to get what you want."

"What do I want?" Natalie asked in a puzzled tone.

"You want a cat claw painted on your right-hand index fingernail. It'll be clear, which means it's invisible unless I contact you. When I contact you, you will feel your fingernail get hot as the invisible cat claw turns white. It'll last under ten seconds unless I repeat it."

"How will I know how serious it is?"

"When I'm contacting you for no special reason, it will be once. The more times it happens, the more urgent you get to me."

"I think this will be good unless you keep contacting me, and I'm stuck where I can't help. That would be a gigantic living nightmare."

"It would be rare. I can summon help from Draon, the fairies, Wilfred, Jonathan, and others."

"Good. I guess what I'm really looking for is you letting me know you're okay."

"I'm ancient. You're the one with the out-of-control powers, always causing problems."

"True. Maybe you should wear the nail polish," Natalie said, laughing.

For some reason, she visualized Lorcan with brown nail polish to match his shoes. She stopped laughing when she saw Lorcan's expression. He didn't appear to appreciate the comment.

"My golden treasures are enough, thank you."

"Speaking of nail polish," Natalie pretended not to notice Lorcan was offended by her last comment, "my fingernails grow, so wouldn't this grow out?"

"No, it's permanent. It's a spell with potion ingredients; it's not your regular nail polish."

"How do you know this can be done?"

"Easy. I've visited every shopkeeper. I've also read all the books on the history of the Barracks in the public area of the library. I haven't been in the restricted area, but I have had some interesting conversations with Ash, the guardian. You should start visiting the library."

"That'll have to wait until Angus Thornton is gone." Natalie frowned, and her lips pursed in an expression of dislike.

"You shouldn't be quick to judge."

"Draon doesn't appear to care for him, either."

"Draon isn't used to anyone being in authority except for him. He also isn't used to someone flaunting their authority. However, I'm not questioning why Draon has decided to train you here. He has his reasons. All I'm saying concerning you is that first impressions aren't always reliable."

"Well, it will be a surprise if Angus Thornton changes. That guy is full of himself."

Chapter 8

Hexel at the Gatehouse

Natalie couldn't believe how fast the Tuesday elemental training arrived, but there they were, waiting to board the cart headed for the bookstore. Fully loaded with the six mages, the cart rumbled along the tracks. They were used to the sounds it made, the shadows on the walls produced by the red dragon fire crystals in the dusty air, and the unique smell of the tunnel.

Climbing the stairs, they entered the bookstore, where they went to the back and opened an enchanted door. They headed down into the ancient cobblestone tunnel that took them to the Barracks. This never got old. Each time they made their way through the system, they raved at their extraordinary good fortune of being mages.

Connor lifted the heavy black metal handle of the large wooden door that brought them into the Barracks. As he pushed open the door, he stated the usual warning. "Everyone, take a big gulp of air and hold it."

Five mages with puffed-out cheeks held their breath as they walked past Hexel, floating inches above the ground at the gatehouse. She ignored them. Natalie stood near the Barracks door. As the other mages put distance between them and Hexel, they exhaled and took in big gulps of fresh air. Laughter filled the air until they parted ways and headed in different directions for their elemental training classes.

Hexel's ragged black garment swirled around her as she floated towards Natalie. Stunned, she didn't have time to retreat or take a deep breath and hold it. Hexel continued advancing towards her. Natalie took a step back and bumped up to the door. The smell overwhelmed her, but she was too afraid to notice. She had never been this close to her...not even on the first day.

Hexel slowly raised her right arm up. As she did, the black ragged sleeve fell back, exposing a bony black hand with long, bony fingers and even longer iridescent fingernails. The eyes hidden behind layers of black fabric seemed to stare directly into Natalie as her right index finger moved closer to the center of her forehead. Electricity began crackling from the tip of Hexel's shimmering fingernail. Petrified, Natalie squeezed her eyes shut just before Hexel's energy made contact. Purple, indigo, blue, green, yellow, orange, and red colors exploded behind her eyelids. Natalie crashed to the ground.

Dazed, she half opened her eyes to Angus Thornton kneeling beside her. She groaned. *What did he do to me? Where am I? Why am I on the ground? My head hurts. Seriously hurts.* She closed her eyes.

"Natalie!" Angus Thornton called in a frantic voice. He shook her by the shoulder.

From somewhere deep in her mind, Natalie heard someone yell her name. She struggled to wake up and open her eyes. Through slits, she focused on Angus Thornton and groaned again. The very last person in the entire world she wanted to see. She weakly pushed him to go away as she tried to sit up. She fell back and passed out.

Angus caught her just before her head hit the ground. Gently lowering her back down, he let her rest for a few minutes before he called her name. "Natalie!" No response.

He called her name louder and shook her shoulder. "Natalie!"

She gasped and opened her eyes.

She tried again to sit up. This time, she allowed Angus Thornton to help her get into a sitting position. As much as she disliked his help, she wasn't strong enough to support herself. He held her by the shoulders. She rubbed her forehead and temples, trying to calm the massive headache. It didn't help.

"Natalie, what happened?"

Natalie recalled colors flashing inside her head before she answered, "I don't know, but I think I'm going to be sick."

She tried to stay still to get rid of that queasy feeling. Taking shallow breaths, she kept hoping she would feel better.

Finally, the queasy feeling subsided, but the pounding headache did not. She couldn't concentrate. All she could recall was that one minute she was getting ready to go back to the homestead for a lesson, and the next, she saw vivid colors before blacking out.

Angus Thornton continued to hold Natalie by her shoulders to support her while she sat up. She appreciated that he wasn't asking her a lot of questions. She wanted Draon. He would know what to do. She glanced up, looking for him. Surprised, she noticed Hexel floating in front of a large gathering of mages for the first time. She seemed to be keeping them back.

"Natalie!" came the alarmed scream. Natalie looked in the direction where her name had been yelled. At first, she couldn't see who had screamed her name; then, she saw Pru frantically pushing people apart to get to her. Pru stopped at Hexel. Hexel faced Natalie.

"Hexel," Pru demanded, "let me through!"

Hexel turned and faced Pru. For a few tense minutes, Hexel, shrouded in black rags, floated inches from her. Pru knew better than to challenge her, so she whispered, "Please, Hexel."

Hexel moved slightly to the left to let her through. Pru passed, and Hexel returned to her position.

"Are you all right?" Pru asked, leaning down.

"I feel like a Mack truck hit me," Natalie said, embarrassed that she still needed Angus Thornton's help.

"What happened? Did you hit your head?" Pru noticed a red circle on Natalie's forehead. She glanced around. She didn't see anything on the ground that would make that kind of mark on Natalie's forehead.

"I'm not sure what happened. One minute, I turned to leave, and the next minute, I blacked out. Now I'm ready to barf with a side order of a massive headache."

"Does the Barracks have a doctor?" Pru asked the master wizard.

Before Angus Thornton could answer, Natalie said, "I don't want a doctor. I need to get to the homestead. Draon will know what to do."

"We have people and potions here that can help you right now."

"No, thank you." Natalie gave Pru a look that said she wanted out of there.

Uncertain if it was a good idea, Pru hesitated before leaning closer and holding her right hand out. Natalie grabbed her hand and ungracefully got herself up.

"I don't think this is a good idea," Angus Thornton said with concern as he stood up.

"It's what I want," Natalie replied, hoping that would end it.

Besides, glancing at Hexel, it didn't look like she would let anyone else through. She would thank Hexel later when her headache, pounding to the rhythm of her heartbeat, ended.

"Let me help you get to Draon," Angus Thornton said, more as a statement than an offer.

"I appreciate what you've already done, but I can get there with Pru's help."

"Are you sure?" Angus Thornton asked.

"I'm sure," Natalie said, trying to stand tall and not give him a reason to help her.

Reluctantly, the master wizard held the door open as Pru guided Natalie into the tunnel. The door slammed shut.

With a throbbing headache, Natalie hobbled along. Halfway through, she stopped and leaned against the damp wall. With eyes closed and head pounding, she tried to calm her labored breathing. A soft moan escaped her lips.

Pru didn't like what she saw. "Natalie, do you want me to get help?"

Natalie responded with a weak "no."

Pru moved inches from her, studying her without saying a word.

She felt Pru observing her and felt bad for putting her in a horrible predicament: stay or get help. She hoped Pru would stay as she didn't want to be left alone. She wanted to be safely in bed at home. With significant effort, she pushed off the wall and began to inch toward the bookstore.

"I'm sorry, Pru," Natalie whispered, head down and dragging one foot in front of the other.

"I'm sorry this happened to you," Pru said, tears streaming down her face.

Natalie didn't say anything as she focused on moving forward. On and on, she stumbled along the dimly lit path. The closer they got to the bookstore, the slower the pace. After what felt like an eternity, they made it.

"Natalie, stand here while I go get help." Pru helped Natalie lean against the wall before hurrying away in search of Wilfred or Jonathan.

With her wobbly legs, Natalie strained to stay leaning against the wall. Her headache pounded in time with her rapid heartbeats. With each second, her legs shook more violently. She no longer had the energy to stand. As if in slow motion, she watched herself crumple toward the ground with no strength to break the fall.

"Help," she weakly whispered.

Two powerful hands stretched out and grabbed her within inches of hitting the ground. Half dazed, Natalie felt like a rag doll being lifted and placed against the wall. Her legs shook, providing no support. The weight of her whole being rested in the hands supporting her.

"Don't open your eyes. Rest. I'll stay with you until help comes."

Natalie wanted to open her eyes to see who was helping her. She didn't recognize the voice or his peculiar smell, but she needed his help. She did as she was told. With her pounding headache, time seemed to drag until they heard approaching footsteps. He released her and vanished.

"It's as bad as you said," Wilfred exclaimed, rushing over to Natalie. "Let me help you to a chair."

"No sitting. I need to keep moving."

"But you look dreadful," Wilfred cried.

"With your help, I can make it on the cart to the homestead. Draon is waiting there to train me. He'll know what to do."

"I'll call Draon," Wilfred said, already pulling his phone out of his pocket.

"He's not the greatest with his phone. It probably doesn't even ring. Seriously, I'll get there. The headache is subsiding." Natalie said it, but it wasn't true.

"You sure?"

"I'm sure." Natalie glanced over at Pru, "Thank you, Pru. Do you want to return to your lesson?"

"No, I'm staying with you until you see Draon or Lorcan. Anyway, I'm not brave enough to go into the tunnel by myself."

"I can take you after Natalie's on the cart."

99

"Thanks, but no. Natalie's in no shape to climb the basement steps by herself."

Wilfred walked in front of Natalie, and Pru walked behind her into the bookstore and down the stairs. Natalie appreciated that no one talked, but the clomping of three sets of feet down wooden steps didn't help her headache. Each step pained her. Finally, they were at the cart, where Wilfred and Pru worked together to help her get into it.

The cart chugged along the tracks. It was so much more comfortable with only two of them riding in it. Curled up in the seat, Natalie closed her eyes and tried to relax. It was impossible with the pounding headache and the legs that wouldn't stop shaking. At least her stomach had settled.

Docking, Pru stepped out of the cart, through the enchanted door, and up the stairs. Natalie pushed through the charmed door as Draon and Lorcan came to her. Alarmed, they both asked, "What happened?"

"Fireworks! All these colors exploded in my head, and then I crashed. That's all I remember."

Lorcan anxiously looked at Natalie. "Are you sure that's all you remember?"

"Yes, except for waking up to Angus Thornton kneeling over me. The absolute last person I ever wanted to see. That was enough to make me want to pass out again."

"Not funny," Pru chided Natalie.

"Sorry. In truth, he was an immense help." Natalie shuffled towards the stairs. If her head hadn't hurt so much, she would have felt special with all these guardians.

Standing in front of the stairs and peering up, Natalie wondered how she would make the climb. Her legs would not support her, even with Draon by her side. Lorcan must have read her mind. He stepped around the corner and opened the closet under the stairs. He returned with an old push broom.

Natalie eyed the broom. "Interesting thought, Lorcan. However, my legs are close to being gelatin."

"Not to worry," Lorcan said as he rested the broom against the railing. With a flick of his wand, the push broom had a larger base, a thicker handle, and a piece of wood up near the top for handlebars. It also had a center strap to secure her in place.

Draon and Lorcan helped Natalie step onto the push broom and then fastened her to it. Draon started climbing the steps while Lorcan flicked his wand. Natalie held on as the broom floated up the stairs behind Draon. Lorcan and Pru followed behind. Draon opened the door, and Natalie glided inside the homestead.

"I think it would be best to head home," Natalie announced while unbuckling the strap and stepping off the broom.

"No way!" Lorcan exclaimed. He gripped her arm.

"Well, the only room with a couch is the feather collection room. The gaudy, outrageously ugly colors on the couch will only increase my headache to the point that my head will explode. I can't take it on a normal day. Today isn't normal."

"For you, the furniture will be a boring chocolate brown today."

"Thanks, Lorcan."

"It only remains until you're well."

"I think this is going to be a permanent condition."

"Sarcasm gets you nowhere," Lorcan said as he held her arm, and Draon took the other arm to help Natalie get to the couch.

She lay down on the firm couch, resting her head on a soft pillow. Then, she wrapped herself in a plush blanket.

Draon, Lorcan, and Pru quietly watched her for several minutes before they stepped near the door. Still, in the room, they kept their voices low, hoping she would fall asleep while they whispered.

"Anything we can give her?" Lorcan asked.

"We can't do anything until we have a clue what happened. Pru, it seems to have happened right after your group entered the Barracks. Did you see anything?"

"No, I had entered my classroom when the teacher said there had been an accident at the entrance. We immediately left and headed to the front."

"It's amazing no one saw anything," Lorcan said.

"Lorcan, it happened inside the Barracks' door. There is no way Hexel missed what happened."

"You know as well as I do, Draon, that's as good as not knowing. Hexel provides security and delivers punishment. Communication is one-sided with her."

"Then we might never have the answer," Draon said.

They were quiet for a couple of minutes until Pru volunteered her thoughts on Hexel. "Hexel was keeping everyone back except for Angus Thornton. When I got there, I pushed through the crowd and demanded that Hexel let me through. At first, she didn't move, but then she drifted over enough to let me get to Natalie. She didn't let anyone else through. I sensed she protected Natalie."

"Interesting," Draon said, even though he did not know what it meant.

Natalie tuned them out, closed her eyes, and cleared her mind. Taking a deep breath and slowly letting it out, she tried to relax. The headache made that impossible, but she continued to try to calm down and rest. Maybe instead of clearing her mind, she should do the build-a-story sleep game. No, her head hurt too much to make that effort.

Still taking deep breaths and slowly letting them out, the colors appeared in her mind in the same order as when they had originally happened. They weren't just the elemental colors of blue, green, white, and red. She saw purple, indigo, blue, green, yellow, orange, and red over and over. She watched them appear and fade out in a continuous loop. With each loop, they seemed to get lighter. The cycle repeated until they were gone. The headache diminished; she fell asleep.

Golden yellow moonlight streamed through the window, providing soft light from the surrounding darkness. Like fireflies, drifting dust particles flickered on and off in the half-light. Lavender scent gave the feeling of being in an endless field of flowers. Calm and healing were present in the large amethyst gems spread across the fireplace mantle. Warmth and comfort were the finishing magical touches provided by the soft pillow and plush blanket.

Natalie rolled to her side, but she didn't open her eyes. *Don't spoil this perfect feeling. I'm going to enjoy this one shot where everything aligns to perfection.* Taking deep breaths and slowly letting them out, she kept her mind clear and lingered over this amazing feeling.

"How are you feeling?"

Natalie knew the voice. Puzzled, she wondered when she had returned home. "Dad?"

"Yes. Are you feeling better?"

"Where am I?"

"In the old homestead."

"Am I dreaming? Are you really in the old homestead?"

"No dream. You were too ill to move to the house." Karl got up from his chair and sat on the edge of the couch. He brushed his daughter's hair off her face.

Natalie stayed quiet for a few minutes until she whispered, "Wow."

"No, wow. You're my daughter. Once I heard what happened, I came over here."

"Thanks, Dad. No wonder this place feels perfect."

Emotionally caught off guard, Karl kept quiet for a few minutes until he regained his composure. He got up and returned to the chair near the end of the couch.

"Does that mean the headache is gone?"

"I think so. Sitting up should tell me." Natalie pushed the blanket aside and sat up. At the same time, Sunshine Lily snapped her fingers for the lights.

"Ouch!" Natalie exclaimed, shutting her eyes. That was rough.

Taking her time to open her eyes and adjust them to the bright light, Natalie asked, "Sunshine Lily, did you watch over me, too?"

"Not quietly at first. Lorcan had to take her out of the room and explain the rules."

"Thank you." Natalie knew how hard it was for the fairies to stay quiet—a near-impossible feat.

Sunshine Lily happily chattered in her high-pitched, bubbly voice. Neither Natalie nor her father understood a single word. It didn't matter. She said what she needed to say and flitted for the door.

"What time is it?"

"4:04."

"Good; I get to sleep a little longer before getting ready for school."

"You feel up for school?"

"Okay, who took my dad?" Natalie said, smiling at her father.

"Stop, Natalie. You were out of it. It frightened me watching you like that, and there wasn't anything to do but wait. Are you sure you're well enough for school?"

"Yes, today's the first meeting of the Janus Club. I need to be there."

"I have no idea what that means. However, I'll work from home today. If you get tired or feel bad, call me. I'll pick you up."

Natalie dropped down and pulled the blanket over her.

"You okay?" Karl asked with concern.

"Yes. I want to linger here for a few more minutes, enjoying this amazing feeling of utopia."

"Get some more sleep. I'm going out to speak with Draon and Lorcan."

"Thanks, Dad." Natalie yawned. As Karl turned off the light, Natalie fell back to sleep.

Chapter 9

Four-Alarm

Natalie woke to find her father gone, and Lorcan and Draon were nowhere to be found on the first floor. Needing to get ready for school, she left a note letting them know she had gone to the house. She said she would stop back before leaving for school.

Natalie's father still slept when Natalie ventured over to the old homestead. Opening the door, Lorcan greeted her. He pushed her bangs aside and inspected her forehead. He stepped aside as she entered the old homestead.

"What's that about?"

"Yesterday, you had a red circle in the center of your forehead. It's gone. Do you recall anything more about yesterday?" Lorcan said as he motioned for Natalie to follow him to the kitchen.

"Just the colors. They endlessly looped in my mind until I fell asleep."

"Anything unique to the colors?"

"Purple, indigo, blue, green, yellow, orange, and red. Over and over in that order."

"Strange, those are the colors and order of the chakras," Lorcan said as he paused and looked at Natalie.

"Chakras?"

"The seven energy centers in your body."

"Are they real?" Natalie asked in surprise.

"Absolutely."

"Why would they suddenly appear with a vengeance?" She recalled the violent headache.

"No clue. I haven't heard of anyone experiencing what you experienced yesterday. Sometimes the chakras get out of balance, but what happened to you isn't normal. Far from it, I will venture that there's a missing piece to the puzzle. Unfortunately, where we can get the answer will not be possible. Hexel doesn't communicate," Lorcan said as they passed through the Room of Mirrors.

"Do you think Hexel saw what happened?"

"Without a doubt. It happened by the gatehouse."

"I wonder if she stopped what caused it to happen? I know she protected me while I was out."

"According to Pru, Hexel was your guardian angel."

"A strange guardian angel, but appreciated. It might have been more than chakra colors if she hadn't been there. Do you think the chakras are in balance?"

"How did you feel when you woke up?"

"Like I didn't want to wake up because everything felt perfect."

"Seems whatever happened has worked on you."

"Changing the subject," Natalie said as she sat down at the kitchen table. Her focus immediately went out the window with the whirlwind activities of three fairies helping in the kitchen. Leafy Beefy Daylily brought her a bowl, Rosie Poppertop dumped cereal into the bowl, and Stormy Iris poured too much milk into the bowl. The milk hovered at the edge. Leafy returned and plopped a spoon into the bowl. Milk splashed onto the table. Instantly, an uproar of high-pitched, incoherent scolding erupted from the two fairies flitting around the guilty fairy. Finger-pointing, frowning faces, and relentless scolding were too much. In a huff, Leafy flew from the room.

"Thanks," Natalie said, trying to settle the two remaining fairies.

It didn't work. They continued their high-pitched babbling chatter about the spilled milk. Rosie angrily dropped a napkin on the mess and dramatically wiped it up.

As she did, Stormy eyed the spoon. Natalie knew that look. She picked the spoon up before the fairies started feeding her. Next, she'd get a bib, her mouth wiped after each bite, and a jabbering lecture if she didn't eat to their satisfaction. *No thanks.*

"New subject?" Lorcan, so used to the fairies' bickering, had tuned them out.

"There's a way we can stop the Janus Club meeting today. All we need to do is sound the fire alarm after most of them have entered the building. What is the spell to get the fire alarm to blast?"

"You know that will only work one time."

"Yes, but I'm hoping the training class for Saturday teaches us something useful to stop the Janus Club."

"You haven't received training on your ring yet. Give me a minute while I get you a wand."

Lorcan left for his bedroom. Natalie kept eating to keep the hovering fairies quiet. A few minutes later, Lorcan returned with a slender wand with vines carved into it.

"Hold out your hand."

Natalie marveled at the exquisite wand Lorcan placed in her hand. "It's beautiful."

"Your mother received the wand at her graduation. Many hands went into making it an incredibly special wand, so please handle it with care."

"Wow. Thanks, Lorcan." She twisted it around in her hand and then flicked it like she was casting a spell.

"Thankfully, you don't need to flick it in the air. That calls attention to yourself. However, you'll need to touch it to the paper I will give you while you say the words, *Sonus ignis lituus.*"

"*Sonus ignus lituus.*"

"No. The second word is ignis, not ignus. With magic, you can't have your Massachusetts way of saying things. Words ending in er don't become words ending in a; words ending in a don't become words ending in er. It has to be exact. *Sonus ignis lituus.*"

Lorcan wrote it down, touched his wand to the paper while mumbling a spell, and then handed it to Natalie.

"Mom was the one with the accent. I grew up around here and didn't pick up her "er" to "a" way of talking. I just messed up. *Sonus ignis lituus.*"

"Perfect, you've got it. When you're ready, have the wand tip touch the paper and say the words."

"I'm nervous about getting it right. Wish me luck."

"You don't need luck; you're a mage. Now get to school."

She stood up, picked up the cereal bowl and spoon, intending to rinse them and place them in the sink. Rosie grabbed the bowl. As she did, the spoon flew out and crashed to the floor. Stormy raced over to retrieve the spoon. High-pitched, annoyed voices filled the air. Natalie rolled her eyes and made a direct line for the front door.

She looked at the note and silently recited the words. It would be cool if Joel could add a minor fire, except he hadn't tapped into his elemental power yet. She hadn't tapped into the fire element, either. She shook her head, noting she had enough trouble with the earth element.

Heading out of science for their next class, she caught up to Connor. Wearing his black jacket hood, he didn't know Natalie walked beside him until she spoke.

"Connor, I have a plan for this afternoon. Can you meet me near the auditorium after school gets out?"

Connor kept looking straight ahead as they walked to their next class, but he answered her. "I'll be there."

Walking into algebra at the same time as Joel, she said in a hushed voice, "I've got a plan for this afternoon."

Joel turned and glanced at Natalie. "Wait for me outside the door when the bell rings." She nodded, and both quickly took their seats. Once the class ended, she met Joel, and they headed to their next class.

"Joel, Lorcan gave me a spell to use. Can you meet Connor and me at the auditorium after school gets out?"

Joel glanced at Natalie, gave her a quick nod yes, and then headed in a different direction for his next class.

All three were nervous as they met on the east side of the auditorium. From a safe distance, they watched as a steady stream of excited students headed for the auditorium. Connor lifted his face skyward and imitated the sound of a cow. "Mmmmooooo!"

Joel whacked Connor on the shoulder. "Knock it off."

"All the pep talks and promises have worked not only on the students but on the teachers. Mr. Parrish sounded like he wasn't giving us a choice on whether we wanted to join."

Just as Natalie finished talking, they spotted Mr. Parrish heading for the auditorium.

"Hide," Connor exclaimed as he ran for the back of the auditorium. Joel and Natalie followed right behind him.

When they regrouped behind two trees, Natalie said, "I don't know how close we need to be in order for a spell to work."

"We can see the auditorium; I think that's close enough," Joel said.

"Do you think it will carry more weight if we all say it together?" Connor asked.

"We can try. Do you want to practice before we say it?" Natalie pulled the folded paper out of her pocket. The others leaned in and looked at the words.

"Let's do it before any more people get in there. We don't want a wild stampede with people getting hurt while trying to exit the building."

"Good point, Connor." She reached into her purse and pulled the wand out. Surprised, the two boys glanced at it and then at Natalie.

"Where'd you get the wand?" Connor asked.

"It was my mother's graduation wand. Lorcan said it needs to touch the paper as we say the spell. Are we ready?" Natalie touched the wand to the paper and held it at an angle that made it possible for them to read the spell.

At the same time, all three said, "*Sonus ignis lituus!*"

Wide-eyed, hearts pounding, they covered their ears as every single fire alarm in the school blared. Seeing the sprinklers activated, they nervously glanced at each other. They stepped further back behind the trees as they watched a swarm of soaked people run out of the building towards the front of the school. Natalie dropped the wand and paper into her purse.

"This is even better than we hoped," Connor yelled over the loud alarms. "All their material is going to be soaked."

"I think we need to move," Natalie said as some students started heading towards the parking lot.

"Not move, we need to leave!" Joel exclaimed.

They watched the Janus Club security briskly march towards the front of the school. Separated from the others gathered there, the nine guards, three in each row, marched in unison. Turning their angry faces at the same time, in search of what caused the fire and sprinkler systems to go off, alarmed them.

"That's creepy! Move!" Connor exclaimed. The three turned their backs to the eerie scene and cut across the grass to the students' parking lot.

"I don't have a way home unless I call my dad," Natalie whined.

"You're in luck," Connor said with a big smile. "I just got a car."

"Just in that you haven't been driving too long?" Joel asked.

"Yup, you're my first passengers," Connor informed them as they approached an older, black, compact car.

"Great," Joel said. "I'm not sure which will be more dangerous...you're driving with passengers for the first time or the Janus Club."

"You're about to find out," Connor laughed as Joel opened the front passenger door and Natalie opened the door to the back seats. Connor didn't need to remind them to buckle up.

They turned left onto the main highway as the blaring of sirens filled the air. Two blocks north of the school, they saw fire trucks, emergency vehicles, and Sheriff's vehicles responding to the call as if it were a four-alarm fire.

Joel nervously laughed. "It's kind of scary what we did."

"It's small potatoes if we can stop the Janus Club," Connor said.

"Still scary in my book when they find out it was a false alarm, but all the sprinklers went off. I hope Dad doesn't find out." Natalie watched two more fire trucks go by in the opposite direction from where they were headed.

"Look on the bright side," Connor said. "We did our first spell. We're awesome!"

It seemed more and more emergency vehicles were responding to the call. All the way home, they kept seeing fire trucks. Suddenly, it struck Natalie why they were seeing so many emergency vehicles.

"What if the three of us saying the spell caused the overhead sprinklers not to shut off?"

"Cool," Connor replied, glancing back at Natalie. "That means no school tomorrow."

"Seriously, Connor, pay attention to your driving before we need an emergency vehicle, and one isn't available!" Joel demanded as Connor ran a very amber light that turned red before they cleared the intersection.

Trying to take the focus off Connor's driving, Natalie asked, "What's our story if anyone questions the three of us standing together outside the auditorium?"

"How about we keep it simple and say we all live in the same neighborhood; Connor was taking us home."

"That's great, Joel. If they get nosy and ask why we were there, we can say there was a lot of interest in the club. We were curious what kind of response it would receive," Connor said.

"That should cover us. If it doesn't, we can get Natalie angry and have her send one of her cyclones to take care of the entire school," Joel laughed while looking back at her.

"Ha, ha!" Natalie sourly directed at Joel.

Connor dropped Joel and Natalie off at Joel's house before heading to his home in the northern section of the subdivision. They no longer heard sirens. Whew, that gave Natalie hope that things were under control. Still, she gave Joel a "yikes" look before heading to her house. On her way to the old homestead, she couldn't believe how successful the spell had been. Unfortunately, it was probably overly successful to the point that Draon and Lorcan would consider it one of her disasters.

Walking up to the gate at the old homestead, the scarecrows faced her direction and seemed to stare at her. She looked away. After all this time, they still bothered her.

"So you've heard what we did?"

She wasn't sure how that was possible, but they were enchanted. She took their focus on her as a bad sign about what waited inside the old homestead.

She opened the door. There was no chance of sneaking in as the old door creaked. She stepped in and glanced around. With no one on the other side of the door, she sighed in relief. Facing the door, she slowly closed it, hoping it wouldn't make a sound. It didn't work. The door squeaked as Draon and Lorcan walked into the room.

"Eventful day?" Lorcan sarcastically asked.

"The spell worked extremely well." She could tell by their expressions and how they stood that they weren't happy.

"Please elaborate on how well it worked," Lorcan said.

"Right here, or would you like to go into the kitchen?"

"Right here is fine."

Natalie looked at Lorcan and then at Draon. Wondering if she would get kicked out, she stood there trying to figure out how to make her actions seem like the right decision.

"Joel, Connor, and I met near the auditorium after school got out. We watched in amazement as students kept flooding into the auditorium. Then, we saw one of my teachers, who wanted us to join, heading for the club. Before being spotted, we ran behind the auditorium. Connor suggested we do the spell before too many people were in there, and someone might get hurt trying to escape. Together, we chanted the words. Just once. The fire alarms for all the buildings went off. Right after that, there was a massive exit of wet people running from the building. Then, we saw several members of the Janus Club security heading

114

towards the front, looking for revenge. We took off for Connor's car. He brought us home."

"Connor drives?" Lorcan asked in amazement.

"We were his first passengers," Natalie responded, relieved that was the first question asked.

"I suppose it's my fault that I didn't tell you the spell was for one person to recite. Three reciting the spell caused every fire alarm in the entire school to go off...not to mention the entire sprinkler system."

"I'm sorry. I hoped one of us would get the spell correct and get it to work. I didn't think it would multiply the results, especially since we only had one wand."

"You got lucky. Draon went there to see if you could stop the meeting. When he saw what you three did, he created small fires in a few areas that looked like electrical issues."

"That's why we kept seeing fire trucks going by us as we headed home."

"Yes. I feel you'll be doing e-school for a few days."

"I would prefer e-school. My father would never let me do it except for the one e-school course required each semester."

"It's a good thing you attend school. You need to be there to see what's happening. It's the same reason Madison and Skylar will attend school next year," Lorcan said.

"Hopefully, next year, we'll have control of our elements and know several spells."

"Expect to spend a lot of time with Draon or at the Barracks. You'll be training full-time during the summer."

Draon had been quiet all that time. She looked over at him and tried to read him. She gave up. When he wanted it to be, he was impossible to read.

She changed her thoughts to the fires. Good thinking on his part. The fires made the whole thing look real. The

Janus Club wouldn't be looking for someone who attempted to shut down their club.

Draon took his hand out of his pocket. Opening it up, she saw a Janus Club ring.

Immediately, the Variegated Orb Weaver bracelet started flashing along with the crystal pendant vibrating. Stunned that Draon could get a ring, Natalie ignored the bracelet and the crystal, but Lorcan focused on the bracelet's reaction to the ring.

"How did you get it?" Natalie asked, wide-eyed.

"As people fled the auditorium, I flew into it. At the back of the auditorium, there were interview tables with chairs. Behind the interview tables were tables with mounds of rings ready for distribution to new members. I swooped down and collected a few rings."

Afraid to touch it, Natalie put her hands behind her back and leaned closer for a look. The silver ring with a large blue gemstone didn't look evil. It looked expensive.

She knew most people would enjoy wearing the stunning ring, especially since the ring was free. They only needed to join the club. And then, they didn't even need to stay in the club to keep the ring. It made no sense not to join. A beautiful ring, and if they stayed, the club offered ways to earn money.

"It's beautiful," Natalie said, finally taking her eyes off it and looking up at Draon.

"Indeed," Draon stated, putting the ring back into his pocket. Lorcan noticed the bracelet had stopped flashing.

"Is it safe to have the ring here?"

"What do you mean?" Lorcan asked, focusing back on the conversation.

"What if it has a tracker? What if you take it to the Barracks to study it, and it shows the Janus Club where the Barracks is located?"

116

Natalie watched Draon's eyes widen, realizing that the rings might have trackers.

"I need to leave," Draon abruptly stated. Without another word, he disappeared.

She watched Lorcan bring out his wand and start walking around the house. She heard him mutter several words, with the first words sounding like *purifico venit domus*. She couldn't hear the rest of the spell as Lorcan moved throughout the house, waving his wand and muttering the same words. When he finished, he returned to Natalie. "Thank you."

"For what?"

"We didn't even consider that evil thing can track. I don't think it does because there are hundreds of those rings. However, to be safe, the spell has erased any tracking from here."

"How can you do that without the ring being here?"

"We don't need the ring. It's an elementary spell, erasing any trace of the ring ever being here."

"Where will Draon go with the rings? He can't go to the Barracks or Stormfield."

"He'll find some remote, deserted place to perform the necessary tests. It's easy to set up a lab and summon mages that are experts in evil objects."

"Too bad Draon couldn't have taken all the rings. That would have given us even more time to figure out how to fight this group."

"We're lucky to have some rings. Some are better than none, and they won't miss a few rings."

"I agree." She reached into her purse and held out her mother's wand. Lorcan took it.

"Thank you."

"Thank you for loaning it to me; it worked perfectly. I'll be glad when all of this is over, so we can fully

117

concentrate on our training. Draon also promised flying lessons."

"He did?"

"Tears at my first lesson made him uncomfortable. To make me feel better, he offered flying lessons." Natalie smiled at that offer before her mind placed her at the school. She froze as her smile disappeared, her eyes widened, and the color drained from her face.

"What?"

"The school has security cameras. What if the cameras picked us up reciting the spell?"

"I'll take care of it. Go home. There's nothing for you to do here today."

Chapter 10

Wickedly Twisted

Even with school out for the rest of the week, before they knew it, they were gathering at Natalie's house to make the trip over to the Barracks for their Saturday class. Connor casually strolled into the Room of Mirrors as Natalie entered from the opposite direction. They joined Pru, Madison, and Skylar. Natalie glanced behind Connor, expecting Joel to be a few steps behind him.

"Where's Joel?"

"Remember when we were first told how we could get here?" Connor asked with excitement in his voice.

"Not really," Natalie answered, looking at the others to see if they had a clue. They shook their heads no.

"Well, Joel mentioned to me last night that we should be more cautious about showing up to your property so much. All of us continuing to show up at the same time of day makes it look like we're up to something."

"Connor, we are up to something," Madison said with a smirk.

"I know. That's what got Joel thinking about another way to get to Natalie's without being obvious."

"And?" Skylar asked.

"There are tunnels underneath the subdivision. Specifically, the tunnels are from our houses to Natalie's house. Each one of us has a way to this basement." Connor stopped and waited for the reactions.

"You mean tunnels that no one has ever used?" Madison questioned in disbelief.

"I don't think so."

"So, we don't know if the tunnels are dark with spiders and webs, roaches, rats, and who knows what else is in there waiting to eat us?" Madison asked.

"I doubt drooling monsters are waiting to snack on us. Joel would have texted me if he had failed and turned back. We need to go downstairs to see if he's waiting for us."

"We need to go downstairs and see if he survived that tunnel. He can't call if he's the entree at a salivating monster's banquet. What is it with guys?" Natalie turned and led them out of the room towards the basement door.

She took two steps at a time, skipped the last two steps, and there was a thump as her feet hit the floor. She turned to watch all of them do the same thing, except for Pru. Once they gathered at the base of the stairs, they headed over to the door that took them to the railroad cart and stopped. Glancing around, they didn't see any other doors.

Connor moved closer to the wall and looked for an outline of a door. Not finding one, he said, "I don't see any indication of a door here."

"What if the doors are on the cart side?" Madison volunteered.

"This makes little sense. Connor, you live way in the back of the subdivision. That would be an outrageously long tunnel to get you here."

"What if the tunnels connect or intersect, Natalie?"

"A huge maze underneath the subdivision? This is getting crazier by the minute," Natalie said.

"Tunnels intersecting..." Madison stopped as a muffled voice came from the other side of the wall. Moving to the spot where they thought they heard the voice, they stopped and listened.

"Somebody let me in...now!"

"Dude, there's nothing on this side to open a door. Can you push it on your side?" Connor ran his hands along the walls, feeling for a door. He came up empty.

"It has to open both ways, or we can't use the tunnels to get home," Skylar said, joining Connor in the search for a secret doorway.

"We're going to be late," Natalie complained as she turned and jogged to the stairs. Running up the stairs, she reached the door in record time. Swinging it open, Natalie yelled, "Lorcan!"

Lorcan rushed to the door and looked at her wide-eyed expression. "Did something happen?"

"Joel took the tunnel from his house and now seems to be somewhere on the other side where we can't find a door to let him into the basement, and we're all going to be late for class because…"

"Whoa, Natalie. Take a breath!" Lorcan interrupted while slightly turning so she couldn't see him roll his eyes at her drama. He turned back, moved before Natalie, and headed down the stairs. She followed close behind him.

Lorcan walked up to the group. "Did any of you stop to think that everything around us has an enchantment? Most enchanted items from the outside do not simply open by a doorknob. Magic was involved and was involved in getting Joel's door open. It's the same spell."

"Get me out!" Joel yelled.

"Use the spell Murphy gave you."

"He didn't give me a spell. He mumbled some words, and the door opened. I stepped through; it slammed shut." Joel pounded on the wall in frustration.

"Great. Simply great. What was Murphy thinking??" Lorcan said.

"Maybe he had as much information as we did, so he assumed, and yes, I know what that word means, that we were prepared for Joel coming through the tunnel," Natalie grumbled.

"Joel, you need to step back," Lorcan demanded as he moved closer to the area where Joel seemed to be located. The others split to each side of Lorcan and anxiously waited for the door to open. With his hands raised, Lorcan flamboyantly flung them out while yelling, *"Aperta Depraesentiarum!"*

The door swung open. Joel nervously stood in the dark, musty tunnel doorway, holding a small flashlight. The bright light from the basement showed his clothes and hair covered in spiderwebs. Visions of him walking through the tunnel, smashing into one web after another web to reach them, flashed into the minds of those looking back at him.

"You're crazy, dude!" Connor laughed.

"Get in here before the door closes," Lorcan demanded. "Ridiculous!"

Joel, embarrassed, walked in and started brushing the webs off. The others stared at him, all thinking he was indeed crazy going in there alone.

"What were you thinking?" Natalie hissed.

"Obviously," Madison said while glaring at him, "he wasn't thinking!"

Before Joel could defend himself, Lorcan came to his rescue. "It was rash with little to no thought or planning. No doubt about it, but it wasn't a bad idea. Now that I think about it, all of you should explore the tunnel system."

"No way!" Madison exclaimed.

"Yeah, I'm not into creepy crawlers crawling all over me," Skylar said as she backed away from the open door. She jumped as the door slammed shut.

"Look," Lorcan said, "I'll get the Blemish to install red dragon fire crystals so you have lights in the tunnel.

However, it'll be up to you to clean the tunnels." Lorcan bit his lip as he realized what he had said.

What are Blemish?" Pru asked.

Lorcan frowned. "I believe Natalie has already told you she saw one. There are two assigned to take care of the tunnels in use. We'll need two more for the additional tunnels. No need to worry. It's extremely rare to see one."

"That would be heart attack material," Skylar proclaimed.

"Yeah, knowing they could lurk in the shadows isn't a very comforting feeling," Madison said, looking over at her sister, who shook her head in agreement.

"Skylar and Madison, they won't harm you."

"Until they do," Madison said.

"Both of you stop," Lorcan scowled in annoyance. "The Blemish individuals are paying a high price for what they did. They have a job to do and don't want trouble. I assure you, they want nothing to do with you. Now I suggest you get to class." Lorcan stomped off.

By the time they entered the cart, Joel had removed most of the spiderwebs. Even so, the red dragon fire crystals caused the remaining ones in his hair to glow. Skylar reached over and pulled them off. They stuck to her hands. Fascinated with the glowing webs, she studied them while pulling them off her hands and rolling them into a small, sticky ball.

"I wonder if we can use this in a spell?"

"It's possible. My bracelets come from special spiderwebs found in Natalie's barn."

The cart rumbled down the track under the misty lighting from the red dragon fire crystals. Something scurried across the ground in front of the cart—a plump, oversized rat. Skylar and Madison screamed. The boys laughed.

"That's a bad omen," Skylar cried, slapping Joel's shoulder. "We're supposed to clean out the abandoned tunnels. If this one has a rat, what do you think the deserted tunnels have in them?"

"I'm not thinking about that project yet. I'm focused on us walking through the dank, poorly lit tunnel to the Barracks. Fair warning, if I see a rat scurrying across our path in that tunnel, you better believe that my scream will echo off the walls for a week," Natalie said as they headed up the steps to the bookstore.

"Warn us first," Connor said. "We want to keep our hearing."

They entered through one door, walked briefly to the back of the store, and went down some steps into the tunnel that led to the Barracks.

"Too bad the cart doesn't skirt around the bookstore so that it can take us directly to the Barracks," Madison said.

"It would be nice to avoid this walk that seems more like an ancient dungeon hallway tourist attraction," Skylar agreed as she glanced around the shadowy tunnel. The stale air, the tunnel with sconces of red dragon fire crystals, and the long hike made it feel ominous. The tunnel's low ceiling made them feel claustrophobic. They smiled with relief as they spotted the Barracks' door just ahead.

Standing before it, Connor turned and faced the mages. "Time to take in a big breath of air and hold it. Hexel is the next obstacle."

"Thankfully, we're old news, so she doesn't pay us any attention," Joel said before taking in a big gulp of air.

Connor swung the door wide open. Connor and Joel were the first out, followed by Madison, Skylar, and Pru. The group moved forward, but Natalie lingered behind. None of them noticed as they focused on getting as far away from

Hexel as soon as possible. Hexel held her position, floating near the gatehouse.

"Hexel," Natalie said in a whisper. Hexel stayed in place.

"Hexel, I have something for you. There's nowhere to hang it, so I'll place it on the boulder next to your guardhouse." Natalie found a level spot on the rock and placed the Aurora Borealis crystal butterfly necklace on it. Stepping back, she marveled at the beautiful colors radiating from it. It seemed like captured Northern Lights were being released.

Immensely pleased with her gift, Natalie walked closer to Hexel. She stopped and looked up at her. "Thank you for protecting me the other day, Hexel."

Hexel continued to float in the same position, giving no clue that she appreciated or wanted the gift. The air felt icy. Hexel felt indifferent. Natalie felt deflated. She had not only put a lot of thought into the gift, but it was also a treasured item from her mother's collection of crystal butterfly necklaces. She had picked out her favorite butterfly for Hexel. Maybe her kind wanted nothing of this world.

Natalie started to feel uncomfortable. *What if I insulted Hexel? What if she hates my gift? What makes me think she needs anything but her duty to the Barracks?* Feeling rejected, she lowered her head and stepped past Hexel. She picked up her pace, wiped her eyes, and quickly caught up to the others.

As usual, Joel talked about food. "This place is killing me because I'm broke. To smell that amazing aroma from the Flaky Kuchen and know that I can't even afford one amazing donut is killing me."

Joel put Natalie in a better frame of mind as she and the other girls laughed at his dilemma.

Connor smirked. "Seriously, dude, get a grip."

"Easy for you to say as I waste away." Joel sucked in his stomach and tried to hold it.

"I doubt that's your problem." Connor ignored the stomach drama. He opened the door to the classroom; they entered and took their seats.

Mr. Xanders sat at his desk, reading a book. He looked up after they settled. Closing the book, he said, "Did you miss me?"

A loud "yes!" filled the air.

Mr. Xanders smiled. "I'm glad. Angus Thornton learned I needed to cancel the class, so he volunteered to replace me. How could I say no to the master wizard?"

"Please say no next time," Natalie blurted out.

"That bad?"

"That bad," Connor confirmed.

"Well, I guess what the master wizard said about the class and what you would say about it are two different things."

"Ours would be the honest report," Connor sarcastically replied.

"Okay, well then, let's learn something useful." The teacher got up and went to the back closet. Everyone hoped it wasn't another Odi demonstration.

Turning around, Mr. Xanders held up what looked like a marble. He walked closer. With it between his right thumb and index finger, he waved it in front of them. He stopped and held it up in front of his chest.

"Anyone recognize this?"

"Seriously, those were popular before the sixties. My grandmother has jars of them. Not sure why, but she has a fascination with marbles." Connor shrugged, unimpressed.

"This looks like a marble, but it isn't a marble. That's the beauty of it, Connor. Inside this charm is an ingredient that will activate when you say the spell. What happens

126

depends on what's inside. You can only get these made at the Wickedly Twisted Bottega. Have any of you been inside that shop?"

All of them shook their heads no.

"Of course not, because you were bored when you saw endless apothecary jars full of marbles in the front window of the shop. Why would marbles be in a store in the Crossroads Barracks? Because they aren't marbles, but they fool those around you into thinking you have a weird hobby of collecting them. We can use this to our advantage at school. In fact, when you return to school, it will be the perfect time for you to use them."

"What exactly will we be doing with them?" Joel questioned.

"You'll be disrupting the next Janus Club meeting," Mr. Xanders boasted.

With that statement, he had their full attention.

"So, what do we do to complete this mission?" Joel asked.

"When school opens back up, only Natalie, Joel, and Connor can be at school, so I'll focus on you three. Let's start out with something simple that will disrupt the meeting. Any suggestions?"

They all sat there thinking for several minutes until Skylar said, "Itching."

"Good, what else?"

"Something that causes an allergic reaction that makes the area around the eyes swell and the nose to run nonstop," Natalie volunteered.

"Good, what else?"

"Non-stop farting with smell," Connor laughed.

"Always the one consumed with smells," Joel groaned, but he laughed at the vision playing out in his head.

"And why is that, Joel? It's because we smell Hexel as soon as we open the door. Then, right off the bat, we drink that putrid protection concoction. Oh, and let's not forget smelly Odi. So, yes, I complain because the smells seem endless."

"Try concentrating on the Flaky Kuchen's tempting smells wafting through the air," Joel said, inhaling a deep breath as if he stood before the bakery.

"Speaking of the Flaky Kuchen," Natalie said, interrupting them, "I'm sure the meeting will have refreshments. What if those attending become obsessed with the food and drinks and can't consume enough?"

They all laughed at the visual of a pig fest, and then Mr. Xanders answered the question. "Maybe, but what we want to do is inflict something that doesn't seem too out of the ordinary. Unusual things may suggest that someone is intentionally trying to stop the club from meeting. Pick which one you want to try."

"Oh, I'm going with my suggestion," Connor said, pleased with his idea.

"Connor, we need to start simple, as in itching. Not overly itching, but enough itching that no one can concentrate."

"Of course, Natalie, you would suggest something practical," Connor smirked.

"You can try your suggestion in a class. Just not a class that I have with you," Natalie said.

Pru had been quiet the whole time. She raised her hand.

Mr. Xanders sighed with relief when he saw Pru's raised hand. "Do you have something you would like to add?"

"We're unsure what's happening at the club. Maybe the club leaders don't even care if the members come down with itching or other issues, as long as they wear that ring. We need to discover what the real motive is for the club. While we're figuring that out, maybe the itching, black mold from the overhead sprinklers drenching the place, or whatever it is, involves the entire school. The day before and the day of, so that keeps students away."

"Great idea, Pru," Mr. Xanders beamed.

Connor looked over at Pru as if she had ruined all his fun.

"Okay, here's what we'll do. Natalie will use the itching and black mold potions, and Connor will use his smelly potion. I'll give the order to the Wickedly Twisted store. I'll let you know when the order is ready to be picked up. Joel, hold off. Too many things happening at once will make it look suspicious. If the club isn't meeting until school opens again, there's no rush. However, if we hear the club is meeting somewhere else, then we go there and activate the inflictions."

Madison raised her hand.

"Do you have a question, Madison?" Mr. Xanders asked.

"Can we all go to the Twisted store and learn about the marbles? If you don't want us using one for a plague, we could pick something innocent."

"Good idea, Madison. Of course, each of you should learn where to place the marbles, the instructions to release the infliction, and how to avoid the infliction. Give my name, so they charge the cost to the class."

Before Madison could thank Mr. Xanders, Connor blurted out, "How is it possible to put a potion inside a marble?"

Mr. Xanders turned his focus to Connor. "It's quite fascinating to watch. The potion is created, suspended in the air, and then a shell is spun around the potion. It's extremely complex, with marbles made one at a time. Few people have seen the process; I'm one of the lucky ones."

Connor thought about it for a moment before responding. "So, the marble you are holding and the jars of marbles at the store are just marbles?"

"Brilliant observation, Connor. Yes. Like your grandmother, someone at the store has a fascination with marbles. That fascination resulted in creating a potion and a shell resembling a marble."

"Okay, thanks."

Mr. Xanders walked to the closet and dropped the marble back in the jar. He reached into the back of the first shelf and grabbed the next item. Turning around, he held up what looked like a piece of driftwood. Everyone stared at it, wondering what magic it held.

Walking over to Skylar, Mr. Xanders placed it in front of her. "Any idea what this is?"

Skylar stared at it for several moments. "It's something like a squirrel."

"Good observation, Skylar. Now, pick it up and carefully examine it. When you're done, pass it on to the next student."

Mr. Xanders watched with interest as each mage picked the driftwood up, studied it, and then passed it on to the next mage. After Connor looked at it, Mr. Xanders picked it up.

Standing before the class, he held it so each student could see it, and then he commanded, *"Expergiscimini!"*

Instantly, a brown squirrel the same size as the driftwood sat in his hand. As it sat still in the teacher's hand, it seemed more like a stuffed animal.

"Is it real?" Joel asked, confused at the lack of movement.

"No, it's not. However, it's an especially useful tool when trying to disrupt activity in the mageless world. If I were to give the command to attack, it would chew every wire within this room within minutes. Think how much damage it could cause at the next Janus Club meeting."

"I don't understand," Madison said in a puzzled tone, "how are we supposed to get it into the auditorium, tell it to wake up, and then, without being spotted, it chews all the wiring?"

"It looks harmless, so the custodians wouldn't remove it. With Odi, you need to be close to ask to use his powers, but with the driftwood, you don't need to be over it. You simply need to activate it. It can chew the wires before the meeting. That will slow the entire program down. That is, if they need the attention of the members."

"What shop sells driftwood?" Madison asked.

"This is in the restricted area of the Wickedly Twisted store. A teacher would need to purchase the item for you. After all, we can't have these squirrels running around chewing wires."

"Isn't there a chance it would do far more damage?" Pru asked.

"Hence, the restricted area," Mr. Xanders replied. "Since you can't witness what is happening, time is your guide. Even if you could watch it, it moves so quickly, you wouldn't be able to follow it."

"That one seems a stretch," Connor said.

"That's the beauty of it, Connor. No one would expect it. However, we may or may not need it. If and when we do, I'll give the attack spell at that time. For now, we'll work with the marbles."

"I'm looking forward to putting some marbles in pockets," Connor said before bursting into laughter.

"You know, Connor, I've thought about it. I'm still going with the itching and black mold potions, but I'd like a couple of your marbles. There's a certain jerk I'd like to pay back for hitting me with rubber bands."

"Who would that be?" Joel asked.

"Gary."

"Gary Toppleman is your bully?" Joel asked in surprise.

"Yup."

"He's one of the best players on the football team. You sure you want to mess with him?"

"Oh, I definitely want to mess with him, Joel. He's going to be my personal guinea pig. I can't wait."

"Natalie," Mr. Xanders said, "Gary is the reason we made it to the state level."

"Don't care."

Mr. Xanders let out a deep sigh.

Chapter 11

Rafflesia

Natalie asked Lorcan if he would cast a spell to clean up the tunnels. He flat-out said no. She then asked Draon and received the same answer. For a moment, she considered the fairies, but they couldn't leave the homestead. Sneaking them out might give them the idea to do it on their own, reinforcing their reasons for always breaking the rules. *Darn it, I don't have any other options.*

Still dark outside, Natalie got up, showered, and slipped into an old pair of paint-splattered jeans and a black shirt that had seen better days. She brushed her teeth and zipped through combing her hair. She made as little noise as possible because her father was sleeping. Coal squawked.

"Shh! You can't come with me."

Coal flew up to her shoulder. Reaching over, she removed him and placed him on the pillow on his chair. "Stay!"

Tilting his head, he studied her.

"Stay! I mean it!"

Coal made chirping noises of disapproval as he settled down on the pillow.

Stepping into the darkness, she turned on her flashlight. The long, narrow path between the house and the old homestead was as creepy as always. She turned her flashlight this way and that way to make sure nothing slithered under the palmettoes or dangled from the low-hanging branches above her. Rustling and scratching sounds produced scary images inside her mind. It was probably an armadillo, but she couldn't be sure. She quickened her pace until the barn came into view. A sigh of relief escaped her lips.

Turning left, she walked past the barn and headed towards the old homestead. The scarecrows faced her, but she ignored them. They were nothing compared to her dread of what lurked in the dark, unused tunnels. Even the rusted metal gate, ominously creaking as she opened it, didn't bother her. She had a feeling this would be the better part of the day.

Natalie kept her flashlight on as she entered the dark and eerily quiet old homestead. She was used to babbling fairies, endless squabbles, and Lorcan threatening to bring out his wand. She didn't think the mischievous fairies ever slept. Her flashlight scanned the room. Nothing. It was so quiet she could hear each footstep as she made her way into the kitchen. She sat down and waited. Nervously, she pulled the cleaning bag off the table and went through it.

Several minutes later, Pru entered the house with Madison and Skylar right behind her. Joel came next, and then Connor. All of them marched directly into the kitchen. Loaded with their own bags of cleaning supplies, brooms, and flashlights, they were ready to tackle cleaning the unused tunnels.

"Ready to do this?" Joel asked, looking directly at Natalie.

"No, but there doesn't appear to be a choice." Natalie stood up, pushed her chair in, and grabbed her sack of supplies. On the way out of the kitchen, she grabbed the broom leaning against the pantry.

"I think soprano Joel should be the lead in the tunnels," Madison chuckled.

"Hey, that spider was a disgusting, gooey mess. All of you would have sounded like a screaming soprano if it splatted on you."

"Nope," Madison cringed. "I'd have fainted and crashed to the ground."

Joel laughed while opening the door to the basement. They slowly and reluctantly made their way down the stairs. They kept that snail's pace as they headed to the invisible door. There they stood. No one wanted to say the spell that opened the door. Quiet. No movement. A lump of six mages staring at a blank wall.

"Really?" Connor exclaimed. "Are we really going to spend our entire morning staring at the invisible door?"

They avoided answering.

"I'll be the man here and step up."

The girls giggled. Connor turned and looked at them with annoyance, which only made them laugh harder. Turning back, he yelled, *Aperta Depraesentiarum!*" The door swung open.

Connor turned his head halfway and, still annoyed, yelled, "Come on! The door's going to close!"

They barely made it into the tunnel, dimly lit by newly installed red dragon fire crystal sconces, before the door slammed shut. Six flashlights instantly turned on.

"Okay, Joel," Madison said, "we've volunteered you to go first since you're the tallest."

"Clearing the spiderwebs for a path isn't my idea of a fun time."

"It's a good visual," Natalie said. "However, you have a broom, so you can swing it in front of you to get them before they get you."

"Good idea," Joel agreed, getting his broom ready.

Before them was an immense tunnel with a cobblestone floor and large stones jutting out and forming the walls. The dim red dragon crystal lights and the light from six flashlights highlighted the tunnel's magnificence.

The damp and chilly atmosphere highlighted its foreboding side. Connor brushed his hand against the rough wall.

"Damp," Connor stated as he wiped his hand on his pants.

"Meaning the place is perfect for spiders and more spiders and even more spiders," Madison whined.

"Stay behind me," Joel said.

"Like that worked last time," Madison said with a pfft.

"Then stay in front of me," Joel joked.

"That's not happening."

"Enough bickering. We'll be here all day and get nothing accomplished," Pru scolded. "We can see endless webs. Joel, you brush the ceiling. Madison and Skylar, you take this side of the wall. Natalie and Connor, you take the other wall. I'll sweep the floor. Sound good?"

"Sounds good to me." Natalie walked over to her side.

With each swipe of the broom, webs came down and added to the sticky pile in the large garbage bag. Spiders scurried for hidden crevices. Further into the tunnel, where it bent to the northwest, the webs were more elaborate and hung lower to the ground. The spiders were more enormous and only reacted when the broom landed on the web. All scurried away except for one. On a wall at eye level, it looked ready to pounce.

"Take that," Connor yelled as he ran up and sprayed the spider. He backed away as the spider wildly jerked around.

"Want more?" Connor taunted the spider, moving closer with the spray in hand.

"Don't!" Joel yelled. "We won't be able to breathe with that smell. The smell has no place to go."

Connor pointed the can within inches of the spider. The spider scampered away.

"Smart spider."

"Whatever, Connor. By the way, that lingering bug spray smell is on you," Joel said as he reached his broom up to swat down another large web.

Three hours later, they had cleaned the main tunnel past the first intersection that went south to Madison and Skylar's home and north to Joel's home. All were filthy and tired. Joel's arms ached as he continually reached up and swung the broom. Pru had blisters forming on her hands. The rest had ripped up hands from the rough walls.

"How about a break?" Pru asked.

Immediately halting what they were doing, they stepped over to Pru.

"Music to my ears!" Connor grinned.

"Lorcan said he would have lunch for us. Hopefully, the fairies are busy with something else," Natalie said, but she knew no such luck.

"They'll be like locusts when they see us," Connor replied.

No one said anything, but they all agreed. They strolled across the basement and trudged up the stairs.

Each mage took in a big gulp of fresh air as they came through the door and stepped into the house. Each one passed Lorcan until Natalie stopped before him and smirked at his expression. She knew he saw a dirty, disheveled lot, and he bit his lip not to laugh. Natalie laughed, which caused Lorcan to roar with laughter. He gave Natalie a light push to catch up to the others heading towards the Room of Mirrors.

"While you worked, each mentor prepared food and drinks for you. In the Room of Mirrors, you will see a spread of delicious food and desserts. Enjoy your feast," Lorcan said, trying to stay serious. He stayed back as Natalie and the others entered the room.

"Feast," Joel exclaimed, "now you're talking my language."

Feast was an understatement. There, they stood in awe of the immense table loaded with sandwiches, fresh fruit, and various ice-cold drinks. The center section of the table had mounds of desserts. The mages couldn't take their eyes off the abundant assortment of foods and beverages. Six fairies excitedly floated around the table, waiting to serve. Joel and Connor turned their attention away from the food and looked at each other.

"How long?" Connor quizzed.

"Within ten minutes."

"You're on."

"Can we wash up first?" Pru asked as the guys moved closer to the table.

Lorcan took his wand out and muttered "*purigi omnis*" at the mages. Instantly, the mages were clean. "Thanks, Lorcan," they said, feeling better.

Wasting no time, they plopped down on the chairs. Each fairy brought a fresh, wet cloth for each mage to wipe their hands. Joel reached for a sandwich before wiping his hands. High-pitched scolding erupted from Lavender Moonflower as she waited on him. He tried to ignore her and continued reaching for a sandwich. She smacked him with the wet cloth. Stunned, he looked up, saw her expression, and burst out laughing. She frowned and raised her hand, threatening fairy dust. He wiped his hands.

Joel looked across at Connor. "Does that count?"

"Nope, that's an everyday annoyance." Connor grabbed a sandwich and the mayo.

Natalie only wanted to drink. Consuming one drink after another, she sipped her third drink when Leafy Beefy

Daylily encouraged her to eat something. She shook her head no. Exhausted and hot, she didn't want food.

Facing Natalie, Leafy's high-pitched voice demanded she eat something. Natalie said no. Angrily, the fairy buzzed around her while nagging her to eat. Natalie ignored her, finished her drink, and reached for another cold beverage.

In a huff, Leafy flew over to the sandwiches and grabbed the one on top. Bright red with heavy breathing, she struggled to hold on to the sandwich as she flew above the plate.

Connor and Joel looked on in amusement, Pru, Madison, and Skylar looked on with concern, and Natalie stayed oblivious to the situation.

As Leafy roughly flew towards Natalie, the sandwich fell apart. With a thud, it hit the table. Connor and Joel burst out laughing while the girls felt sorry for the fairy. The other fairies furiously zoomed over. Surrounding Leafy, a high-pitched scolding erupted.

"Knock it off," Natalie shouted above the gibberish and complaining voices. Her head pounded from those shrill, nagging voices.

Turning on her, they directed their anger at her. Flying around her, they changed to high-pitched nagging with little fingers pointing at her. She looked over at Joel and then Connor. They were enjoying the ruckus aimed at her.

She picked up an extra icing fudge cupcake and threw it at Joel. Joel ducked. The cupcake went sailing towards a mirror. Horrified, Rosie Poppertop zoomed to intercept it. Too late! Splat! Rosie turned and screamed something at Natalie before furiously wiping it off the mirror. With a gooey mess held in her tiny hands, she made a direct line for Natalie.

Lorcan walked into the room as Rosie closed in on her. "*Duratus!*" The fairy with the gooey chocolate mess in her hands froze in the air over the table, within inches of Natalie. Her angry face lined up with her eyes. Nope. She scooted her chair closer to Skylar. Skylar pushed her chair closer to Madison. Natalie moved a couple more inches towards Skylar.

Before Lorcan could even ask what happened, the other fairies angrily flew up to him and began complaining about Natalie. Lorcan looked over as she reached for another drink. Stormy Iris flew over and slapped her hand. She ignored her. She placed the can on the table and popped the tab. Fuming, Stormy kicked the can. The soda splashed on the table and flowed into her lap. Natalie shrieked and jumped up.

"Enough!" Lorcan yelled.

Startled, the five fairies glanced at Lorcan and saw he was serious. In a huff, they stormed off. Their high-pitched complaining filled the air until they slammed their bedroom door shut.

"How long was I gone before it turned into mayhem?" Lorcan growled in annoyance as he sat down.

"Under ten minutes," Joel laughed. He pointed at Connor, made the dollar sign in the air, and then he pointed to himself. Connor rolled his eyes.

"They are the worst helpers ever," Lorcan complained as he scooped fruit into a bowl and ignored the fairy frozen inches above the table.

"They try," Pru said to support the fairies.

"No, Pru," Natalie frowned, "it isn't possible for them to behave. Pixies have a bad reputation, but they usually do their own thing. The fairies want to be fully involved, which always ends in a disaster. Well, I take that back. There was the one time they saved the day. They rescued me from Lorcan the Giant."

"A giant?" Skylar said in surprise.

"Lorcan, when he morphed into giant status."

"Oh, the thing that caused the spider problem in the basement," Skylar said.

"Yup."

Wanting to change the subject, Lorcan asked, "How far did you get today?"

"We're past the first intersection if you don't count the side tunnels at the intersection. We worked on the main tunnel," Joel answered while he reached for a double chocolate cupcake.

"The choice is yours. Work another three hours today or come back Monday afternoon."

"Seriously, Lorcan, is there a reason this is a priority?" Natalie asked, picking up a cheese sandwich.

"Yes, there needs to be an option to get to this homestead. The sooner, the better."

"I'm for continuing today," Madison said. "I don't want to fret about having to come back on Monday."

"Ditto," Connor stated as the rest nodded in agreement.

They stalled getting up. They continued eating and drinking. Joel twirled the frozen fairy in his direction, tapped her nose, and received an annoyed look from Lorcan.

"Natalie, since the suspended fairy is off limits, why don't you entertain us with the story of Lorcan morphing into a giant?" Joel asked.

"Don't you need to get back to the tunnel?" Lorcan asked.

"It'll be quick," Natalie said and then laughed when she saw Lorcan resign himself to an embellished story. Natalie did that as she reenacted him, screaming in a soprano

141

voice as spiders dropped all over him until he headed to the front door and smashed into Draon.

"Enough!" Lorcan said to quiet the laughter. "If you delay any longer, you'll return to an empty table."

Those magic words had them getting up, heading down to the basement, and entering the tunnel system. With full stomachs, they struggled to get interested in the project.

They ambled to the intersection and picked up where they left off. The spiderwebs grew thicker and longer the further into the tunnel they went. Spiders and webs were the only things they saw. They wondered if the spiders ate everything that ventured into the tunnel system.

"I wonder how the Blemish installed the dragon lights without disturbing the webs?" Skylar asked.

"Good question. It doesn't look like anyone has been in here for an exceptionally long time," Joel replied.

"I wonder if the spiders ate them," Connor ventured.

"Not funny," Pru scolded as the others considered his statement.

"I hope our flashlights don't quit on us. I wouldn't be happy heading back in this dim red light," Madison said. She looked at the beam streaming out of her flashlight. It stayed good and strong.

"Safety in numbers," Pru reassured them.

"Besides, we have Natalie," Joel commented. "If she gets scared enough, her powers will take over. We're safe."

"Safe from the spiders, but probably not what I whip up. You know I have little control when anger or another powerful emotion takes over."

"True," Joel agreed.

They talked about the Barracks, Angus Thornton, Saturday classes, Odi, and Hexel. Everyone teased Connor about his constant complaining about smells, particularly since they could still smell the bug spray. They talked about what they liked best about magic. Each of them rattled off the names of their twelve fairies and marveled they didn't know the names of their pixies. The constant conversation made them less aware of the many webs and spiders that grew larger the further they entered the tunnel system. Before they knew it, they were at the second intersection after three hours.

"We're out of here," Connor announced as they gathered all their supplies and returned.

They quickly made it back to the first intersection. Natalie focused her flashlight down the southern tunnel to Madison and Skylar's old homestead. Something glowing red caught her attention.

"Wait!" Natalie yelled. The others turned to face her.

"Something's down that tunnel."

"Can't it wait for another day?" Connor asked.

"No, what if it's something caught on a web?"

"Seriously, Natalie, survival of the fittest," Connor said, walking away.

"You go on. I couldn't sleep knowing something struggled on a web, and I did nothing about it."

"I'll go with you," Pru said, returning to Natalie. The others followed.

With six flashlights shining down the tunnel, they focused on the red glow coming from the massive web. As they moved closer, they saw a ball of green leaves with something resembling a red tail stuck in the center of the web.

"Weird," Connor said as they approached it. They flashed their lights around, looking for the spider. No spider. Connor and Skylar took out their bug spray.

Natalie slowly approached the web and studied the leaves above her head. They heard a scraping movement in the tunnel. She reached into her bag and pulled out scissors.

She tried to cut around the leaves, but it wasn't working, and the scraping sound got louder.

"We need to leave now," Madison cried in a frantic tone.

"I can't cut it out," Natalie yelled as she frantically worked on getting it off the web.

Red eyes appeared. Madison screamed. Then, they saw the rest of the monstrous spider. The leaves were too delicate. Natalie couldn't pull them off. The spider moved closer. Madison, Skylar, and Pru backed out of the southern tunnel.

"Natalie, now," Joel yelled. Connor stood behind Joel with his can of bug spray.

Natalie grabbed her broom and raised it above her head. The spider moved directly behind the web. Terrifying clicking noises warned of an imminent attack. For a fleeting moment, she wanted to run. In panic mode, she slammed the broom down on a section of the web away from the leaves. The spiderweb stuck to the broom. She twirled the broom to catch the leaves on it. The spider advanced.

"Duck!" Joel yelled as a fireball appeared above his right hand. She moved against the wall. Joel aimed. The fireball flew at the spider—a direct hit. The spider screeched and retreated.

Natalie held her broom up as they fled the southern tunnel. They continued that pace until they met up with the rest of the group.

"When did you get the ability to do fireballs?" Connor exclaimed while trying to catch his breath. He couldn't believe what he witnessed.

"Just now," Joel said in a surprised tone. "I've worked on it for weeks, and there wasn't a clue I was any further along than day one. Not even an encouraging sign of a bit of smoke."

"What did you do?" Madison asked.

"He came to our rescue with a fireball," Connor exclaimed. "It was a direct hit."

"A fireball? I'm impressed," Skylar said.

"That spider probably has family that'll come for us." Madison shuddered at the thought.

"Can we keep moving?" Pru pleaded.

"I hope that ball of leaves was worth it," Connor muttered.

"You saw Joel's first fireball. Wasn't that worth it?" Natalie said, trying to keep the broom up and away from the others.

"I give you that; it was cool."

"Natalie, you go in front of us, so we don't get hit with your broom or the spiderweb," Joel said as the others made way for her to take the lead. They stayed close together and hurried towards Natalie's basement.

They didn't hear any strange noises, but they stayed on high alert as they visualized an army of humongous spiders marching towards them. They didn't want to become a meal. Finally, Connor shouted, "*Aperta Depraesentiarum!*" They scrambled through the door and headed for the stairs.

Plopping their supplies on the kitchen table, they turned and headed for the Room of Mirrors. Desserts and drinks were still on the table, but Rosie Poppertop was no longer there. Joel looked disappointed. The others ignored his pout and sat down to enjoy the break without fairies.

Natalie sat at the end and slowly lowered the broom. Except for the red tail, it looked like leaves that had gathered in the wind to form a circle. She pulled one piece after another of the web away from the leaves. She constantly wiped her fingers on napkins to get the gooey web off. It was a slow process.

"Kind of disgusting doing that while we're eating," Connor grumbled as he reached for a chocolate cupcake.

"Don't watch," Natalie countered as she continued to remove the spiderweb from the leaves.

"Congratulations, Joel, on your first fireball," Pru beamed, trying to take the focus off Natalie.

"Thanks. Unfortunately, it was a scary scene, so it falls into the same category as what happens to Natalie."

"It doesn't matter. You've had success. That's more than the rest of us can say," Pru said as the others nodded in agreement. Connor gave Joel a thumbs-up.

Before Joel could respond, Lorcan walked into the room. The others turned to look at him while Natalie finished removing the last piece of webbing. She heaved a long sigh of relief. It was done. Now, she needed to check it for damage. She held it up.

"Thank you for your hard..." Lorcan stopped and stared at the leaves in Natalie's hand.

Natalie wasn't paying attention. She studied the leaves and red tail. It became too quiet. Glancing at the others who focused on Lorcan, she lowered her hand to the table and tilted her head in his direction. Wide-eyed, Lorcan stared at the leaves. His eyes moved to Natalie and then back to the leaves.

"You okay, Lorcan?" Natalie asked.

"Wh-where'd you get th-that?" Lorcan stammered.

"In the southern tunnel. It was stuck on a spider web."

"It's not possible," Lorcan said as he walked over to her and held his hand out. She placed the leaves in the palm of his hand.

"Is it an animal?" Natalie asked as she watched Lorcan study it.

"We thought they were extinct." He marveled at the creature.

"What is it?" Natalie asked.

"It's a Rafflesia. She's an Earth sprite." Lorcan gently rolled the leaves around his palm.

"What does she do?" Connor asked.

"I'm not sure. We never learned about them because we thought they were extinct for hundreds of years. I can't believe our good fortune." Lorcan sniffed, a tear running down his cheek.

"Do you want to hear some other good news?" Natalie asked.

"Quickly, as I need to contact Draon and Angus," Lorcan said, never taking his focus off the leaves in his hand.

"Joel used a fireball to save us from this hideously humongous spider coming to claim it."

"That's great, Joel. You helped save the rarest of creatures. She might be the only one still alive," Lorcan absently answered. He bumped into the door on the way out. He didn't even seem to notice.

"Well, I see how I rate," Joel kidded.

"You're our hero!" Madison and Skylar exclaimed in an exaggerated tone as they clinked their soda cans together in a toast to Joel. They both broke into laughter.

Before Joel could respond, Lorcan turned around and came back into the room.

"If there was one Rafflesia down there, there may be others. That means an elite group of wizards and witches will go down into the tunnel system to search for them. The good news for you is they will take over cleaning and securing the tunnels." Lorcan turned back around and left to contact Draon and Angus.

"Wow," Connor muttered. "It's a good thing we went back and checked out the southern tunnel."

The others all gave him a "really" look before breaking into laughter. Now, they had three reasons to stay at the table and celebrate.

Chapter 12

Marbles

Connor and Natalie took big gulps of air and held their breaths. Connor swung the Barracks' door wide open. Like horses right out of the gate, they bolted towards the gatehouse and Hexel. Natalie nodded towards Hexel as they continued their rapid pace. They stayed at that pace until they could breathe again.

"She gets a shower gift set for Christmas," Connor declared as they headed towards the Wickedly Twisted store.

Natalie laughed at the idea. "It wouldn't help. She's a Fury. Or maybe she's a Grim Reaper. I'm not sure there's a difference. However, neither would use your thoughtful Christmas gift."

"Yeah, they don't teach about Furies or a Grim Reaper at school or here. We should ask our mentors about her and why she smells so bad."

"She makes the Barracks safe. That's all that counts." They turned a corner and headed towards the Wickedly Twisted store.

In front of the store, Natalie asked, "Why haven't we ever noticed this shop before?"

Connor peered into the front window. All he could see were endless rows of apothecary jars filled with marbles. Glancing over, he stated the obvious. "Because the only interesting part of this store is its name. Endless marbles come under the heading of boring."

"But marbles can be something other than marbles."

"We just found that out." Connor opened the door to a wildly loud cackling sound. The cackling continued well after they shut the door. They started laughing. They still laughed when they approached the red-haired girl at the front counter.

"Wow, I didn't think any of the shops had young employees."

Natalie looked at Connor and asked, "Are you for real?" Connor ignored her and concentrated on the blue-eyed cashier.

"You'd be surprised how many of the shops have young owners. We prefer to work behind the scenes, developing our businesses." She leaned against the counter and waited.

"All we ever see are old people."

Natalie turned and gave Connor an "I don't believe you" look.

"Those would be our parents or grandparents," she laughed.

"I'm Connor, and this is Natalie," Connor announced, pointing to Natalie as if the girl behind the counter couldn't figure out who was who. She laughed again.

"I know who you are. Natalie is a frequent topic around the Barracks. Way to go, girl." She reached over to give her a high five.

"Thanks. My trainer and mentor aren't so happy with all my disasters. However, they make good stories."

"Truthfully, this place has come alive since your group started training here. Not only that, but the discovery of a Rafflesia is astounding. The news has traveled worldwide." Her excitement increased as she mentioned the Rafflesia.

"I hope it's well. The web entangled her in an almost impossible task of freeing her."

"I've seen her. She's doing great."

Natalie's eyes went wide in surprise. Lorcan had told them the Rafflesia might be the only one alive. Why were people allowed to see her?

As if reading her mind, the cashier said, "I'm Twilight Thornton."

"You're Angus Thornton's daughter?" Natalie asked, dropping her mouth open in surprise.

She laughed before answering. "No, Angus is my uncle and much younger than my dad. He's the youngest of five brothers."

She saw her look and smiled, knowing what Natalie was thinking. "Being the baby brother and having the high honor of master wizard has made his head a little too big at the moment. He's really a good guy. Give him time."

"I hope you're right."

"Yeah, he was a first-class jerk to Natalie in the class he taught with Odi."

Natalie looked at Connor in surprise. He slightly smiled before returning his focus to Twilight.

"Sorry about that. He's retired from the Army Night Stalkers. He definitely has a no-nonsense side to him. My dad's working on him to soften his interactions with mages."

"Night Stalkers," Connor exclaimed. "Cool! I was thinking of flying for the Air Force, and here's your uncle, a Night Stalkers aviator. Wow!"

"It is a big wow. Being the master wizard is a big wow. He's not even forty, and he's accomplished a lot. I'm proud of my uncle. Let me get your marbles," Twilight boasted as she turned to head into the storage room behind the front counter.

Natalie noticed Connor's reaction to Angus Thornton being in the Night Stalkers. She knew Angus Thornton had risen to hero status in Connor's world. In her world, she remembered being picked on in his class. She didn't want to think about him.

She glanced around the front. It was a small but tidy store with tall, wooden shelves holding large apothecary jars full of marbles. The floor and front counter were made of mahogany wood, and Tiffany lights added to the warm and cozy atmosphere. Over to the right stood a table for two, which held a thick binder of potion suggestions.

"Since Mr. Xanders placed our order, do you want to look through the binder for more ideas before we leave?" Natalie asked Connor.

He shrugged his shoulders in disinterest. "I have the winning formula." Then he glanced back at the binder.

She watched him and laughed.

"What's so funny?" Twilight asked as she entered the room.

"Connor is wondering if his stinky potion is in your binder."

"It isn't a common request, but it's there." Twilight handed a bag to Connor and a bag to Natalie.

"Good luck. I hope you can stop it."

"One way or another, we're going to end it," Connor said.

"Good to hear. Whatever way I can help, let me know."

"Thanks, Twilight," Natalie said.

"I hope we see each other again." Twilight smiled while leaning against the counter.

"Once school gets out, we'll be here more often for training and, hopefully, Draon will give us flying lessons," Natalie said.

"Really?" Twilight exclaimed. "I'm seriously jealous. No one teaches flying anymore."

"Does Angus Thornton or your father know how to fly?" Natalie asked, surprised that not all mages had learned how to fly.

"Long ago. They say there are better ways to get around."

"Wow, they grew up and became old unless they are talking about the Chinook or Black Hawk helicopters."

Twilight and Natalie looked at Connor in surprise, but his comment made sense.

Walking in the tunnel towards the bookstore, Connor asked, "Do you really want to seek revenge on Gary?"

"I'm going with karma and not revenge."

"What did he do to you that has you wanting revenge?"

"Karma, Connor, karma."

"Okay, so tell me what has traumatized you for life."

"He's constantly mean. He enjoyed hitting me with rubber bands in class. Not only was it painful, but it was embarrassing, as several students laughed at me. He always makes snarky remarks when he sees me, but the most humiliating thing was when he approached me and handed me an envelope. He said he was tired of seeing me in the same cheap shirt, so he started a collection to help me buy a more expensive one. The envelope had five dollars in it."

"Wow! That's seriously messed up."

"I cringe every time I see him heading in my direction. Truthfully, as soon as I spot him, I turn around and go completely out of my way to avoid him."

"Understandable. Now that I see it from your point of view, my plan makes sense. I'm going to place the marble on Gary, but you'll be near when it activates. You'll get to see it in full operational mode. I definitely want a report."

"Absolutely! I guarantee you'll be the first to hear about it." Natalie sighed with relief.

As they continued walking, she smiled to herself. Payback without her involvement. She glanced over at Connor.

"You have no inkling how I dreaded going anywhere near Gary or his chair. This eliminates me getting the nerve up to place a marble on or near him."

"No problem. I've got this."

"That's awesome! A little marble is about to inflict instant karma on a first-class jerk. Gary may be an excellent football player, but he's a spoiled brat. He needs to learn to empathize."

"And if he doesn't?"

"Well, he'll end up being my primary guinea pig."

"You're brutal!" Connor laughed at the thought of Gary experiencing his potion.

Natalie got up early. Coal didn't bother to get up. It was a school day. She walked over and gave him a couple of crackers. He gobbled them down before she even left the room.

Twelve marbles were in her pocket. Before classes started, she would slip two into each hallway and the cafeteria. She planned to activate them one pair at a time as she walked through the school. As the day wore on, more and more students would itch, and black mold would appear. It was the first day back, and mold would be the culprit of an itching problem. She assumed the school administration would consider it a health issue because of the fires that activated the sprinklers throughout the school.

She looked at her phone for the tenth time. Where was the bus? It was already ten minutes past the scheduled pickup time. She would be late for science. That meant all eyes would be on her when she entered the class. She dreaded it. This had to be a bad omen.

As soon as the bus driver opened the door at school, she jumped up and hopped down the steps. She ran down the sidewalk, swung the front door open, and flew into the lobby. Taking a sharp turn, she jogged down the science hallway until she came to her class. Taking a deep breath to calm her nerves, she swung the door open and entered. Mr. Parrish stopped talking and turned towards Natalie. She avoided looking at him or anyone else, dashed to her seat, and sat down. Mr. Parrish cleared his throat before he started speaking again.

Connor met Natalie outside of science. Wringing her hands and glancing around nervously, she looked flustered.

"What's going on?"

"Of all days, the school bus was late...really late. I'm going to need to change my plans," Natalie complained as she opened the back door, and they headed outside.

"Chill. Things are about to get interesting," Connor said with a huge, mischievous smile. She couldn't help but smile. She relaxed as they headed towards her World History class.

"Gary is in my next class."

"I know. That's when the fun begins."

"You sure you can make it, so it only happens to Gary?"

"Just Gary. I know his before-school routine, so it's already on him. Actually, he has two on him."

"That's awesome."

"Yes, it is. Now pick up your pace so you'll beat me to your class."

"Thanks, Connor."

Natalie rushed towards her class. Nervous and excited, she entered the classroom, hurried to her seat, and plopped down. With her seat in the front, his in the back, and noisy students, she might miss him entering. She desperately wanted to watch the door, but she knew better.

Where was he? It was close to the bell ringing when she finally heard his voice as he came through the door. As usual, he bragged about himself. Natalie smirked.

Mrs. Reinheart took attendance and reminded everyone that their homework must be put in the basket on her desk. Natalie half listened to her. Shouldn't the potion already be working? The suspense drove her crazy to the point that she had forgotten to look at the "Do Now" project on the board.

She reached into her bookbag for her homework and notebook, but instead of pulling things from her bookbag, she thought about sticking her head in there. She got a whiff of something that smelled like rotten eggs...a boatload of rotten eggs.

Nervous giggling erupted from the back of the class. Mrs. Reinheart stood up to see what was happening. Just then, a ridiculously long and loud fart let loose, followed by several toots.

"Excuse me," the teacher hollered, heading down Natalie's aisle, looking for the culprit.

Halfway down the aisle, she stopped and looked horrified as another ridiculously long and loud fart filled the air. The smell was horrendous. Several toots followed. Gagging, Mrs. Reinheart hurried back to her desk. She grabbed a tissue to cover her nose. With her nose covered and breathing out of her mouth as little as possible, the angry teacher stomped towards the back of the room.

Looking at Gary, she shouted while pointing at the door, "You foul, disgusting creature, depart my room now!"

Gary Toppleman noisily bolted from the room.

Mrs. Reinheart stomped back to her desk and brought out the odor-neutralizing spray. Walking around with her nose covered and angrily muttering, she heavily sprayed the room. Students ducked to avoid getting sprayed, but the spray did nothing to cover the smell.

Standing at the door, Mrs. Reinheart seethed, "I'm not paid enough to teach in a room that smells like a manure factory. This is ridiculous. Class dismissed." The teacher was the first one out the door.

Early dismissal was perfect. Trying hard not to laugh at what happened, she took a yellow marble and a black marble out, sat down on a bench in one corridor, and secretly placed the marbles. Getting up, she found a place to laugh before going to the next spot to place the marbles. The teacher's words and Gary running out the door in his hurry to escape made her stop and laugh before hiding the next marbles. Finally, she had placed all the marbles. Before her fourth-period class, she activated them.

It didn't take long for black mold to appear, and soon everyone at school scratched endlessly, leaving them covered in red scratch marks. They were miserable. Over the PA system, an announcement of an emergency drill came. Everyone swarmed out of the school and stood far from the front of the building.

Loud complaining and angry voices drowned out the administrator speaking in front of them. Students with cars left for the parking lot. More followed, and soon, only students using alternative transportation remained. The administrator flung her hands up in the air in frustration. Still itching, some students walked across the highway to the restaurant. Connor met Natalie as the crowd dwindled.

"Come with me," Connor said as he scratched his arm. Joel was already waiting at Connor's car.

"Let's get out of here," Joel exclaimed as he opened the passenger door and jumped into the car.

"Is there a remedy besides time?" Connor asked.

"Good question. The instructions Twilight gave me didn't mention a remedy. Let's hope our mentors have the answer."

Turning onto the highway and heading north, Connor asked, "How'd it go with Gary?"

"It was absolutely a hoot, or with Gary a toot," Natalie roared with laughter.

"Tell us," Joel demanded.

"The first one must have been silent, as there was this huge smell of rotten eggs. It consumed the whole room. The teacher got up to find out who was causing the problem. As she went down the aisle, Gary let out the longest and loudest fart ever, followed by several toots. We could hardly breathe when the next round hit. Chairs were dragged across the floor as his friends tried to escape him. The teacher retreated to get a tissue to cover her nose. Stomping back to Gary, she yelled, "You foul, disgusting creature, depart my room now!" Gary and his obnoxious activity bolted from the room. The teacher sprayed the room, but it still stunk. Fuming, she ranted that she couldn't teach in a place that smelled like a manure factory, so she dismissed us. It was priceless." Natalie laughed so hard she could hardly get the words out. Connor and Joel were laughing hard at the visual in their heads.

"Man, to have been able to see it," Connor chuckled while scratching his left arm.

"He deserved it. I'm thinking of buying a can of room freshener, putting it in a brown bag, and walking up to Gary. While handing it to him, I'll tell him he needs this more than I need a new shirt, so I spent his money on him."

"What's that about?"

"That was the final straw, Joel. Gary told me he was tired of seeing me in the same cheap shirt, so he wanted me to take the envelope he handed me and buy a more expensive shirt. The envelope had five dollars in it."

"Wow! That's low, even for Gary."

"Yes, it is. I think today humbled him, even though I'm puzzled about why he stayed in the room after the first one escaped. Maybe he isn't all that bright, or maybe he thought if he left the class, he'd stink up the entire school." She laughed at the visual.

"Now that's hilarious," Joel roared with laughter.

"Remember, I put two marbles in his pocket."

"It reacted as a double load," Natalie laughed. "So incredibly awesome. If you see me laughing for no particular reason, you know what I'm replaying in my head."

"The teacher's reaction is what I would have enjoyed seeing," Connor said.

"Me, too, Connor."

"Being an ancient teacher, all prim and proper, it was hysterical. I wonder if Gary will return to class. If so, I can't wait to see how Mrs. Reinheart deals with him. Anyway, that's his problem. Hopefully, he's learned a lesson. If not, and he picks on me again, he will find other horrendous things happening to him."

"I still have three marbles," Connor laughed.

"Where'd you put a marble?" Joel looked over and studied Connor's face.

"A jerk that likes to bug me."

"Joel, he isn't going to tell you. It doesn't matter. Gary's antics caused early dismissal, which gave me time to set up my marbles. It worked out perfectly."

"Let's hope the black mold and itching cause the school to close for a few more days. We need time to plan our next attack."

"I think our next attack should be on the Janus Club leadership."

"Good idea, Natalie. Any ideas?" Joel said as he tried to reach his arm down his back to scratch.

"No, I have nothing."

"I'm thinking of anonymously calling the Health Department on the school," Connor said as they stopped at a traffic light.

"Great idea," Joel said.

"It's an excellent idea. Maybe I can get some more black mold marbles from Twilight and have Coal place them at the school. We can keep it going for a couple more days."

"If you go, let me know. I'll go with you."

"For the marbles or to see Twilight."

"What do you think?"

"Should I see Twilight?" Joel asked.

"No!" Connor immediately replied. Natalie laughed.

"Now I'm curious."

"Joel, Twilight said something interesting while we were there. She said several of the stores have young owners. Maybe your beloved Flaky Kuchen has a young owner."

"With my luck, it's probably Hexel's twin."

"Dude, there's no way the pastry smell could cover a Hexel twin smell." That got all of them laughing even though they were still scratching.

Finally, Connor stopped in front of Joel's house. Doors flung open. They jumped out, slammed the doors shut, and immediately headed to their homesteads, looking for relief from the endless itching.

"Lorcan!" Natalie yelled before she had even stepped into the homestead. No reply. She jogged towards the kitchen. Passing through the Room of Mirrors, Lorcan met her. Where she had rolled up her sleeves, exposing her arms, he saw long red scratch marks.

"Successful day?"

"Too successful. Can you do something about this itching? It's driving me nuts."

Lorcan took his wand out and pointed it at Natalie. "*Alleviate!*" Still holding his wand out, he waited. Natalie waited. Nothing. The itching was gone.

"Thank you. I feel sorry for the others who have to suffer with the itching."

"Taking a shower will end it."

"Really? That's all it takes?"

"It's a potion to disrupt, not to injure. It's a temporary annoyance." Lorcan put his wand up. He studied her. She already looked more relaxed.

"Come get a drink," Lorcan said, returning to the kitchen.

Natalie found a lemon-colored punch in the refrigerator. After making drinks for both of them, she sat down and took a big gulp of the punch. Before Lorcan could react, she stood over the sink. It took a minute before she could speak.

"That, whatever that is, desperately needs sugar." She filled a glass with water and rinsed her mouth out.

Lorcan laughed. "With the fairies, it is always a hit or a miss. It is never mediocre."

"In all ways." She sat back down, hoping her throat would soon recover.

Joel called. Lorcan could tell by Natalie's expression that the news was good—no guessing needed. He waited.

"Joel said no school tomorrow. However, if it needs to be closed on Thursday and Friday, they'll send us instructions on how to attend e-school classes. Looks like the Janus Club won't be meeting tomorrow."

"Good, now you have more time to come up with another way to stop it."

"Let's hope."

Lorcan pulled a photo out of his pocket and placed it on the table. She leaned in to get a good look at it. At first, all she could see were green leaves. Then she noticed the red triangle. She grabbed the picture and pulled it closer to her face. It was similar to, but not as close as, a bird. It had leaves. The eyes were the same color as the tail. She couldn't believe it. It was the leaf ball.

"That's Rafflesia?"

"Yes, you found her in her protective state."

"Wow."

"The amazing thing is we found another Rafflesia in the northern tunnel near Connor's homestead."

"What does that mean?"

"There's a chance they don't become extinct. They now live in Stormfield."

"Good. A magical place where they won't need to hide. Speaking of hiding, how do we know the tunnels will stay clear of spiders?"

"For your discovery, the council placed bug zappers throughout the tunnel system."

"Mmm, I'm curious now. Are these bug zappers anything like Pru's sarcastic candles?"

Lorcan's eyes lit up as he laughed, but he didn't answer the question.

Getting up, she looked down at the mischievous smile on Lorcan's face. She wanted an answer, but she wasn't brave enough to venture down into the tunnels without the rest of them. No school tomorrow meant it was the perfect time to check out the bug zappers.

Chapter 13

Tunnel Guardians

"I can't believe Pru chose Angus Thornton's project over us," Skylar whined as she clomped down the homestead's basement stairs with Madison and Natalie.

"They aren't that different in age," Natalie said.

"Ew, Natalie, are you saying what I think you're saying?"

"Maybe. Lorcan said Pru impressed Thornton by standing up to Hexel. This is Pru's chance to be with someone closer to her age."

"But she's part of our group," Skylar whined.

"Which she cherishes, Skylar, but there's more to life than hanging out with teenagers."

"But it's Angus Thornton."

"I'm surprised I'm saying this, but there's hope for him. Twilight, his niece, says he's full of himself at the moment. Pru will put him in his place. You know how often Pru says "not funny" to our group. I wonder if Thornton will break our record."

"Probably the first day," Skylar countered as they walked towards the door to the tunnel system.

"I'm more disappointed with Joel and Connor," Madison fumed.

"They're in the doghouse with their lame excuse for not being here," Skylar agreed.

"When it comes to video games, you know how they can be. No school meant they stayed up and planned to sleep in today. They'll probably just make it in time for their training."

"And be useless," Madison remarked as they stood in front of the door that would take them into the tunnel system.

"True. Who wants the honor of opening the door?" Natalie asked.

"I'll do it," Madison volunteered. "I need to practice getting the words right."

Standing close together, Madison stretched out her arms and hands and shouted, "*Aparty Depressionitarium!*"

Natalie and Skylar burst out laughing. "Sis, this isn't a depressing party. Say '*Aperta Depraesentiarum*' correctly," whispered Skylar. The door shook slightly at hearing the spell words whispered by Skylar.

"Isn't that what I said?"

"Not even close, and you don't need to be so dramatic. Loudly and clearly saying the spell will work." Skylar and Natalie giggled while imitating Madison's dramatic hand movements without saying the words.

"Stop it! I know what to do, but why can't Lorcan come with us?"

"Madison, you're stalling. We're the only ones who could make it this morning. Do you want to see what's in the tunnels now or wait until all of us can get together?" Skylar asked.

"No waiting," Natalie exclaimed. "We're here. Let's see the tunnel zappers."

Madison shouted, "*Aperta Depraesentiarum!*" The door immediately swung open. Skylar gave Madison a gentle push to get her inside the tunnel. Natalie went in after Skylar. The door slammed shut.

The red dragon fire crystals dimly lit the tunnel. Even so, the three girls immediately noticed an enormous blob of translucent slime on the rugged wall.

"Disgusting," Madison said, cringing at the slimy, jiggling blob attached to the wall.

"You're disgusting!"

The three girls screamed, turned around, and yelled, "*Aperta Depraesentiarum!*" but nothing happened.

"Calm down. I'm a tunnel guardian. My purpose is to protect you by keeping the tunnel free of pests. You're the exception."

Turning back around, the three girls ignored the last statement and stared at the wiggling blob. A gigantic protruding circle with orange glowing eyes, a large mouth, and slime that seemed to be in constant motion. A frightful sight.

"Lorcan wouldn't tell me if you were like Pru's candles. Are you?" Natalie asked.

"I, we, have never met the candles. Our job is to keep the tunnels clear of pests."

"I'm afraid to ask, but how is that accomplished if you're stuck to a wall?" Natalie asked, still not comfortable with the jiggling blob.

Instantly, a tongue shot out and splatted against the door. Before the girls could react, the tongue splatted against the ceiling and then down toward the next tunnel guardian.

"Hey, knock it off!"

"Sorry, my demonstration got out of hand," the tunnel guardian yelled to the other guardian.

"Good grief!" Natalie cried. "How far does your tongue stretch out?"

"As far as it needs. I zap, I eat."

"What if it's a super gigantic spider?" Skylar asked, keeping her distance.

"We feast."

"Gross! Not a vision I want in my head." Natalie shook her head as if trying to clear the image out of her mind.

"It's what happens if you don't want to be the feast. We're here to keep you safe and the tunnels clear of pests."

"Thanks, I think. To finish the meal, do you eat a treat?"

"No, but we do like salt and pepper. Do you have any on you?"

"Of course not! We had no idea what Lorcan and the council had cooked up for bug zappers. I was thinking about those yellow, sticky things that hang from the ceiling," Madison said.

While Madison answered the tunnel guardian, Natalie stepped closer to get a better look at the bug zapper. Slowly raising her left hand, she was close to touching it.

"Don't!" Its eyes bulged out as it incredulously stared at her.

The freaky look had her jumping back to Madison and Skylar. "I'm curious if you're cold and slimy to the touch."

"I'm curious if you have any manners." It narrowed its eyes and studied Natalie.

"Sorry. We've seen nothing like you before. I guess we'll be speaking with Lorcan."

"You do that. All you need to know is we are here to keep the tunnels free of pests. We'll do our job so you can safely travel the tunnels. If you want to do good, bring some salt and pepper."

"If we do that," Skylar said, "we'd need to bring it for all the guardians. How many are there?"

"We total 26."

"Wow! There's a lot of you." Skylar glanced down the tunnel.

"The number needed to protect the tunnels. Now, if you have any more questions, ask Lorcan. I'm busy."

"We can see you're overwhelmed. What to do next?" Natalie rolled her eyes and turned away from him.

"Should we check out your tunnel?"

Skylar shook her head yes.

Heading straight and then taking the southern tunnel, they moved toward Skylar and Madison's old homestead. The tunnel lit by the dragon crystals appeared clean and bug-free. The three tunnel guardians remained quiet, but their eyes followed the mages. They arrived at the entrance door to their old homestead.

"Do we want to go in or turn around?" Madison asked.

"Would Breccan be okay with us just showing up?" Natalie asked.

"I'd be more worried about the fairies. I'm sure they're fluttering around the first floor right now."

"Oh, right, they're worse than the tunnel guardians. Let's go back," Natalie said, already turning around.

The southern tunnel guardians remained quiet, but the guardians followed the girls with their eyes as they walked back to the main tunnel. After a turn and a short walk, they reached the door to Natalie's old homestead. Madison stood, ready to say the password. Suddenly, the first tunnel guardian's tongue flew past them and stuck to the door.

In horror, the girls turned around and faced the angry tunnel guardian.

"Aren't you going to say goodbye?"

"What? I thought you wanted us to move through the tunnels without making any noise. Which one is it?" Natalie asked, confused.

"It would be good manners, which you appear to be lacking, to acknowledge us by saying hello or goodbye."

"We'll keep that in mind," Natalie said. "Goodbye for now."

Turning to face the door, Madison yelled, "*Aperta Depraesentiarum!*" The door opened, and they walked through well before it slammed shut.

Heading towards the stairs, Madison burst out laughing. "Natalie, you really do need to work on your manners."

"One minute, he's too busy for us, and the next minute, my manners are lacking because we aren't saying goodbye."

"You can make it up to him with salt and pepper," Madison smirked.

"It'll be a start. I may name all of them so that he can see how friendly I can be."

Climbing the creaking stairs, Skylar developed a plan. "There are 26 of them, so let's give each one a letter from the alphabet."

"Sounds good. Grumpy pants can be Agar," Natalie said.

"Agar?" Skylar questioned.

"The meaning is close to slime."

"Seriously, Natalie, you really do need to work on how to win friends and influence people," Madison laughed as she opened the door to the first floor.

Standing by the stairs that led up to the bedrooms, Natalie said, "Thank goodness we don't have to go from snarky tunnel guardians to annoying fairies. The new battery-operated car has been a smashing success."

"Good choice of words, as I can hear them crashing into each other," Madison laughed.

"They've been at it all morning."

"A pleasant break from their all-consuming role of disastrous helpers," Skylar commented.

"Definitely, a much-needed break," Natalie agreed and then focused on the guardians. "Getting back to the tunnel guardians, I'm thinking A through Z; each name is four letters and no flowery names. I'm sure I won't have a problem coming up with unique names."

"No," Madison insisted, "we get half the names. You take A through M. Skylar, and I will take N through Z. We'll follow your rules."

"Fine by me. Lorcan finally put a larger table in the kitchen. Do you want to work in there? I can get some paper and pens. While we're working, anyone brave enough for a glass of fairy punch?"

Madison and Skylar laughed before Madison said, "Isn't it amazing how they can make the most amazing punch or the most disgusting punch? There have been times when I wanted the whole pitcher. There have been other times I was afraid that if we poured it down the sink, it would eat the pipes."

"So true. The other day the punch burned all the way down." Natalie recalled the burning sensation in her throat. "It was close to qualifying for pipe-eating status."

"I'm not taking any chances. I think water will be fine," Madison said.

"Good. You want to take care of the water, and I'll go get paper and pens?"

They were there for over an hour, laughing at some of the names they had suggested and rejecting many others. Finally, the list was done. It was time for Madison and Skylar to head to their elemental training class.

"Lorcan can look over our list. If he's okay with the names, I'll ask him to put a big, glowing letter by each guardian."

"Why not use their full name so we won't need to memorize this list?"

169

"Good idea, Skylar. I'm sure Joel and definitely Connor would just call them A, B, C if the names are not down there."

"Speaking of those two, look who just showed up for training," Madison said.

As Joel and Connor headed over to the girls, Joel asked, "Were you brave enough to check out the bug zappers?"

"Yes, no thanks to you and Connor," Madison fumed.

"You're still mad at us for taking time to play video games?" Joel asked.

"It would have been nice to have both of you with us. However, we managed without you."

"So, Madison, you can tell us all about the tunnel guardian adventure on the way to the Barracks."

"Nope. You get to experience the bug zappers on your own."

"Not on my own. Connor will go with me."

"Sure. We can go right after our training."

"See. Solved."

They headed for the basement door. Natalie stayed behind and cleaned up the kitchen. She left the papers on the table. *Where is Lorcan? I want him to see the list before Draon arrives for my training.*

"Lorcan!"

He didn't answer. Natalie walked through the first floor, but Lorcan wasn't anywhere to be found. The fairies made too much noise with their cars for him to be upstairs. Walking outside, she saw a black tail sticking out from underneath the front porch.

"Lorcan? Jericho? You okay?" Natalie walked over and peered under the porch. Jericho backed out and shook the dirt from his fur. He didn't make eye contact. Instead, he headed for the steps. Bouncing up the steps, Natalie followed and opened the front door. Jericho transformed into Lorcan. She felt he was doing something she didn't want to know about.

"Are you okay?"

"Fine." Lorcan brushed the remaining dirt off his pants.

"Okay, I was worried. However, I think it's best I don't know what you were doing."

"What do you want?" Lorcan grumbled, still avoiding eye contact with her.

"We met the tunnel guardians today. The council may have placed them, but the personalities are like the candles."

"True. You like Pru's candles. I kept that in mind while creating the bug zappers. They have attitude."

"Putting it mildly. After our brief visit, we decided to name them. The list is on the table. If you're okay with the names, can you place a name for each guardian? We purposely kept the names short."

"Do you want Joel and Connor to have a say?" Lorcan looked up at her.

"Nope. They lost their chance when they decided video games would be a better use of their time."

"Okay. While Draon is here for your training, I'll review the list and handle placing the names by the guardians."

"Thanks, Lorcan." Natalie hesitated. "Lorcan?"

"What?"

"You have roach legs stuck in your braid."

"Go get ready for your lesson with Draon."

Chapter 14

Laughing Hyenas

Natalie enjoyed being in her pajamas as she attended e-school on Thursday and Friday. This was much nicer than getting dressed and hiking to and from the bus stop. She smiled, knowing Gary couldn't harass her. Then, she thought about her last encounter with him. She laughed.

Without a doubt, she knew he favored school via a home computer instead of sneering and joking about his odorous activities. Fortunately for him, the familiars, excluding Joel's bird, hid black marble potions throughout the school. Black mold would continue for more weeks.

She woke up early on Saturday and did her outside chores in her pajamas. After a nice warm shower, she traipsed through the palmetto-bordered path toward the old homestead. No longer fearing the scarecrows, her eyes were on them as she headed towards the gate. Out of the corner of her eye, she spotted Skylar and Madison using the gravel road on the north side of the property to reach the homestead.

"I can't believe we're already heading to Saturday's class," Madison said as they all reached the gate.

"I prefer these classes to school classes," Natalie said.

"Definitely!" Madison and Skylar agreed.

The three girls stepped into the house. Immediately, twelve excited fairies, squealing in high-pitched voices, swarmed the girls. Enthusiasm mounted as the fairies split up and, in groups of four, they flew around each girl. Soon, pushing and pulling had the fairies maneuvering the girls into the kitchen. Stormy Iris and Sunshine Lily opened the refrigerator door and pointed at the purple punch. Shrill, high-pitched voices showed they wanted the girls to taste their punch.

"I trust Sunshine more than the other fairies, even so." Natalie hesitated to get a glass.

Stormy's voice turned into a nagging tone. The girls laughed, and each grabbed a glass. Natalie poured the punch. Turning to Sunshine, she asked, "Have you tasted this punch?"

Sunshine happily shook her head yes.

Holding the glasses up so they could smell the punch, each sniffed. It smelled sweet. Small sips turned into big gulps.

"Yum," exclaimed Madison, holding her glass out for more.

"Wow, you outdid yourself on this punch. It's awesome!" Natalie gushed as she refilled their glasses. The girls had consumed all the punch by the time Joel and Connor arrived.

Madison and Skylar plopped into the cart and sat across from Natalie. Leaning in, they whispered and giggled as the railroad cart lurched forward. Rumbling noises from the cart as it slowly made its way toward the bookstore had the girls raising their voices. Their nonsense conversation had them endlessly laughing. Natalie kept bouncing into Connor. Connor kept pushing her off. The girls laughed as Natalie pushed him back. Extremely annoyed, Connor and Joel reached their limit.

"What's so funny?" Connor asked in frustration.

"We don't know," Skylar giggled.

The walk in the tunnel to the Barracks echoed with the sounds of stumbling, laughter, endless whispering, and more laughter. Joel stayed behind the girls, and Connor stayed in front of them. Reaching the door to the Barracks, Joel moved to the front and stood with Connor. Crossing their arms in front of themselves, they stood as guards blocking entry into the Barracks. Both angrily glared at the girls.

"What were you whispering about that had you laughing the entire trip?" Joel stared at them as if all three girls were drunk.

"I don't remember," Skylar chuckled, with Madison and Natalie joining in the laughter.

"Can you count to ten and touch your nose each time you say a number?" Joel asked as he touched his nose with his index finger.

"Can you count and twirl like a ballerina each time you say a number?" Natalie asked.

All three girls roared with laughter while awkwardly twirling and ending up facing in different directions.

"I'm dizzy," Skylar complained, trying to hold onto Madison.

"Should I open the door?" Joel asked Connor.

"Sure, let Hexel deal with the Laughing Hyenas."

Joel pushed the door open. Connor turned the girls so they faced the door. One at a time, he walked each one through the doorway. The door slammed shut, and the girls burst into laughter. Hexel floated over and hovered by the girls. As Madison shouted, "What's that smell?" the boys took off.

"Did you forget to shower today, Natalie?" Madison said, holding her nose.

"I thought it was you, Madison!" Natalie pushed her nose up like a pig's nose and went, "Oink, oink!"

"Can we get by, Hexel? Pretty please with a cherry on top," Skylar laughed.

"Why didn't you like the butterfly necklace I gave you, Hexel?" Natalie said, beginning to cry.

Hexel floated closer to Natalie and hovered in front of her.

"I meant it as a thank you. I hope I didn't hurt your feelings." Natalie continued to cry.

Skylar and Madison grabbed her and tightly hugged her. Skylar whispered, "You still smell, Natalie."

"You smell, but not as bad as Gary Toppleman." Natalie laughed. With her mouth, she made a loud fart noise and then several smaller fart noises. The girls roared with laughter.

Hexel backed up and continued to float around them. Angus Thornton walked out of the Water elemental building and spotted Hexel floating around the girls. Curious, he walked over to them.

"Is there a problem?" He looked at each girl and then at Hexel.

"Seems Hexel doesn't want us to attend class today!" Natalie shouted as the other two dramatically nodded their heads up and down.

"We even said pretty please with a cherry on top," Skylar blurted out.

"Have you been drinking?" Angus Thornton's tone changed to one of annoyance.

"Nope. We're not old enough, but we had some incredibly awesome-tasting fairy punch before coming here. It was truly delicious. The three of us drank the whole pitcher…in minutes…without sharing one single drop with the guys." Skylar stumbled as she pretended to chug the punch down.

Madison and Natalie caught her, causing the three to knock against each other, split apart, and stagger a few steps to regain their balance. They giggled.

"You're drunk!" Angus confirmed while pointing at them.

"We are? Natalie, I thought you said we could trust Sunshine Lily?" Madison pouted.

Natalie wobbled in place as she watched Joel and Connor walk up with Mr. Xanders.

"Oh, goodie," Natalie slurred, "Mr. Xanders is going to talk with Hexel."

"No, he's not. He's going to be speaking with me," Angus Thornton replied.

"Party pooper," Natalie said. She made the fart noises again. Madison and Skylar roared with laughter at Natalie.

Angus Thornton looked on in disgust. "It appears they consumed a whole pitcher of fairy punch before heading over here. They're drunk. Hexel won't let them pass."

"It's obvious," Mr. Xanders said, trying to keep a straight face, but he couldn't stay serious. He burst out laughing. Joel and Connor joined him.

"What do you propose?" Angus Thornton said, folding his arms in front of him and waiting for an answer.

"Send them home," Mr. Xanders stated. "If they can stand here under these circumstances and not sober up, there isn't anything that will help but time. We'll have class tomorrow."

"You sure?"

"Definitely. Joel and Connor take them home," Mr. Xanders said, watching as they rounded up the three drunk girls.

Natalie woke to a monstrous headache and stomach-turning nausea. Without questioning why she still wore street clothes, she released the top button of her jeans. It didn't help. Eyes closed and frozen in place, she waited a lifetime until the nausea abated. The hammering headache did not. Jericho walked in and jumped on the bed.

176

"Don't do that! My head is going to explode."

She took a pillow and covered her face. Her father walked into the room.

"Do you remember what happened?" Karl pulled the pillow from Natalie's face and sat on the edge of the bed.

"I remember drinking that awesome fairy punch and then waking up here." Natalie tried to reach for her pillow, but it pained her to move.

"Joel and Connor brought you home. You've been sleeping most of the day."

"It was the fairy punch, wasn't it?" Natalie groaned.

"I'm afraid they put something in there that made you, Skylar, and Madison drunk."

"Great. Did we make fools of ourselves in class?"

"You didn't get that far. Hexel wouldn't let you pass."

"So, we missed class, and now my head is going to explode."

"Mr. Xanders has agreed to teach the class tomorrow."

"Good. Can I have something for this headache?"

"You need to sit up and take an aspirin with water. I'll come back in a few minutes with toast and orange juice." Karl got up and waited for Natalie to sit up.

Struggling to stay sitting up, she took the aspirin and a sip of water. Once the pill went down, she took a bigger sip and then fell back on her pillows. That's the last thing she remembered from Saturday.

"Notice how quiet it is in here?" Natalie asked the other four as they gathered in the Room of Mirrors.

"Of course," Connor smirked, "the little flying evildoers are in hiding."

"Good. I'm sure whatever was in the punch was a rule-breaker. Brats."

"I can think of several other names to call them, Natalie. We were drunk all day with miserable headaches. To top it off, our parents considered not allowing us off the property. They think you're responsible, so that you can imagine their displeasure with you."

"Oh, great, Madison. Now I'll want to avoid your parents," Natalie complained as they headed towards the basement door. Lorcan waited in the kitchen.

"Wait a minute," Lorcan called out. Reaching them, he looked over each girl. "How do you feel?"

"Embarrassed," Natalie said. "I trusted Sunshine Lily, and yet she and the other fairies made a concoction that made us act like total fools. I hope they stay in hiding for a long time."

"Yeah, we don't want to see them, either. They almost cost us from ever coming over here again," Madison exclaimed as Skylar shook her head in agreement.

"They got into the potions. Since they can't read, they thought they were using a flavor enhancer, but they used Loonypox instead. Those potions are the same color and texture. Again, they are forbidden from entering that room, but they thought they were giving you a treat."

"Why is there always a but with them?" Connor said, "You tell them no. However, they think they're coming up with a great idea, so no doesn't apply. It always, and I mean always, leads to a disaster."

"I agree," Lorcan said. "They have restrictions in their room for a week. Hopefully, this time, they will learn that no and off-limits have no exceptions."

"I'm betting not."

"I'm betting with you," Joel agreed with Connor. "Want to bet?"

"Sure. Within two weeks of being off restrictions, they'll break a rule."

"Mmm, I may lose this one as I think they won't make it for five days."

"You want to pass?"

"Nope. The loser takes the winner to the Flaky Kuchen for two donuts and a drink."

"You're on, Joel."

"Enough of this nonsense. The fairies may surprise you," Lorcan said, defending the fairies.

Joel and Connor burst into laughter.

"I'm sure they'll surprise us," Connor said, still laughing.

Annoyed, Lorcan cut their laughter short. "Head to class. Mr. Xanders has some important announcements."

"Will Pru join us?" Skylar asked.

"No."

"When will she be back?" Skylar asked.

"Go to class and get that information. You're going to be late if you don't go now." Lorcan walked away.

Just before Joel opened the door to the Barracks, he looked back at the girls. "It'll be interesting to see how Hexel reacts to you being here. Yesterday, she stopped you at the gatehouse."

"Thank goodness that's all she did." Natalie cringed, thinking about what might have happened if they had annoyed Hexel.

Hexel waited at the gatehouse. Natalie noticed she showed no interest in Joel and Connor as she let them walk past the gatehouse. Hexel moved to block the girls. Natalie quit holding her breath and moved closer to Madison and Skylar. Glancing over at Joel and Connor waiting at a safe distance from them, she thought, *Lucky them.*

Hexel floated before each girl. She stopped before Natalie. At first, Natalie kept her gaze fixed on the ground. Hexel approached her, moving closer. She looked up.

Between the veil and the layered coverings, she couldn't see Hexel's face, but Hexel could see her face. For a few tense minutes, Hexel observed her. The others watched the strange encounter but were too afraid to speak or move. Finally, Hexel turned and floated back to the gatehouse. With an enormous sigh of relief, the three girls joined Joel and Connor.

Walking into class discussing Hexel's strange behavior, they became quiet as they saw a dark-haired boy their age already seated. They exchanged glances but quietly took their seats.

Mr. Xanders, already at his desk, observed them as they came in and sat down.

"How are you feeling?"

"Today is a different answer from yesterday. Today, we're back to normal. Lorcan told us when leaving that the fairies accidentally gave us Loonypox."

"Yeah," Connor smirked, "if the flying dudettes ever considered following the rules, we'd have less stressful lives."

Mr. Xanders laughed. "True, but that's not possible. They're mischievous by nature."

"Believe me, they frequently remind us of that trait," Connor said, shaking his head.

"You don't realize it, Connor, but you're fortunate to have fairies in your life. Very few people get to experience what you do daily."

"I guess."

"Okay, let's move on. Before we address an upcoming magical event, let me introduce Dillon Westbay. Dillon and his family have been living in the Barracks for the last ten years. With Pru working on a special project with the master wizard, Dillon will help your group."

"Good. We're no longer outnumbered," Connor grinned.

Then, he leaned forward and asked Dillon, "What's your element?"

Dillon leaned out to answer Connor. "Alchemist."

Connor pointed at his chest and gave a thumbs-up.

"Depending on how things go, Dillon and his family may move to your subdivision."

"In Pru's home?"

"No, Natalie, Dillon would be next door to Connor."

"That's empty acreage," Connor said.

"Not for long. If Dillon and his family decide to move there, the house and old homestead will be ready and available. At a minimum, they'll be able to use the address for attending school."

Disappointed, Natalie asked, "Pru isn't coming back?"

"I don't know. All I know is she's staying here for now."

"What about the candles?"

Mr. Xanders leaned back and laughed. "Lorcan said you would ask about them when you found out Pru is living here. What do you suggest?"

"I'd say Dillon's place if he lived there, but we don't know that answer yet. We each already have things guarding our old homesteads. I don't know."

"What about Natalie's basement? She always feels guilty if she doesn't go over to Pru's and stuff those dudes with candy. This way, they'll be around us more."

"You do know they aren't real, Connor."

"Tell that to Natalie."

"Natalie?" Mr. Xanders asked.

"Would Pru be okay if they moved to the basement? What will protect her place while she's gone?"

"The protection would be a different form of protection. It would most likely be a spell, so you wouldn't need to worry about getting attached."

"We could have them inside the tunnel system with the tunnel guardians. Can you see the candles and Agar insulting each other all day?" Connor laughed.

"And take it out on us. No thanks." Madison shuddered at the thought.

"Okay, we need to cover other things today, so think where you want the candles, Natalie, and get back to me."

"I'll try to find a good fit for them."

"Good, Natalie."

"One other thing, Mr. Xanders, while we were naming the tunnel guardians, I gave each candle a name. Castor and Pollux. They don't know it yet."

"Okay, I'll pass it on. Again, Natalie, they're not real."

"I know, but they have so much personality."

"Dillon, do you have any comments?" Mr. Xanders asked.

"Other than wanting to see these candles and the tunnel guardians, nope."

"Changing subjects. The good news is that the Janus Club has issued a statement that they will not be meeting at the school until April. With the black mold continuing to surface, the school will remain closed. Your familiars will make sure the black mold stays active."

"Don't give Joel's bird credit," Connor said with a snicker.

"I agree. My bird's useless."

"He may surprise you one day," Mr. Xanders said.

"Lorcan said the same thing about the fairies this morning," Joel said.

"The fairies and familiars may surprise you one day, but that isn't the point. The point is, for now, the familiars are keeping the black mold active, so the school can't open."

"The black mold has to end at some point. Do we have any new methods to stop the Janus Club?" Madison asked.

"We're thinking the marbles will still work to stop future meetings. However, Connor, your marble potion was a one-time event."

"We could always inflict Gary with loud, garlic burps," Natalie laughed.

"Give Gary a break, Natalie."

"It depends on whether he gives me a break. In fact, I'm going to visit Twilight and order some garlic burping marbles. If Gary continues to be a bully, Gary will soon gross everyone out with his garlic burps. Maybe he produces garlic bubbles that float and burst throughout the classroom. I can see Mrs. Reinheart marching down the aisle to oust the foul creature."

All the students, except Dillon, burst into laughter.

Dillon raised his hand. "I'm not following this. Can someone bring me up to speed?"

"It's a hilarious story. Joel and I will meet with you after class and bring you up to date," Connor said.

"Sounds good. We can meet at the Flaky Kuchen."

"I'd love to," Joel frowned, "but we're broke."

"No problem. My parents own the Flaky Kuchen."

Before Joel could respond, Natalie peered around Skylar and Madison and focused on Dillon. "Is Candace your mother?"

"Yes, why?"

"She made a deal with Oxley for pictures of us. They weren't pictures we wanted out there."

Dillon roared with laughter. It took a minute for him to catch his breath. "Those are hilarious. They're actually up in my study." He continued to laugh.

"Glad you enjoy us looking like monkey butts," Natalie grumbled.

"And here we go again," Connor interjected. "If the fairies had followed the rules, we wouldn't have looked like spider-splattered monkey butts, but no. They can't behave for ten minutes. Add to that my sweet-tooth mentor, and you have fairies and Oxley traitors."

"Seriously, you all need to lighten up. You have brought so much energy to the Barracks. We're your biggest fans. In fact, when Angus Thornton came to me asking if I wanted to join your group, I jumped at the chance to become a member."

"Glad to have you with us, Dillon," Joel said.

"Don't let Joel fool you, Dillon. He's in love with the pastries at Flaky Kuchen. His happiest time here was when the elves' twisted scheme required sugar-loading us over at your shop," Connor stated, while Madison and Skylar shook their heads in agreement.

"I remember that day."

"All right, we're seriously off-track. Your undivided attention up here. Does anyone know what is special about March 2?" Mr. Xanders asked.

Natalie immediately answered. "It's a full moon."

"Correct. It's also a feast, but not for us. We're the ones to prepare the feast and then distance ourselves from it."

"We do all the work and someone else has all the fun?" Connor grumbled.

Mr. Xanders ignored Connor's remark. "Each one of you has a familiar, correct?"

"Our birds," Madison and Skylar answered.

"Do you know what your birds are when they aren't birds?"

"Oh, no," Natalie said. "They aren't like Lorcan, who can morph into an angry giant, are they?"

"No, but once a year, they have a feast and return to being hobgoblins. This feast is in honor of their service to their mages."

"My familiar is a hobgoblin?" Connor tried to envision Jackson as a hobgoblin.

"Yes, as strange as it seems, it's true. Every year, the first full moon of March is the Feast of Service."

"So, we prepare food, provide drinks, and let them go crazy the night of the full moon?"

"Yes, and this year the party takes place in the Earth elemental building. Wizards and witches will work on the interior to make it look like a campsite. Each of you will bring food. We need Shepherd's Pie with gravy, mashed potatoes with gravy, homemade chunky applesauce, cupcakes, and s'mores. Adult mages will bring the drinks."

"Obviously," Dillon offered, "I will bring the cupcakes."

"I won't get away with making anything without my parents being suspicious," Joel said, frowning in frustration.

"The old homesteads have stoves and refrigerators, Joel," Madison said.

"Oh, right, I'll get the fairies to help me. Maybe my nonstop yakking Rose-Breasted Cockatoo knows how to read recipes, even though he may be too busy deciding what to wear to the party."

"Guess you better stick with buying the ingredients for the s'mores," Connor said, trying to contain his laughter.

Mr. Xanders ignored Joel and Connor's exchange and continued. "More than one of you can do the same thing. It's your familiars and the familiars in the Barracks."

185

"Hexel is going to allow this to happen?" Natalie asked in disbelief.

"This has happened many times. Hexel approves it each time."

"Does she sneak a drink?" Connor asked, laughing.

"I believe Hexel can do whatever she wants without sneaking anything," Joel laughed.

"I can make Shepherd's Pie. My mother has an amazing recipe for Shepherd's Pie with gravy. My dad knows what I am, so that I can make it in the kitchen without those disastrous fairy helpers."

"We'll do gravy and potatoes. Can we do it over at your house, Natalie?"

"Sure, Madison. It'll be fun to make this stuff together."

"Can I join you?" Joel asked.

"Sure, the more the merrier. We'll need to start a few days before, so we have it all done in time," Natalie said.

"Question, Mr. Xanders."

"Yes, Joel."

"What do our familiars look like when they're hobgoblins?"

"Beefy, hairy men about Natalie's height. They usually have long red hair, green eyes, and yellowish teeth. They dress like ancient warriors, idolizing a fighting spirit, even though they are normally quiet. This night is the exception. This night they party from sundown until 2 a.m."

"Avoiding traditional guidelines, my familiar will probably have pantaloons, a pirate shirt, and a pirate hat with one of his long pink feathers sticking out of it," Joel sighed.

"You do have a unique familiar, Joel," Mr. Xanders agreed with him.

"Well, he may surprise you and end up being the life of the party. When we hear a loud and drunk voice singing

99 Bottles of Beer on the Wall, we'll know it's your squirrelly bird," Connor laughed.

Natalie ignored the exchange. "Are mages from the Barracks bringing food to the feast?"

"Yes, but many of them will focus on beverages."

"Then add to my list chocolate, marshmallows, and crackers. My dad will volunteer to pick them up when he knows it's for Coal. Strangely, my father and Coal are best buddies. Coal sits with my father, watching television. It's a scream when it's football. If Dad yells, Coal squawks." Natalie laughed, visualizing her father with a glass of wine and Coal sitting next to him with his plate of crackers.

"Changing direction," Connor said, "Natalie mentioned after the marble event at school that we should focus on the Janus Club leadership. Even though they won't be meeting soon, should we go after them now?"

"Do you know who the leaders are?" Mr. Xanders asked.

"I've been going through last year's yearbook and figuring out some people," Natalie volunteered. "We definitely know Victor Mountebank is one of them."

"When you know something, let me know. If it sounds like it'll work, we'll do it unless Draon and Angus have broken the curse."

"What curse?" Dillon asked.

"Every member of the Janus Club receives a ring. Each ring has a beautiful blue diamond, but the beauty ends there. An old story tells of an enormous, cursed diamond that destroys lives. We believe each Janus Club ring has a fragment of that diamond."

"What rubbish," Connor said, interrupting the teacher.

"Not so, Connor. Recently, Draon and Angus have validated that the curse is real. They don't know how it works and they haven't been able to break the curse, but the curse is real."

"Every time my Variegated Orb Weaver bracelet is near one of those rings, the bracelet flashes," Natalie said.

"Variegated Orb Weaver?" Dillon was confused.

"Pru makes bracelets out of a special spiderweb." Natalie got up and walked over to Dillon. She showed him her bracelet. "When there is nearby danger in the magical realm, it wildly glitters."

"Wow! I've never seen anything like your bracelet."

"Pru has made hundreds of them. She could probably sell them here."

"No doubt!" Dillon exclaimed.

"Okay, we've gotten off track. Dillon obviously has a lot of catching up to do. Joel and Connor, when you go to the Flaky Kuchen this afternoon, be sure to cover what's happened since your team came together."

"More time to enjoy donuts."

"All you can eat, Joel."

"You'll live to regret that offer, Dillon," Connor countered.

"Again, we're off topic." Mr. Xanders got up and stood before the class. "There's one more thing before you go. I have your wands and a paper with a couple of simple spells to practice."

"Aren't we going to stand out wearing wand rings?"

"No, Joel, mageless wands are for sale in a few stores. They look identical to the wand you will be wearing. Once you put it on, keep it on. Natalie and Dillon already have their wands. Joel, come up."

Joel put the wand on his finger, took the assignment, and sat down. Next were Connor, Skylar, and Madison.

"Okay, when we meet next week, you should have already mastered those spells. Class dismissed."

Natalie watched as Joel, Connor, and Dillon headed over to the Flaky Kuchen while the girls headed to the front of the Barracks.

"Have you been in the tunnels since our first trip in there?"

"There are two of us, so we have ventured in there a few times. The tunnel guardians at our entrance are quiet. They're nothing like Agar," Madison said.

"I wish that were true of Agar. He's snarky, whereas the candles are boisterous. The candles make me laugh; Agar makes me cringe. If he weren't snarky, I might think about venturing in there. In reality, it isn't a big deal. The tunnels lead to my place. I don't need to use the other tunnels."

"That sounds lucky for you," Skylar said.

It was the usual trek walking through the tunnel, to the bookstore, and the ride in the railroad cart to Natalie's basement. Trudging up the basement steps to the first floor, Natalie swung the door open and held the door for Madison and Skylar. She spotted Lorcan sitting in the kitchen.

"Lorcan, do you know if Pru is returning to our group?" Natalie asked as the three gathered in front of him.

He looked at the concerned expressions. "I can't honestly answer that question. However, if I had to make a guess, I would say no."

"We were worried about that," Skylar cried, wringing her hands together.

"I'm sorry. It began as a short-term project, but Pru is highly skilled and valuable to Angus."

"Next, he'll marry her, and we'll never see her again," Skylar whined.

"What? That's crazy." Lorcan shook his head in amazement.

"So, are we really getting Pru's candles?"

189

"It's up to you, Natalie. I can remove my spell, and they will strictly protect Pru's property. No personality. No communication. Or we can keep them as they are and move them."

"You can't remove your spell. It would seem like they died. However, I'm not sure where they should call home. Can I think about it? If they're at the basement door, it might be too much. There must be a place where we see them often enough, but not every day."

"Sure. There's no rush."

Lorcan spotted the wands. "Great, you're now ready to learn spells."

"Mr. Xanders gave us a couple of spells to practice. We're practicing when we get home."

Natalie headed out to lock up the chickens while Madison and Skylar headed home to practice. Completing her outside chores, she wondered if Joel and Connor were still sharing their adventures with Dillon. She laughed, thinking about Joel prolonging it for the enjoyment of stuffing himself with endless Flaky Kuchen donuts.

Chapter 15

Night Hollow

Exhausted from five trips down the basement stairs, lugging heavy boxes of food, Natalie, Madison, and Skylar took a quick break beside the stacked boxes waiting to be loaded on the railroad cart. They barely had time to wipe the sweat from their faces before Madison startled Natalie and Skylar with, "Time's up!" They groaned.

"Since you're so full of energy," Skylar said, "you stand inside the cart. We'll hand you the boxes to stack."

"Fine with me." Madison jumped inside.

Natalie and Skylar handed box after box to Madison, watching her struggle to keep up. Sweating, Natalie didn't say a word. She huffed, puffed, and started groaning near the end of loading the boxes. Finally done, she watched a weary Madison climb out of the railroad cart.

Their faces showed satisfaction as Natalie reached inside and pressed the button that started the cart on its way to the bookstore.

"Whew, that was a lot of hard work," Skylar said while using her sleeve to wipe the sweat from her brow.

"It was, but we're done. Now we can chill as Wilfred and Jonathan handle getting the food over to the Feast of Service." Natalie lifted the front of her shirt, lowered her face into it, and wiped away dripping sweat from her beet-red face.

"Good," Skylar said, "because I'm ready to chill. I'm so over cooking in bulk, endless clean up, and getting the heavy pans of food down to the cart. The guys were lucky to get reassigned to the Barracks and not have to cook. However, they're probably still working. Thank goodness our part is done, and the Feast of Service only happens once a year."

Natalie laughed. "When I told Dad that we would cook a lot of food over a couple of days, he asked why. I explained the Feast of Service. You should have seen my father's face when he realized Coal is a hobgoblin."

"I'm sure a genuine surprise for someone who doesn't want to know anything about magic," Madison smirked.

"It did shock him, but only for a few hours. Dad actually came back later, saying maybe that's why Coal likes football. He's thinking of letting Coal have a small taste of beer while they watch sports. Can you believe it?"

"Never try to figure out guys. It's impossible." Madison rolled her eyes.

"And they say we're the ones that make no sense," Skylar said.

"To the point, my dad may get Coal a tiny team scarf."

"Go figure," Madison laughed.

"That sounds adorable." Skylar smiled, visualizing a tiny scarf on Coal.

Natalie called Wilfred. "It's on its way over to you…you're welcome…bye."

"Mission accomplished. Hopefully, the guys finish soon and get home before our familiars become hobgoblins," Madison said as the three headed to the stairs.

"Have your familiars been absent the last two days? I haven't seen Coal."

"Now that you mention it, I haven't seen our owls. Madison?" Madison shook her head no. "Do you think there's a pre-party before the actual party?"

"Wow, Skylar, I'm having a hard enough time imagining our little owls being hobgoblins, and now I need to add a party animal. What happens if the party animal doesn't want to revert to a familiar after the Feast of Service?"

"That's an interesting question. If one of ours decides he doesn't want to be a familiar, I'm betting that it's Joel's bird. Lorcan fumed when Joel's hobgoblin decided to be a Rose-Breasted Cockatoo," Natalie said as she pulled the basement door open.

A few hours later, Natalie and the sisters were overcome by curiosity. Sneaking out of her house, she quietly entered the old homestead and made her way to the basement. Madison and Skylar traveled through their tunnel to join Natalie at her homestead.

It was almost 9 p.m. when they swung the door to the Barracks open and came face-to-face with Hexel. The three jumped back and stared at the agitated guard. She moved within inches of Natalie, hovered there, and then moved on to Madison and then Skylar. Too scared to move or speak, they stayed frozen as Hexel hovered over each girl again. They gave up holding their breaths. After several tense minutes, Hexel moved aside and let them enter.

"What was that about?"

"No idea, Madison. Maybe with this party, Hexel restricts who can get in here. It's a lot more work for her. It makes me wonder if she tires of constantly being on guard." Natalie said, surprised and disappointed, that she had overlooked the fact that Hexel was on duty 24/7 year in and year out.

"We kind of take her for granted," Madison said, thinking how Hexel's always there but unable to talk or touch.

"Big time," Natalie agreed as they approached the courtyard.

"Look!" Skylar exclaimed, pointing at the Earth elemental building. "The building's surrounded by wizards and witches."

Standing shoulder to shoulder, the entire building was circled with stiffly standing mages. Natalie, Madison, and Skylar became uncomfortable with their statue-like appearance. Nervously glancing from one mage to the next, the girls looked for movement, conversation, or anything that would make this a typical scene. Nothing.

"You'd think with this being early in the event, they wouldn't be standing so tight. It makes you wonder how often the Feast of Service gets out of hand," Natalie said.

"Even Hexel acted odd…odder," Madison said.

"Do we want to stay or leave?" Natalie was unsure. She wanted to see if they could hear the hobgoblins partying, but uneasiness hung in the air.

"I'm a little uncomfortable with the stiffly lined-up mages. If it gets more uncomfortable, let's leave."

"You okay with what Madison said, Skylar?"

"Definitely. I'm curious if some hobgoblins will attempt to expand the party area. I hope they do. I want to see some action after all the work we put into this event."

"Maybe the mages are conserving their energy for such an event. If that's the case, it would be fun to watch," Madison replied as they walked over to the Flaky Kuchen and plunked down at one of the outside tables.

The large, full moon shone brightly down on them. Hundreds of stars twinkled as small clouds leisurely moved across the night sky. Breathtaking but artificial, it reminded Natalie of the elves trying to steal their powers. She sighed and hoped it wasn't a bad omen.

"Isn't it amazing how many mages are here?" Skylar mused.

"Maybe this is a first feast for some of the hobgoblins, and the mages don't know how they will act. Worse, maybe they know how they'll act with encouragement from the repeat partiers. We need to ask Mr. Xanders if our familiars have been familiars to other mages."

Natalie stopped talking and uncomfortably glanced around. Shoulder-to-shoulder mages surrounded the building, yet they remained silent. She shook her head, trying to overcome the uneasiness of the unnatural silence.

"We should also ask him how they're selected as our familiars. Would it be an ancient honor ritual or something as simple as the one that picks the shortest stick gets the job?"

"Madison and Natalie, you're missing the point. What I meant is that there are a lot of mages surrounding the Earth elemental building. Where did they all come from? Did they ask Wilfred, Jonathan, and Mr. Xanders to help guard? Would they include our mentors?"

"Our mentors are supposed to be inside, hosting the hobgoblins. Maybe they asked outside mages to come and help. What I find odd is that with all those mages outside and the hobgoblins inside partying, you would think we would hear some type of sound. However, it's oddly quiet, which is making me anxious. Let's go for a walk." Natalie got up, and the other two joined her.

Their footsteps were the only sounds as they walked along the isolated streets. Darkened shops cast unfamiliar shadows. Uncomfortable, they made their way to the back of the Barracks, intending to circle back to the Earth elemental building. As they approached Natalie's apartment building, she had an idea.

"Let's go up to my apartment. It's safer in there. We'll also have a better view from there; we can open the window to hear if anything is happening."

Natalie moved two brown recliners to the window overlooking the Earth elemental building. Madison and Skylar sat down. She opened the window and looked out.

"These are comfy. How'd you get them up here?" Skylar asked as she snuggled into the chair.

"They're a gift with delivery from Lorcan."

"What a thoughtful gift," Skylar said.

"A perfect gift, as they're great for sitting or napping."

Madison changed the subject. "Do you think something's going to happen soon? We can't stay much longer without the risk of getting caught outside the house."

"Same here." Natalie looked back at Madison as she spoke to her.

Turning back to the window, she stared at the scene and grew alarmed. The moonlight faded, and the twinkling stars diminished in number.

Natalie quickly closed and locked the window before pulling the curtains together. She turned to Madison and Skylar. "Stay here. Keep the door locked. If someone knocks, don't answer it. I have a key. Something isn't right."

She ran down the two flights of stairs. Slowly opening the front door, she peered out and looked around. Nothing. She tried to stay in the shadows as she made her way over to the Earth elemental building. An unsettling silence lingered in the air. Why weren't the mages talking to each other?

The moon continued to lose light. Within a few feet of the wizards, she watched them. Nothing. They seemed frozen in place. She moved closer. Nothing. Moving right in front of a wizard, she touched him. He stared straight ahead.

Backing away, her heart pounded in her chest as she turned and ran as fast as she could to the front. Hexel, floating in her usual spot at the gatehouse, seemed unaware of the sinister signs.

"Hexel," Natalie whispered. She turned and floated towards her.

"Hexel," Natalie tried to keep the alarm out of her voice. "The mages seem frozen in place. They aren't guarding, and it's getting dark in here. Something bad is happening."

Natalie watched Hexel glance upward and study the sky before she drifted closer to her. *Does Hexel understand what I said? She seems more focused on me. I can't wait any longer.*

Natalie turned around to go back, but Hexel grabbed her left arm. Even wearing a jacket, coldness crept through her. A numbing coldness consumed her before she blacked out.

With that touch, the moon doubled in size, and bright light lit the Barracks like it was the middle of a warm summer day. Holding Natalie up by her left arm, Hexel reached over and grabbed the back of her jacket. Releasing her grip on Natalie's arm, Hexel used the jacket to slow her fall to the ground. She hit the dirt with a soft thump. Hexel circled her before she floated towards the Earth elemental building.

Hexel floated to the front of the building before moving to the side facing the courtyard. Under the bright moonlight, a mage awkwardly twisted. Before he could recover, Hexel floated in front of him. Her right arm came up. The ragged sleeve fell back, exposing a black bony arm and hand. Her long fingernails glowed. Planting her hand on top of the wizard's head, his squirming body turned into a skeleton fully dressed. It dropped to the ground. Wizards and witches slightly stirred as Hexel floated out of sight.

197

She floated mere inches from Angus Thornton's face, impatiently waiting for him to become alert. He blinked twice, smelled an offensive odor, and focused his eyes. He jumped and backed up to the building. Hexel moved closer. Pressed against the building, he stared at her.

She floated a short distance away and then turned back to stare at him. He didn't move. She floated back to him and then moved a short distance away. He grasped she wanted him to follow her. Hexel moved to the side of the building in front of the skeleton. Angus ran over and knelt down. Other nearby mages leaned in to see what was happening.

Angus looked to the left. "Who stood beside you?"

"Wilfred from the bookstore."

"Are you positive?"

He nodded yes. Angus looked over at the mage to his right. "Do you know who stood next to you?"

"Yes, it was Wilfred."

Angus got up. Turning around, he almost bumped into Hexel. He took a quick step back. Hexel moved forward, and then she moved away. This time, Angus understood her. He followed her to the gatehouse.

As he got closer, he saw Natalie sprawled on the ground. Running to her, he fell to his knees. Cold to the touch, he turned her over and desperately searched for a pulse. Over and over, he pressed his fingers against her neck. Finally, after what felt like an eternity, he found a faint pulse.

"I wish you could talk, Hexel," Angus muttered, pulling his cloak off and wrapping Natalie in it.

She began to shake. Angus pulled his cloak tighter around her. He brushed her hair from her face and panicked at her blue lips. Alarmed at her weakening state, he wasn't sure of the next step when Madison and Skylar came running up.

"What happened?" Madison and Skylar screamed as they raced to Natalie and knelt beside her.

"I don't know. Hexel brought me to her."

Madison and Skylar turned to Hexel. "Hexel, did you do this? We saw what you did to that wizard!"

"You saw what?" demanded Angus Thornton.

"We saw Hexel kill a wizard!" Madison and Skylar cried.

"Get up and go home!" Angus commanded as he backed away from Hexel.

"We're not leaving Natalie!" Madison cried.

"Yes, you are! Go now!" Angus reached down and picked up Natalie. Hurrying towards his office, Hexel followed.

"Get back to your post," Angus commanded, sounding braver than he felt.

Hexel stopped. Angus ran across the grounds, through the lobby, up the elevator, and into his study, carrying Natalie. He lowered her onto the oversized couch. She was freezing. He brought out blankets and placed them over her. Her arms uncontrollably shook. He put her arms under the blankets. Crouching down, he held a fireball in his hand close to Natalie's face. It didn't help.

Panicking at her condition, Angus paced the room. As he paced, he recalled Draon's golden charm. Running over and retrieving it from his desk, he flipped it high into the air and summoned Draon. Halfway down, it froze in place. With a sigh of relief, Angus knew Draon had received his summons. He checked Natalie before running out of his office to meet him.

"Draon, thank you for coming. Natalie is unconscious, and we have a body. There are claims that Hexel killed Wilfred. Follow me to Natalie."

Shocked at all that happened, Draon didn't say anything as they ran for the elevator.

Draon went directly to Natalie and became alarmed by her blue lips and ghostly skin. He pulled the covers back and became more concerned as he saw the uncontrollable shivering.

"What has been going on here?" Draon muttered to himself as he brushed Natalie's hair from her face and moved her head from side to side, observing her neck. She had no marks, but she was ice cold. Draon grabbed her right hand and pushed her sleeve up. Nothing. He did the same with her left hand. He saw purplish-red marks on her arm.

"Hexel needed Natalie. This is where Hexel grabbed her; this is where Hexel connected to Natalie." Draon pointed to the purplish-red marks on the left arm.

"I don't understand?"

"What has been happening since the Feast of Service started?"

"I don't know. Two girls said they saw Hexel kill a mage. The wizards on each side of the body said it was Wilfred."

"Nonsense."

"Honestly, I can't remember what happened in the last hour."

"Get me these ingredients," Draon demanded as he scribbled a list of ingredients.

While waiting for Angus, he pulled the blankets up to Natalie's chin. Taking his cloak off, he placed it over her. Dropping into a nearby recliner, he watched Natalie as he waited for Angus. It seemed like an eternity before he returned with the ingredients, mortar, and pestle.

"We need a towel."

Draon pulled a small bottle containing sparkling violet-colored slime from his pocket. Adding all the slime to the ingredients, he mixed them together. As he brought Natalie's left arm out from under the cloak and blankets, Angus returned with a towel. Draon placed it under her arm before spreading the potion on the markings.

"Contact with Hexel's hand is dangerous. It is deadly for most mages. Hexel must have been desperate to put Natalie in this life-threatening situation."

"Hexel killed Wilfred."

"You do not think it is strange that you cannot recall the last hour?"

"I don't know what to think, but those two girls said they saw Hexel kill Wilfred."

"They know it was Wilfred?"

"They didn't say Wilfred; the mages on either side of the dead mage said Wilfred."

"Before we get up in arms over Hexel, we must get the story."

Draon saw movement in Natalie. Color returned to her face. She moaned and pushed the covers off her. She felt feathers. Feeling around, she traced feather after feather.

"Draon?" Natalie whispered.

"I am here, Natalie."

"Where is here?"

"In the master wizard's study."

"Oh," Natalie slowly opened her eyes and looked at Draon. Draon sharply inhaled and took a step backward in surprise. She closed her eyes.

"Natalie, look at me!" Draon demanded as he moved closer, leaning within inches of her face.

She opened her eyes and glanced at Draon before shutting them. Puzzled, Draon shook his head as if doubting what he thought he saw. He turned and looked at Angus to see if he had spotted anything unusual.

"Something wrong?"

"No, it appears the potion is working," Draon said, straightening up and moving back a few feet.

"What did you add to the potion?"

"Unicorn snot."

"Would that have cured Natalie without the other ingredients?"

"She needed the entire potion, but it played a vital part."

"Would you be willing to give us a vial or two?"

"Next time I am here, I will bring it."

"Thank you."

Natalie moved her right hand up to her forehead and rubbed. "I have a colossal headache…again."

"I am sorry. Are you well enough to talk?" It bothered Draon that he could not help her.

"Keep your voices soft. My head wants to explode."

"Do you remember anything?"

"Lots of bad omens. I can't concentrate; there's so much pain." Natalie kept her eyes closed as tears ran down her face.

"Because the headache is from Hexel touching your arm, we cannot do anything to help with the pain. I wish we could."

She stopped rubbing her forehead and glanced at Draon. "Did Hexel stop it?"

Draon and Angus stepped closer to Natalie. "Stop what?"

"Everything was off. Hexel hesitated to let us inside. The mages were weird; they were almost like statues. We went up to my apartment to watch, but then the phony moon became less bright."

She stopped and tried to get comfortable. Draon and Angus waited until Angus thought they had waited long enough. He opened his mouth to tell Natalie to go on, but

Draon motioned for him to be quiet. After several more minutes, she started talking.

"Madison and Skylar stayed behind as I made my way over to the Earth elemental building. The mages were in a trance. I ran to Hexel and told her what was happening outside the Feast of Service. That's all I remember."

"Madison and Skylar said that Hexel…"

"Stop!" Draon angrily interrupted Angus.

"Stop what?" Natalie turned her head to look at Angus.

"We do not have the full story." Draon gave Angus a withering look.

"I can call Madison. Would that help?" Natalie focused on Draon.

"Yes."

"Can you take these covers off me so I can reach my phone?"

Pulling the covers off and throwing them on the recliner, Draon watched as Natalie squirmed to bring her jacket up and reach into a pocket.

"Wow, even this little movement makes me feel like someone hit me with a ton of bricks."

She grabbed her phone and called Madison.

"Are you okay?" Madison cried before Natalie could speak.

"Yes and no, but I'll be okay. I'm with Draon and Angus Thornton. I'm putting you on speaker. Would you tell them everything you saw after the moon lost light?"

"Sure. We watched you head towards the mages. We couldn't see what you were doing when you arrived, but you were only there for a few minutes. You looked like you were heading for the entrance. It got darker. We were getting nervous about staying when, suddenly, the entire Barracks became flooded with light from a gigantic full moon. All mages were still rigid except for one squirming in the light. We watched Hexel float over to that mage and put her hand on his head. The next thing, he was gone. A pile of bones in his place. It was awful. It's something we won't ever get out of our heads. However, Hexel seemed unfazed. She left. Petrified, we fled the apartment and ran to the front. That's when we saw the master wizard leaning over you."

It stayed quiet for a moment.

"Was the mage squirming before the moon turned bright?" Draon asked.

"I'm not sure. I only remember seeing the squirming when the moon burst into brilliant light."

"Thanks, Madison."

"Tell Natalie we hope she gets better soon."

Draon gravely turned to Angus. "You had a Night Hollow. A shapeshifter waited for the familiars and mentors to get drunk enough to have his own feast. The outside mages protecting the building were under his trance and were already useless at protecting those inside. It was only a matter of an hour or two before he attacked."

"That's horrible! How's it possible with Hexel guarding the Barracks?"

"The shapeshifter took on the form of Wilfred. Identically matching Wilfred, Hexel would not know the difference. The more frightening aspect is that there is only one way for a Night Hollow to enter the Barracks. The Night Hollow needs to be invited. You have a traitor."

"I can't think of anyone who would want to cause that kind of destruction here," Angus said as he dropped into a chair.

Draon looked down at Natalie and then over at Angus. "You are fortunate that Natalie and her friends came to the Barracks tonight. Hexel, whom you wanted to blame, knows her touch is the kiss of death to most mages. She also

204

knows Natalie is a powerful witch. With Hexel being a punisher and not a creator, she needed to tap into her powers to create the brightly lit, enormous moon. A Night Hollow cannot take bright light. Frankly, it is amazing that Hexel quickly figured out it was a Night Hollow. They are one of the foulest magical creatures to exist."

Natalie again rubbed her forehead. The headache remained as bad as when she first woke up. "I can't believe anyone here would be that vicious. You're sure the elves aren't doing it to get even?"

"I do not think so. It is not how they operate. Besides, they know summoning a Night Hollow comes at a high price if it does not succeed. They are rare creatures. Family honor. Another Night Hollow will attempt entry into the Barracks and feast on the mage that summoned the first one."

"Oh, that's gross!" Natalie wanted to bury her head in the blankets and forget about this whole evening.

Chapter 16
Go stuff it, Leona!

Everyone was friendly one minute, and the next, everyone was suspicious. Other than family members, there wasn't any trust. Most businesses didn't open up. Everyone was on edge until they captured the mage that invited the Night Hollow to the Barracks.

Seeing Hexel floating the entire Barracks several times a night was unsettling, but the unknown concerning the Night Hollow was even more disturbing. Angus assigned seven teams of mages to walk the entire complex at various times of the day. With the Flaky Kuchen, Wickedly Twisted Bottega, and the Mystical Pets Treat Store the only stores open, it felt more like a ghost town. Unless patrolling, most mages stayed in their apartments.

Gertrude Cunningham sat outside her Mystical Pets Treat Store, watching the advancing patrol. Her old, wrinkled face showed disgust.

"If Angus didn't let every Tom, Dick, and Harry in here, we wouldn't be in this mess." She spat the words out at the three mages walking by her.

Leona turned and walked back to Gertrude. The two men stayed back. "I don't believe the Night Hollow has anything to do with the new mages, Gertrude. We don't…" Gertrude cut her off.

"Go stuff it, Leona!" Gertrude got up and yanked the door open to a loud squawking bird that cut off in the middle of a squawk as the door slammed shut.

"She's always, and I mean always, pure joy to be around," Malcolm said as they continued their walk.

"Be nice. She's nastier than usual because of the Night Hollow. Heck, we're all anxious," Leona said.

"What are you two talking about? That was Gertrude's everyday charming self." Leona smacked Nathan's shoulder. They all laughed.

The last leg of their patrol was the Water elemental building. As they walked along the Alchemist shops, they saw Twilight sitting outside of her Wickedly Twisted store. She smiled and waved as soon as she spotted them.

"Hey, guys, how's it going?"

"Getting our exercise," Malcolm replied as they walked up to her.

"Thanks for making the rounds. I really appreciate you going out several times a day. Just the same, it'll be awesome when you can go back to your regular jobs, and Hexel is back up at the gatehouse full time."

"Definitely. Right now, it doesn't even feel like the Barracks."

"True, Nathan. If this continues, I may need to go topside for a job."

"Us, too!" Leona exclaimed.

"Don't worry, before we know it, this will pass," Malcolm reassured them as they started walking again.

Several feet away, Nathan commented, "I'm glad we end our patrol with Twilight and not Gertrude."

"Yup," Malcolm said, "it's the difference between a fresh apple or a mushy, worm-infested, rotting apple." All three burst out laughing.

Day after day, the patrols made their rounds. Hexel continued to patrol the entire community by night. Nothing unusual happened. Toward the end of the second week after the Feast of Service, most businesses had reopened. Even with an undercurrent of uneasiness, everything returned to normal.

Tightly gripping her wand, the old woman in the long white dress and blue robe stormed into the center of the Barracks' courtyard. Eyes ablaze, she pointed her wand toward the sky. One after another, multi-colored fireworks burst across the compound. Curious mages gathered in the courtyard.

Once a crowd gathered, the old woman screamed, "What does it take to get rid of the riffraff? Ever since they arrived, it has been nothing but trouble."

Twilight stepped out of the growing crowd. "Gertrude, we're all upset about the Night Hollow..." Gertrude aimed her wand at Twilight's forehead. Eyes wide, Twilight stopped talking and slowly stepped back into the crowd, which also backed up.

"I am not upset about the Night Hollow; I called it!" She screamed at the top of her lungs.

A collective gasp of shock escaped the frightened mages. They backed up some more. A few mages ran away, yelling what was happening in the courtyard.

Terrified, the crowd anxiously watched as Gertrude shouted, "I am the matriarch, having been here for decades, but no one listens to me. I warned Angus those new young mages were nothing but trouble. He wouldn't listen to reason. We need to revert to the old ways."

Angus heard every word as he ran into the courtyard from the Air elemental building. Stepping in front of the growing crowd, he stood facing Gertrude. She pointed her wand at him. He remained still, but his wand ring activated.

"You...you! This is your fault!" She leaned forward as she spat the words. Hatred distorted her weathered face.

Angus tried to remain calm and reason with her. "Gertrude, why? Your friends surround you, and you have your business. The new mages have done nothing to you. Why invite a Night Hollow to destroy lives?"

"Angus Thornton, you pillock, they're just the beginning. More rabble will come, and the Barracks will no longer be safe. The mages here will have no protected place because of you and them."

Her furious eyes erratically shifted from one mage to another and back to Angus. The distressed crowd backed up. Angus stood his ground.

"Gertrude, you're wrong. You were in the meeting in my office when the Oracle came through with her prophecy. The prophecy named the very mages you want to destroy as our champions."

Gertrude interrupted the master wizard. "The Oracle has been wrong before. She's wrong now."

"Not true, Gertrude. Circumstances can sometimes alter an outcome, but the Oracle was adamant we needed these mages. However, you didn't want to hear it because it didn't fit your agenda. You're the one who made a deadly decision when you invited the Night Hollow into the Barracks. You're what caused the Barracks not to be safe. We have no choice but to arrest you for your involvement in the endangerment of mages, mentors, and familiars."

Angus stepped forward. Before he could get close, Gertrude pointed her wand at her chest and recited a spell; she vanished.

Stunned, Angus glanced around but didn't see her or anything scurrying away. He picked her wand up and snapped it in two. Unfamiliar with the spell, he didn't know what had happened to her. Whatever it was, she was stuck with it.

Uncomfortably standing there, nervously shifting, the crowd of mages waited for Angus to reassure them that everything would be all right.

Angus turned slowly to look at them. He hesitated about what to say. Everyone knew Gertrude. As a founding member of the Barracks, she was a friend and a mentor, even with her sour disposition. Unfamiliar with providing comforting words, he struggled to address the crowd.

"Frankly, I'm at a loss for what to say. Gertrude didn't want new members, but she never came across as so opposed to them that she would summon a Night Hollow. It may have been a rash decision. Once in motion, she couldn't stop it. When it failed, it fell on her. I have to believe that the last weeks of waiting for the Night Hollow to come for her sent her over the edge. We need to remember all the good Gertrude did for the community. It's a sad day." Angus patted some shoulders as he walked through the group.

He wasn't good at comforting. His weaknesses included being stiff and limited in expressing compassion, but he struggled with this one. He visited with the mages every day, listening to their concerns. He had missed the signs. Feeling responsible for failing Gertrude, Angus needed to verbalize his thoughts to someone he trusted.

Reaching the second floor of the apartment building, his eyes widened when he saw six-foot-tall candles with carved faces on each side of Pru's door. Angus paused. The candle to the left shifted his eyes to him. "I hope you brought candy."

"What?" Angus walked closer. The one to the right shifted his eyes to Angus. It was unnerving as the candle to the left licked his lips in anticipation.

"Are you deaf? I said candy as in C A N D Y," the left candle raised his voice. "No one gets through unless we say they get through. Where's the candy?"

"Good grief," Angus grumbled. "I don't have any candy."

"I guess you aren't getting through. Now run along until you figure out how to pay the piper." The candle to the left rolled his eyes and turned his attention to his brother.

Angus, flustered, rummaged through his pockets until he produced a small package of mints.

"Will this do?" He held it out for them.

"This time only. Next time, bring some tart candy for my brother and me."

Flicking his tongue out, he snatched the package. Angus jumped back in surprise. Both candles roared with laughter. Their flames lit, and the door unlocked.

"We're back," they laughed.

Angus continued to stand there.

"Duh, the unlock sound you heard means you can enter."

The candle to the left shifted his eyes from Angus to his brother. "With some people, you have to do everything for them!"

Angus stepped through, and as he did, he laughed. Those two clowns were just what he needed to relax. He called for Pru.

Chapter 17

Dreamcatcher

Depressed, Natalie sat at the dinner table, pushing her food from one side of the plate to the other. She could still feel Hexel's connection on her arm. Sometimes, she would turn to see if someone had grabbed it. That event was surreal, and the reason for it hurt her to the core. She couldn't wrap her mind around someone being so against them that they summoned a Night Hollow. Would she ever belong? She sighed and fell deeper into her melancholy mood.

Natalie's father sat across from her, watching her push food around her plate. The hurt on her face tugged at his heart. He stopped eating. "Do you want to talk about it?"

She looked up. "It relates to magic, Dad."

"I can manage it." He put his fork down and waited.

"You sure? The house rule is that magic is off-limits. I don't want to upset you."

"I've been dealing with a cat that's a gnome before you were aware of your powers. A few weeks ago, what I thought was you was a yellow-dressed fairy. And last but not least, there is a hobgoblin disguised as a crow who watches sports with me. I'm adapting to your world."

Natalie smiled at the visual of her dad and Coal watching a game together. Her dad is yelling, and Coal is squawking at a terrible play or call. A Cuban sandwich and beer for her dad, while Coal has crackers and a tiny bottle cap filled with beer. Surreal, and yet it seemed normal in their house.

"Before I start, promise me you'll stop me if it's too much."

"I'll let you know." Karl leaned forward, ready to listen.

"Someone invited a monster into the Barracks to go after our mentors and familiars because of her hatred for us. She called us riffraff."

Karl interrupted her. "What kind of monster?"

"It was a Night Hollow shapeshifter that looked like Wilfred. Wilfred frequents the Barracks, so no one thought anything about him being there to help guard the Feast of Service."

"What would he have done to Coal, Lorcan, and the others?"

"Without graphics, they would be gone."

"That, Natalie, is pure evil."

"That's why it's so twisted. It's ripping me up inside, Dad. We could have lost all our mentors and familiars."

"It isn't your fault. It's the actions of a deranged person."

"Maybe, but I've created disastrous situations since the first day we entered the Barracks. I can't help but feel responsible and the reason we don't belong. Without me, the others are fine. I'm the one that doesn't belong. Will I ever fit in, Dad?" Tears welled up in her eyes.

"The mages here are good friends. You have Draon and Lorcan. Draon has been around for centuries. I would venture Lorcan has, too, even though I have heard the rumor that when a four-leaf clover pops up over a potato in an Irish potato field, a gnome is born."

Natalie's eyes widened. "Lorcan comes from an Irish potato field?"

Karl smiled. "No, it's my pathetic attempt to cheer you up. The point is that Draon and Lorcan have been around for centuries. They're excellent judges of people. Both of them mentor and protect you. The same isn't true of the person who wanted to harm others."

"Sometimes I feel I'm tolerated but not liked."

"I feel that way sometimes. Probably, the vast majority of people have experienced that feeling. I'm not trying to minimize your feelings, but you can't dwell on it. It isn't good for you. You need to talk with someone or find something positive to do."

"I used to speak with Pru. She's the one person I could talk with about anything, and she would keep it a secret. I guess Angus Thornton has discovered that Pru is an amazing person. Right now, she's living at the Barracks and helping him on projects."

"Can you still talk with her?"

With a vision of Pru's two candles, Natalie smiled before answering. "Yes, I can. It isn't as easy as before, but I suggested her talking candles guard her apartment. Wait until the no-nonsense Angus Thornton encounters those two wise guys. I would love to see that exchange."

"I'm glad you're feeling better. I'm not comfortable with emotional issues. That was your mother's department. However, if you need to talk, let me know."

"There is one thing, Dad."

"What would that be?"

"I'm having strange dreams that blur in the morning. It leaves me with the feeling that they aren't dreams but things I've blocked. Would you mind if I borrow the dreamcatcher that's over your bed?"

"When your mother and I opened wedding gifts, the last gift, wrapped in green paper, didn't have a name on it. Unlike normal wedding gifts, your mother held up the dreamcatcher. We never knew who gave it to us, but I figured it had to be one of her mage friends. I don't do magic, so please keep it."

"Do you mind if I get it right now? I want to use it tonight."

"All yours."

Natalie hung the giant dreamcatcher on the south wall over her bed and noticed the red crystal beads within the webbing. Not paying much attention to them, she focused on the black feathers at the end of the beaded strings, which hung slightly above her headboard. Coal flew over to study the feathers.

"You think they're feathers from one of your ancestors or buddies?" Natalie asked, throwing the covers back so she could climb into bed.

Coal squawked and pecked at the feathers before he lost interest. He flew to his chair and settled down on his pillow.

"I guess the dreamcatcher doesn't compare to the Feast of Service," She yawned.

Coal squawked as if he answered the comment.

"Good night, Coal."

One final squawk and Coal settled.

Natalie's mind went into overdrive. Trying to sleep so she could get the needed answers wasn't working. Thoughts bounced all over the place, from the Night Hollow to the blacking out at the Barracks to the goofy tunnel guardians. Uninterested in her build-a-story, it was going to be a long night. Minutes turned into an hour. Finally, exhausted, she fell asleep.

The dreamcatcher's red beads glowed.

Dank and musty smells assaulted her nose as she stood alone in the icy darkness. The red dragon fire crystals didn't light the way, but she had to be in a tunnel. A dragging sound moved at some distance through the black void. She envisioned an enormous spider coming for her. She placed her hand on the wall and took a couple of steps forward. Was she moving toward the bookstore? She didn't know. She took a few more steps and still did not know where she was or where she was going. The dragging sound moved closer. She shouted in her mind to wake up and get out of there. Looking around, she couldn't decide if it was real or not. One wrong move and she would go deeper into the endless tunnel. Fear took over. The dragging sound advanced. She screamed and woke up in a sweat.

Coal squawked and flew over to the bed. He hopped closer to her face and squawked again.

Breathing hard from the nightmare, Natalie didn't answer Coal. Instead, she grabbed the extra pillow and pulled it to her. With eyes closed, she tried to figure out how the nightmare related to her real world. She couldn't think of anything but knew she wouldn't go back to sleep with that thing hanging over her bed. She got up and took the dreamcatcher down. Coal chirped.

"Shh, I'm going to move the dreamcatcher so we can get some sleep."

She took it into the music room, removed a picture, and placed the dreamcatcher on the east wall. Back in bed, she fell asleep without dreams. The alarm clock beeped.

Dragging herself out of bed, she stayed in her pajamas as she logged into her e-school classes. Nothing exciting happened, and time dragged on. Finally, school was over, and they were out for Spring break.

"Anybody come up with some ideas for sabotaging the Janus Club in two weeks?" Natalie asked as they all climbed aboard the railroad cart.

"Not a thing," Connor said.

The cart creaked and groaned as it rumbled down the tracks toward the bookstore. It made enough noise that they kept quiet until they crossed over and walked in the medieval tunnel towards the Barracks.

"Did Connor ever mention to you his idea of getting Hexel a Christmas shower gift set?"

After they all stopped laughing, Joel agreed. "It sounds like the perfect gift. In fact, the more, the better. Maybe we should all pitch in and get her the jumbo deluxe set."

"I wonder what makes her smell like she is decaying," Natalie said.

"Probably the fact that she never washes her clothes or takes a bath. Maybe instead of a shower gift set, we buy her a colorful, modern pantsuit, fluffy white blouse, and top it off with some dangling silver earrings." Connor laughed at his own joke.

The vision of his absurd comment had the others laughing, too.

"I like Hexel hides her face behind layers of fabric," Skylar said.

"We all do. Besides Connor, if she is a Fury, the smell probably relates to the reason for the birth of Hexel and her two sisters," Madison said.

"Did you read up on it?" Natalie asked.

"I did, except nothing tells the whereabouts of her sisters. Actually, I'm curious how we know her as Hexel. None of the reference books refer to a Hexel."

"She was probably wearing a name tag on the first day." Connor laughed as they rounded the corner and headed to their classroom at the back of the building.

"Stop, man. Your jokes are lame."

The girls nodded their heads in agreement.

"I wonder how she ended up at the Barracks. She's a vengeance spirit that could float around the world, yet here she is with us," Madison said.

Natalie felt sorry for Hexel. "It has to be an awful, lonely, and frustrating life. She has no friends. Everyone is afraid of her. She can't change that because she can't communicate, and her touch is lethal. She's stuck at the gatehouse 24/7, where we all make a big deal about how bad she smells."

"You're forgetting that Hexel grabbed you," Connor said.

"I haven't forgotten. I can still feel where she grabbed me. The powers that cause my problems are also the powers that saved me that night."

They opened the classroom door to find Mr. Xanders standing near four tables with all the makings of brooms. His expression showed he expected an entertaining class today.

Dillon sat, waiting for the others to settle down. They quickly took their seats.

"No need to explain what is up at the front of the class. It's obvious what we will do today. Put your best effort forward because we will learn to fly on Monday."

Madison raised her hand.

Before she could ask her question, Mr. Xanders answered it.

"No, you may not use the brooms you and Skylar made. Not yet, anyway. All of you will be on an equal playing field. Well, maybe. If you build a poor broom, you will experience a poor ride."

Natalie, Madison, and Skylar immediately looked in Connor's direction and laughed.

"I'll show you. Fair warning, I'm all business if it involves a competition."

Mr. Xander ignored Connor's comment.

"Madison and Skylar will recognize these are traditional besom materials. We're using ash for the handles and twigs from birch trees. We're using thin pieces of willow wood to secure the twigs to the handle, but there's twine if that proves too hard."

218

"We spend considerable time sanding, varnishing, and assembling each broom. Our brooms also have engravings and gems," Skylar beamed.

"I'm sure your brooms are masterpieces, but today it's a DIY project. Take your time, otherwise you might not have a sturdy and reliable besom on Monday."

"Be some falling off the brooms on Monday," Connor chuckled.

"If you keep it up, I'm going to knock you off your broom," Joel threatened.

"Connor, Joel, focus on class. Dillon, pick up what you need and take it to a back table. One at a time up here. You have all afternoon to work on them; if needed, you can return for more supplies. The brooms stay here."

Mr. Xander sat down as each student went up and grabbed the needed materials. Focused on assembling their brooms, it stayed quiet until Natalie asked Skylar, "When allowed, would you be willing to sell one of your brooms to me?"

"Sure, we have twenty of them made. If anyone in here wants a broom, we'll sell them one."

"How much?"

"Madison and I have already agreed on $50."

"Thanks, that's a fair price."

Natalie turned toward the teacher. "Mr. Xanders, if we agree, can we buy a broom from Madison and Skylar?"

"Does everyone want a broom from Madison and Skylar?" Mr. Xanders asked the class.

Immediately, everyone yelled yes.

"What's the cost?" asked Mr. Xanders.

"$50," Skylar answered.

"That's very reasonable for a custom broom," Mr. Xanders said. "Can everyone manage that price?"

"It'll take me a couple of weeks to come up with $50," Joel said.

"How about I buy your broom, and you pay me back as you can?" Natalie offered.

"That would be great," Joel said, pleased with that arrangement.

Connor looked over at Natalie and then pointed at himself.

"Same deal for you, Connor." Connor grinned and did a double thumbs-up.

"It looks like the class favors Madison and Skylar's brooms, Mr. Xanders," Natalie said, relieved she wouldn't be flying on what looked like a questionable broom.

She glanced at Connor's broom and Joel's broom. Their brooms almost made her broom look good.

"All right, here's the deal. Keep working on your brooms. Come Monday, you'll be test-driving them. Madison and Skylar, if you bring your brooms in on Monday, we'll get them personalized, and on Tuesday, we'll start training for a competition."

"Is there prize money?" Connor asked.

"No money, but there will be awards for the winners."

"Free donuts from the Flaky Kuchen are good," Joel said. Dillon laughed.

By the end of class, the only brooms that looked good were those made by Madison and Skylar. The other brooms looked like embarrassing rejects.

As they headed out, Connor said, "Thankfully, we only need to survive one day on our brooms."

"Let's hope we survive," Joel said.

Just before bedtime, Natalie retrieved the dreamcatcher from the music studio. Coal flew over and watched her mount it over her bed. Nervous and hoping for a different dream, she climbed into bed and pulled the covers tightly around her body. Her head rested on one pillow while the other pillow pushed against her back.

She yawned from exhaustion. The broom-making had been long and frustrating, so she gave up on the willow strips and used the twine. Even so, it took her several attempts with the twine to secure the twigs in place. All that annoying work produced one pathetic broom.

Closing her eyes, she tried to fall asleep, but the dream from the night before kept her nervous and awake. She didn't want to experience that nightmare again, so she changed her focus to the broom project. Almost to the end of reliving the making of her broom, she fell asleep.

The dreamcatcher's red beads glowed.

Dungeon smells swirled in the air as she stood in the darkness. She stood once again in a tunnel, but which one? Why wasn't there the glow of the red dragon fire crystals? If this was a past event, the crystals should light the tunnel. She heard the dragging sound again. No tunnel guardians meant she had to be in the medieval tunnel to the Barracks. Natalie moved slowly in the direction she thought would take her away from the Barracks and get her to the bookstore. She could hear the dragging sound getting closer, but she slowed down instead of picking up the pace. The dragging sound grew louder. Instead of escaping, she leaned heavily against a wall. A deformed creature loomed over her. She screamed and woke up.

Coal flew to the bed and chirped as she sat up.

"It was a nightmare, nothing more."

He flew to her right shoulder. She pushed the covers and pillows away. Sitting at the edge of the bed, she tried to relax. She couldn't settle down. Getting up, she went over to Coal's chair. Lifting him off her shoulder, she placed him on his pillow. "Stay."

She went into the kitchen for a drink of water. Still anxious, she sat in the family room and watched a movie on the DVD player. Her mind kept going back to the nightmare. Somehow, it felt familiar. This time, she knew she was closer to the forgotten truth. Taking two big gulps, she finished her drink. Standing up, she stretched and decided she would try one more time.

She tried to relax and focus on anything but the nightmare, but her body vibrated with nervous energy. Tossing and turning, fluffing her pillow, and pulling covers over her only to push them off finally wore her out. She fell into a restless sleep, triggering the red beads to glow.

As before, she stood in a dank and musty tunnel. Red dragon fire crystals faintly lit the tunnel. This time, she wasn't moving. She tried to get to the bookstore, but she had no strength. Leaning against a wall, she felt herself falling and was unable to stop herself from landing on a large two-pocket pouch filled with glowing dragon crystals. Within inches of crashing on the sack, two powerful arms grabbed her. She saw the shadow of a hunched-back person lifting her. She heard a voice telling her not to open her eyes. She closed her eyes. As she closed her eyes in the dream, she woke up. She remembered. When Pru went for help, she lost her strength, and one of the Blemish helped her.

Now, knowing her rough shape and the Blemish preventing further injury, she didn't know what to do with the information. She didn't want Lorcan or Draon to find out and get the Blemish in trouble.

She got up and removed the dreamcatcher. Coal chirped his approval. She moved it back into the music studio. While climbing into bed and pulling up the covers, she decided she would dwell on the new information tomorrow. Right now, she needed sleep.

Chapter 18

Give It a Good Name

The cool early morning air seeped through Natalie's jacket as she walked over to Madison and Skylar's property. Cringing, she thought it wasn't as cold as the arctic reception she would receive if Madison and Skylar's parents found her on their property.

"Pain-in-the-butt fairies," Natalie muttered as she paused at the front gate and glanced around. She didn't see anyone outside. With a deep sigh of relief, she jogged up the driveway, across the front lawn, through the Halloween path, and over to the old homestead.

She rapidly banged on the door, hoping to enter before their parents spotted her. Breccan opened the door. Without a word, he motioned her in and directed her towards the kitchen.

Walking through the Room of Mirrors, she couldn't help but notice mirrors covered the walls in a similar pattern to Lorcan's collection of mirrors. She wondered if it was another trait or obsession of a Ruiri gnome.

"Hey, Natalie," Madison said as she stood up to take her dishes to the sink.

"Where are your helpers?"

Madison laughed. "Thanks to your suggestion, the helpers are upstairs, playing with their battery-operated sports cars. I think it's more bumper cars, but it's keeping them entertained."

"I can hear them. They sound like they're having the time of their life."

"It's mainly because they enjoy crashing into one another. I'm not sure what will top the cars."

"Maybe we can change it to a different mode of transportation. If they rode battery-operated giraffes with long swinging necks, they would have a whole new experience of whacking each other off their mount."

"That would be a sight."

Skylar walked into the room. "Hi, Natalie. I've taken the last of the brooms downstairs. We agreed that using the tunnel would avoid neighbors wondering why we carry fancy brooms."

"Good idea. It also rescues me from a scary encounter with your parents."

"True, they're still furious with you for getting us drunk," Madison said.

"You won't ever catch me offering fairy punch again."

"Or us drinking it again," Skylar laughed.

"Enough chitchat. The tunnels are beckoning us."

"Wow, Madison, you say that like you're comfortable with the tunnels."

"We are."

"Let me guess. You've been using the tunnel system for flying practice."

"Guilty as charged," Madison laughed.

"The tunnel guardians are okay with your practice sessions?"

"It's a change of scenery for them."

"Great! Do you think I could fly in the tunnel?" Natalie asked, excited about the prospect of zooming over to her homestead.

"Mmm, it isn't going to be easy to fly and carry a broom," Madison said. "We need to wait on that so we don't damage the spare brooms."

Disappointed, she bit her lip and focused on the ground.

"When we get downstairs, you pick your broom. While they're identical, you may like one more than the others," Skylar said, hoping to cheer Natalie up.

"Thanks. There won't be a problem selecting one. All of your brooms are winners. I can't say the same for the brooms we made in class. Those are disasters waiting to happen."

"True," Madison said. "I'm glad Mr. Xanders is letting us use our brooms after today."

Standing in front of four brooms, Natalie picked each one up and mounted it as if she were going to ride it. Nothing happened until she mounted the last broom. As soon as she sat on it, it lifted off the ground. Startled, Natalie thought down, and it brought her back down.

"Congratulations, Natalie!" Madison and Skylar beamed, "Now, you must name it."

"Name it?"

"Name it and take good care of it," Madison said.

"Wow! Getting a broom feels like adopting a pet."

"It's remarkably similar. Give it a good name," Madison said.

"I'll think about it."

Natalie paused. Madison and Skylar raised their eyebrows, questioning the puzzled expression on her face.

"What's up?" Madison asked.

"Your brooms are stunning and unique. When Mr. Xanders sees them, he's going to want one."

"You really think he'll want to buy one?" Skylar asked.

"Definitely. You two underestimate your brooms."

While riding the cart to the bookstore, Natalie thought about the honor of selecting her broom. "Are you going to let the others try each broom to see which one they like best?"

"No, you're the only one with that honor. For the others, the broom will adapt to the rider," Madison said.

"We wanted to give you special treatment, as you're the one who brought us together," Skylar said.

"Thanks, Madison and Skylar. You don't know how much this means to me, especially after we were called riffraff. I took that to heart."

"The riffraff was that evil woman," Madison said.

"Good riddance," Skylar exclaimed.

The loud railroad cart creaked and moaned along the tracks, making it difficult to talk. Natalie spent the time admiring her broom. Before she knew it, they were standing with Joel and Connor at the back of the bookstore.

"How about picking your broom before we enter the tunnel?" Madison said.

"There's an extra broom," Connor observed as he walked closer to the brooms.

"It gives you more choices. Now pick a broom," Madison answered.

With no thought, Joel and Connor each grabbed one. Entering the tunnel leading to the Barracks, Connor asked, "Can we test drive them?"

Madison hesitated for a moment before answering him. "If you go slow, and you do nothing stupid."

"I have no intention of doing anything stupid the first few times we practice flying."

"What a relief," Madison said. "Skylar and I will carry the extra brooms."

Each mounted their brooms. Madison and Skylar were comfortable flying. Natalie was cautious, Joel was respectful, and Connor was already tempting fate.

"Connor, stop weaving back and forth before you smack into a wall and kill your broom!" Madison yelled in his direction.

"Kill my broom? It's a thing."

The broom bucked. Wide-eyed and horrified, Connor tightly gripped the handle and held on for dear life. Halfway through a buck, the broom switched gears and zoomed full speed down the tunnel.

"Whoa! Slow down! Stop!"

The broom came to a dead stop. Connor flew over the front of the broom and landed face-first on the ground. The broom settled against a wall.

Catching up, Natalie cringed, looking at a dirty Connor pushing himself off the ground. She glanced over as Joel lined up with her.

"Stay back with me; this isn't going to be pretty," Natalie whispered as Madison and Skylar stopped, dismounted, and stormed toward Connor.

"Your broom is not a thing. We put a lot of time, detail, and love into making each broom. Your broom is more like a beloved pet. Name it and respect it, or you will lose it," Madison growled.

"Thanks for asking if I'm okay," Connor said, still shaken from the wild ride.

"We can see you're not injured, but you could have destroyed your broom. It isn't a toy. Treat your broom like it's a family member," Madison said in exasperation with Connor.

"You serious?"

"Deadly serious!"

"Okay, I'll treat Kira with respect," Connor muttered as he pulled the broom from the wall and mounted it.

With no one focused on him, Connor leaned close to the handle and whispered to the broom. "I've given you a revered name, so no more bucking or trying to break the speed of sound or my neck."

Joel held the door wide open as Madison entered with her and Dillon's broom. Dillon, standing near the door, immediately took his broom from Madison. He focused entirely on the magnificent broom. He marveled at its design, its carvings, and its gems.

"It's beautiful. I've never seen a more beautiful broom."

"Thank you!" Madison grinned at him, even though all the brooms were identical.

Mr. Xanders got up from his desk and walked over to join Dillon in inspecting the broom.

"Madison and Skylar, you truly have a rare talent for making beautiful brooms. Can I buy one of your brooms?" He looked hopeful that they would say yes.

Madison lifted her index finger up, showing she wanted a moment with Skylar. Leaning into her sister, they whispered back and forth, making it look like one of them hesitated to sell a broom to him. After a few minutes, Madison looked over at the teacher.

"As long as we don't have to practice on the brooms we made the other day, you can buy one."

"Deal. When can I get my broom?"

"Natalie, you can come in," Madison said with a sly smile.

Natalie entered with the extra broom and handed it to Mr. Xanders. He ignored the setup and studied his new broom.

"This is the best $50 investment I've ever made."

"I don't need to remind you to treat your broom with respect," Madison said to Mr. Xanders as she looked at Connor. "We have made your broom with love and enchanted ingredients. It's like a treasured pet. Name it, take care of it, and it will be loyal to you."

228

"It's a magnificent broom, Madison, but it is just a broom."

"Ask Connor what happens when you disrespect your broom."

Mr. Xanders took his focus off Madison and looked over at Connor.

Connor grimaced. "I called it a thing, and it went berserk before throwing me off rodeo style."

Mr. Xanders looked down at his broom with new appreciation before addressing the students. "I'll have to think of a name for my broom, so for now, it will only have my name on it. Have all of you named your brooms?"

Everyone said yes.

"Good. Madison and Skylar, there's a wizard next door who'll be personalizing each broom via spells. If you want to, you can be there to ensure you like his work."

"We have faith you picked out someone who will appreciate our brooms," Madison said.

"Thank you," Mr. Xanders said, then he focused on the entire class. "Okay, listen up. You'll enter next door one at a time. After you're done, head over to the courtyard. No flying until we're all there."

Lined up in the courtyard, they mounted their brooms and waited for instructions. Connor turned to Joel. "Thank goodness the handles are much thicker than a regular broom. I can't imagine spending much time on a small handle."

"If it were any smaller, we'd have to invest in bicycle seats."

"Wouldn't that look stupid?" Connor laughed. Joel burst into laughter.

"Connor, Joel, can I have your undivided attention?" Mr. Xanders waited until they stopped laughing. "The goal is to lift off, fly to each elemental building column, touch it, and return here without falling off your broom. Stay low in case you have an accident. Questions?"

"How do we direct our brooms?" Dillon asked.

"Think of riding a horse," Mr. Xanders answered.

"I don't know how to ride a horse," Dillon answered.

"Dillon, your broom connects to you. Think what you want to happen," Madison said.

"It takes practice, but in no time, it'll be second nature to you," Skylar said. She moved next to Dillon in case he needed more encouragement.

"This isn't a competition; it's practice. Get ready to go. One, two, three...go!" yelled Mr. Xanders.

All lifted off at the same time. Madison and Skylar went much higher than the others and raced around, touching all four elemental columns before the others reached the first column.

"Hey, watch where you're going!" Joel and Connor yelled as they bumped into each other.

Joel stayed upright, but Connor hung upside down.

Joel laughed as Connor yelled, "Help!"

Responding to his scream for help, his broom went low and hovered. Connor dropped to the ground, jumped back on, and resumed flying.

"Good, Kira." Connor patted the handle.

Dillon yelled "go" to his broom, and it shot out full speed. Tightly gripping the handle, Dillon exclaimed, "Slow down!"

The broom slowed down and wobbled along. Frustrated, Dillon looked around to make sure no one looked at him before he leaned toward the broom handle. "Why can't you fly like a normal broom?"

Natalie didn't enjoy being up high for any reason. She stayed low and on course.

Mr. Xanders stayed so close to the ground that if he pointed his toes, his feet would have touched the ground. He moved at a slower pace than Dillon. Cautiously, he rode the broom like an 80-year-old man.

After each loop, Madison lined up with Joel, laughed, and zoomed off. Skylar did the same thing, except to Connor. Joel and Connor concentrated on staying on their brooms. They ignored the girls. Madison flew out of the courtyard and circled the outer road. Skylar circled the other way. As they passed each other, they reached out and slapped hands. The gathering crowd broke out into wild cheers.

Madison lined up behind Joel, and Skylar lined up behind Connor. Flying at a much slower speed, they both pretended to yawn. Giggling, they went around the boys and flew down to the ground. The crowd ran over and engulfed them.

Natalie knew everyone in the crowd clamored to buy one of their brooms. Flying above Madison and Skylar, she yelled for them to save brooms for Pru and Twilight. They nodded yes, each giving a thumbs-up.

Appreciating their brooms, they stood in a group inside the classroom and reveled in their flying experiences. They teased Mr. Xanders for flying so close to the ground that he could almost walk with the broom. Madison told Dillon the winning combination is believing in yourself. The mages marveled at Madison and Skylar's flying abilities. Amid the celebration, Angus Thornton walked into the room. The room became quiet.

Walking over to Mr. Xanders, he held his hand out. "May I inspect your broom?"

The tone told Mr. Xanders it really wasn't a question. He reluctantly handed his broom to Angus. Everyone stayed quiet and frozen in place, clutching their brooms as the master wizard studied it. After a few minutes, he handed the broom back to the teacher. Then, he focused on Madison and Skylar.

"You have a rare talent for creating beautiful mage brooms. You should sell them in one of the existing shops or consider opening your own shop."

"Thank you," Madison said, "but each broom takes over two months to make. We couldn't make enough brooms to open a shop, nor would we want to be forced into constant production."

"Ask Twilight at the Wickedly Twisted Bottega to sell them for you," Connor blurted out.

"Connor will even volunteer to deliver the brooms," Natalie said with a smirk.

"You bet I will."

"I still need to get in there and meet this Twilight," Joel said.

"No, you don't."

"Oh, but I do."

Before Connor could respond, an exasperated Angus Thornton interrupted them. "Enough! We are off-topic!" He considered reminding them that Twilight was his niece.

"If you plan to sell brooms you have already made, you should have a lottery. Too many mages want your brooms."

"That's a great idea," Madison said. "We have thirteen brooms already made, but eleven are available as we want Pru and Twilight to each have a broom."

"Make it ten. I want a broom."

"Seriously!" Madison and Skylar exclaimed. They had difficulty concealing their excitement over the master wizard wanting one of their brooms.

"Your brooms are masterpieces. Long ago, two young witches owned a small shop in a foreign country that made custom brooms as magnificent as yours. When I returned to purchase a broom, they had closed the shop. Over the years, I've searched for one as magnificent, but I've had no success until now. How much do you want for a broom?"

"Fifty dollars."

"An extremely reasonable price. Do you want it in silver, copper, or paper money?"

"Silver would be good," Madison said.

"Done. I will pay for Pru's broom and deliver it to her."

Madison, Skylar, and Natalie exchanged looks that made Angus Thornton blush. Then, seeing Joel, Connor, and Dillon's clueless expressions, the girls laughed.

Chapter 19

Daft Governor

"Yesterday was interesting, watching each of you fly around the courtyard. Right now, Madison and Skylar have the advantage. In order for the rest of you to get on the same level, we're going to use class time for practice. On Friday, you'll compete in a simple contest," Mr. Xanders said as he stood up and walked around to the front of his desk.

"What happens if Madison or Skylar wins over and over?" Connor asked.

"Let's wait and see if that happens."

"They're Aerials. There's no way we can win," Connor muttered under his breath.

"You might have a chance if you do what we do," Skylar said.

"Pray tell me, what's the secret formula for success?" Connor asked.

"Train in the tunnels," Madison replied.

"That's where you're practicing?"

"I'm surprised the blabbermouths' Yank and Zonk didn't tattle on us," Madison said.

"They're too busy asking for salt and pepper on a big, juicy spider."

"True, Connor," Skylar laughed, "but they also complain that we cause too much dirt to spray up on them."

Before they could continue, Mr. Xanders interrupted them. "Take your brooms and head out. Fair warning, you need to practice purposefully because tomorrow we're adding a glyph to each column."

"A what?" Joel asked.

"Tomorrow, there will be a glowing glyph in the element's color at each column. You'll need to tap the glyph to move forward."

"I'm sorry, say that again," Connor asked.

"Each element has a rectangle with a symbol inside that differs slightly from the other elements. The symbol is a glyph. The glowing symbol will be high near the column. For example, the fire glyph will glow red and float somewhere near the top of the fire elemental column. When you reach that column, you must hit the floating glyph with your hand. If successful, the symbol will disappear for five seconds."

"Oh great," Connor groaned, "Today we're just pitiful against Madison and Skylar; tomorrow, we elevate to total losers."

"That's not the case. Now get out there and practice," Mr. Xanders said as he held the door wide open for them. He stayed at the back of the group as they made the short walk to the courtyard.

Mr. Xanders sat outside on a bench and watched the mages attempt to fly around the courtyard and slap each elemental column. Most of the mages were cautious on their brooms, but he observed Madison and Skylar zooming around the others and tapping the four columns before the other mages were at the second column.

As time went on, he frowned when they tired of repeatedly zooming from one column to the next and switched to annoying the other mages. He stood up and crossed his arms over his chest. He didn't like what he saw, as it proved Connor's point about the Aerials having a natural advantage.

Walking up to Mr. Xanders, Angus said, "I see Madison and Skylar are again outshining the other mages. The others look downright pathetic next to them."

"It's been hard not to laugh while watching Joel and Connor. However, Madison and Skylar have put a damper on it with their showoff antics."

"I agree. I've been watching the practice, and it's obvious Madison and Skylar are naturally talented on brooms," Angus said, watching Joel and Connor fly around the courtyard. He glanced up and saw Dillon flying higher and faster, with Natalie flying at a lower level at the same speed.

"True, but they're being bratty about it."

"We'll fix that with what I have in this box," Angus said as he lifted his left hand up and showed Mr. Xanders a blue plastic lunchbox with air holes punched into the top.

Curious, Mr. Xanders asked, "What's in there?"

"I have brought governors. Each Aerial will have one secured to her broom." Angus snapped open the lid. Mr. Xanders leaned in to look at the tiny governors.

"What are they?" Mr. Xanders looked at the two tiny creatures with long ears staring up at him.

"They're Daft Governors. Once latched onto a broom, they can make erratic and random movements at any moment. The mage loses control of the broom. One minute, everything is fine, and the next minute, the governor is operating the broom."

"Wow, have we always had governors?"

"Yes, but we haven't needed them. Most of us don't fly. We certainly don't enter contests, so even if we used a broom, we wouldn't need to be restrained."

Angus took a governor out and held it in his hand so Mr. Xanders could see it up close. The daft governor purred.

"It looks and sounds too cute to cause Madison and Skylar trouble."

"Oh, they're happy to be here and getting to work. Believe me, they're full of mischief. Madison and Skylar will have a challenge staying on course. In fact, they might be challenged staying on their brooms," Angus chuckled at the thought.

Mr. Xanders motioned for the students to land. Madison and Skylar were the first to walk over to them. Natalie arrived next, with Dillon not far behind. Joel landed with Connor not far behind him; they walked over to the group.

"Master Wizard Thornton and I have been observing your flying abilities. We agree that Madison and Skylar need a challenge." Mr. Xanders paused, giving the two proud witches a few minutes to feel superior.

"That being said, Madison and Skylar, please step forward with your brooms." Mr. Xanders stepped back as Angus Thornton stepped forward.

"Madison, please hand me your broom," Angus Thornton said with his hand already extended out. Madison reluctantly handed him her broom.

Clutching the broom with his left hand, the master wizard had Mr. Xanders open the lunchbox and hand him a governor.

"What are you putting on my broom?" Madison asked, puzzled at the small creature with big fluffy ears hugging the handle.

"It's a Daft Governor."

"What's a Daft Governor, and why does it need to be on my broom?"

"I'll explain it in a minute, Madison," Angus Thornton said, handing Madison her broom.

He motioned for Skylar to give him her broom. She handed it to him. After the Daft Governor wrapped his legs around Skylar's broom handle, Angus Thornton returned the broom to her.

"Madison and Skylar, you now have Daft Governors on your brooms whenever you use your brooms. You'll have control of your brooms until you don't. The governor will not give you notice when it takes control. You'll need to be ready at all times for unusual maneuvers. We're doing this to help level the playing field."

"What is it going to do?" Madison asked.

"Whatever it wants to do," the master wizard replied. "It's going to take a rapid response from you to work through whatever it sends your way."

"This happens whenever we are on our brooms?" Skylar asked, surprised that this happened to them.

"Your broom, under most circumstances, will only fly with the governor attached to it," Angus Thornton confirmed.

"This isn't fair!" Madison exclaimed.

"Maybe you shouldn't have rubbed your superior skills in our faces," Connor countered.

"Hush, Connor. It's none of your business," Madison snapped.

"Oh, but it is," Connor smirked.

"So, you think you have a chance just because we have governors? Well, think again," Madison said, moving closer to Connor.

Mr. Xanders ignored the angry exchange and said, "Madison and Skylar, go back out and fly around the columns a few times to get a quick feel for the governor's actions."

Mr. Xanders and the others walked the short distance behind the girls as Madison and Skylar grumbled about the injustice of having governors.

"This I have got to see," Connor said, giving Joel a high five.

Madison and Skylar didn't wait for instructions. They mounted their brooms and soared towards the columns. Madison flew in one direction, and Skylar flew in the opposite direction, each increasing their speed as they circled the courtyard. Halfway through the third loop, Skylar's governor flipped her upside down. Skylar screamed. As she clung to the handle and dangled in the air, the governor took the broom close to the ground. Skylar dropped to the ground and hopped back on her broom.

While Skylar mounted her broom, Madison's governor increased the speed and aim for the Water elemental building. Madison screamed, and with all her might, she pulled right on the handle to avoid the building. Madison strained, took a deep breath, and she again pulled hard to the right. She missed the building by three inches.

Shaken, Madison and Skylar called it quits and flew to the ground. Dismounting, they carried their brooms over to the waiting group.

"Can we say we're not interested in participating in the contests, and that will get rid of the governors?" Madison asked Angus Thornton.

"No," was his simple reply.

"They could have killed us up there," Madison stated, still shaken from the narrow escape.

"The governors will not get you killed. However, they will present you with challenges," Angus Thornton said.

"I don't like this! I don't like this one bit!" Madison snapped, turning her back to the group and stomping off. She headed towards the front of the Barracks.

"Wait up!" Skylar yelled as she jogged to catch up to her sister.

Connor laughed and slapped Joel on the back. "I think we have a chance."

239

Chapter 20

Now I'm Jealous

Madison and Skylar frightened the tunnel guardians as they kicked up dirt, zooming through their tunnel. Making a rough right turn, they sped through the short tunnel that took them to the door, which gave them entry into Natalie's basement. Screeching to a halt, they dismounted, and Madison screamed, *"Aperta Depraesentiarum!"* The door burst open and slammed against the wall. Still furious with the governors, they were pleased to see the surprised expressions that greeted their angry expressions. Madison and Skylar pushed their way into the room. The door slammed shut.

"It was tempting not to show up today," Madison snapped.

Without waiting for a reply, Madison and Skylar shoved to the front of the group and yanked open the door that took them to the railroad cart. They climbed into the cart; the others waited until those two settled before they entered and sat down.

Once the cart started moving, Natalie gingerly said, "I know it seems unfair, but you're being challenged. The other way would be boring to you in no time."

"It is boring," Skylar agreed, "but it's nice being the winners for a change."

"Is that why this is so upsetting?" Natalie asked.

"Mostly, but also, the governors can take control at any moment. It's frightening thinking what they might do," Skylar said as Madison fumed.

"Can I ask you a question without you biting my head off?" Joel asked.

"Not me," Madison snarled.

"Okay, how about you, Skylar?"

"Go ahead."

"The governors look like they're magical creatures. Living things. Have you fed them since you got them?"

"Nope, not my problem," Madison said, shifting uncomfortably in her seat.

"I never thought about it," Skylar said. "We went home, put our brooms up, and did chores. The poor little guys were probably waiting for us to feed them, but we stuck them in our dark closets all night."

"I'm sure Angus Thornton or Mr. Xanders would have told us if they needed to eat," Madison said.

"I'm not so sure," Joel replied, "as you didn't wait around to see if there were any special instructions."

"After what happened! You're right, we didn't hang around, but they could have contacted us through Breccan," Madison snapped.

"You may be right, Madison, but I don't think so. I think what the governors did surprised them, and they were even more surprised with you two marching off."

"Now I feel awful," Skylar said as she pulled the broom handle closer to her so she could study the governor. He blinked twice and purred. Skylar thought she heard a sound coming from the governor, but the rumbling of the cart made it hard to hear. She pulled the broom handle next to her ear.

"He's purring!" Skylar exclaimed.

"Let me hear," Natalie asked, leaning forward so Skylar could move the governor close to her ear.

"You guys need to hear him," Natalie said.

Skylar moved the handle so Joel could listen, and then to Connor for him to hear.

241

Connor leaned back and said, "Joel, I have a feeling we need to train hard, as the governors are going to become pets and protect them. Now I'm jealous."

Watching what happened, Madison petted her governor. He purred. In an instant, Madison's irritable mood disappeared.

"I think we need to name our governors," Madison said, already trying to think of a name.

"Whoa, where's the grump that entered the cart?" Connor asked.

"Stuff it, Connor!"

As soon as the cart docked, Madison and Skylar jumped out, ran to the back of the bookstore, opened that door, and hopped on their brooms. They flew to the Barracks' door, opened it, greeted Hexel, and zoomed to the classroom.

Madison and Skylar swung the classroom door wide open and burst through. Running up to Mr. Xanders, they smiled at the surprised look on his face and Dillon's. They didn't care. They wanted answers now.

"Are we supposed to be feeding the governors?" Madison asked.

Before the teacher could answer, she asked, "Do they need to drink? How often? What do they drink?"

"Well,…"

Madison cut Mr. Xanders off.

"Are they like dogs, and we need to let them outside, or do they need a litter box, or maybe they know how to use a toilet?"

Before Madison could ask another question, Mr. Xanders stood up and raised his right index finger. "Whoa, Madison, take a seat and let me have a minute to answer your questions."

"I can't," Madison said. "We may have starved our governors last night."

"So, when did the governors go from evil nuisances to pets?" Mr. Xanders asked.

"Do you know they purr?"

"Yes, but that's all I know about them. Sit down, and we'll get the answers."

Madison and Skylar nervously sat down and lowered their brooms to pet their governors as a distraction while they impatiently waited for the answers.

Mr. Xanders connected to the librarian as Natalie, Joel, and Connor entered the classroom.

"No talking while you take your seats," Mr. Xanders directed at the same time Librarian Codex answered the call.

As Mr. Xanders asked questions, Dillon leaned over and whispered to Joel and Connor. "We have a crisis on our hands."

"We know," Connor said. "It was a traumatic trip getting here."

"Stuff it, Connor!"

"Okay, it's up on my screen. Thanks for the help," Mr. Xanders said to the librarian before disconnecting the call.

The teacher took his time reading the material before moving it into a document where he could change some of the information. More minutes passed as he worked on things he wanted hidden from Madison and Skylar.

"Is this going to take long?" Madison asked.

"Not much longer."

Mr. Xanders looked up at Dillon. "Dillon, please run to your store and see if you can get some walnuts and bottled water from your mother."

"On it." Dillon ran out the door.

"Okay, the gist of it is that a governor has a diet similar to a squirrel's diet. They like all kinds of nuts and need water. For sleeping, they like to hang on a bar like a sloth. I'll have copies of the instructions for their care to hand you after class."

"They need to eat before we fly, right?"

"Yes, Madison, we aren't doing anything until they eat." Mr. Xanders said, shaking his head in amazement at how fast the governors turned into pets.

"While we wait, do you have any information on the Friday contest?" Connor asked.

"It'll be close to what you are training for today and tomorrow, except the icons will float instead of staying in place. There may be one more type of obstacle. We're still discussing it. It'll be simple enough that all of you should have an equal chance of winning."

"Not against Madison and Skylar," Connor said.

"The governors will be active on Friday, just as they will be today and tomorrow. It won't be that simple for them to win."

Dillon ran in and handed Madison and Skylar a bottle of water. He then placed a small pile of walnuts on each of their desks. He jumped back in surprise as the governors leaped from the broom handles to the desktops so they could eat. Backing away, Dillon found his seat and sat down.

"Wow, I'd say they were hungry," Connor said as the governors rapidly devoured the walnuts.

"I can't believe no one told us we needed to feed the little guys," Madison said.

"I'm sure they ate yesterday afternoon before placing them on your brooms," Mr. Xanders said.

"Thank you, Joel, for asking us if they eat," Skylar said.

"If it has anything to do with food, go to Joel. If it has anything to do with smell," before Natalie could finish, they all yelled, "Connor!"

"Okay, enough goofing off. The governors have eaten and have had water. Time to fly." As Mr. Xanders said it, the governors attached to the brooms and were ready to work.

Instead of walking out to the courtyard, the mages mounted their brooms and flew there. Mr. Xanders strolled over to where they were standing beside their brooms, waiting for his instructions.

Madison and Skylar looked at each other, gave a fist bump, and waited for Mr. Xanders to say, "Start." They watched as their governors turned around and gave them an all-business look before facing forward.

"I guess business comes first," Skylar said.

"That's okay. Natalie's right about the regular practice being boring. The master wizard said the governors won't kill us, so let's face the challenges."

"This is so going to backfire, as the governors will make us even more formidable!" Skylar exclaimed.

Before Madison could answer, Mr. Xanders started counting down. "3, 2, 1, go."

Madison and Skylar took off and flew level with the glowing blue glyph floating near the top of the Water elemental building column. Madison slapped it; it disappeared. Skylar did a quick circle, waiting for it to reappear. Within her reach, it reappeared. Skylar stretched out to tag it when the broom abruptly reversed and zoomed backward. Yanking hard on the handle, Skylar reversed and flew towards the blue symbol backward. Holding out her hand, she smacked the glyph. Control returned to Skylar as Dillon closed in on the floating icon.

Dillon focused on scoring, leaned in, and increased his speed. Almost there, the glyph suddenly dropped and hovered halfway down the column. Dillon pushed his handle down, directing his broom into a nosedive as Connor pulled close to the floating symbol. Rushing towards the ground, Dillon slapped the glyph and pulled up. While pulling up, he came close to colliding with Connor. Dillon sped away as Connor spun out of control.

Connor counted four nauseating spins before he got his broom going in the right direction. Wasting no time, he lined up with the blue symbol and zoomed towards it. Within reach, the glyph unexpectedly dropped to within six inches of the ground. Connor nosedived towards it.

He misjudged his speed and the distance. The broom handle struck the ground and sent Connor somersaulting through the air. Before Connor hit the ground, Mr. Xanders yelled a spell that had Connor floating down.

Giving Mr. Xanders a thumbs up, Connor ran to his broom, jumped on, and aimed for the glyph. Tapping the symbol just before Joel got there, Connor sped away, leaving Joel waiting for the symbol to reappear.

Joel hovered for five seconds, and then he slapped the symbol. Having witnessed Connor somersault across the field, he wasn't interested in risking his life. Joel meandered towards the next symbol as Natalie approached the blue symbol. Joel moved slowly enough that she soon rode alongside him.

"Joel, I think we're the duds today."

"And we'll live another day all in one piece."

As the others flew by and made daring attempts to score, Natalie and Joel flew around the courtyard like they were on vacation. Sometimes, the symbols would drop to their level, forcing them to speed up and get out of the way to avoid a collision with those in earnest pursuit. By the time

246

they had made it around the courtyard, the others had been around three times. On the second loop, Joel and Natalie picked up their pace, but the others still completed four loops to their one loop. As Joel and Natalie completed the fourth loop, Mr. Xanders broke into a wide grin and motioned for all of them to come to him.

"I'm impressed with the improvement in most of you," Mr. Xanders said as they stood around him. He avoided looking at Joel and Natalie.

"Connor and I get today's top prize. My prize is for the governor spinning me around so many times, it was hard to know up from down. Not to mention, it was hard to hold breakfast down," Madison said.

Then, Connor blurted out, "Mr. Xanders gets the top prize for saving my life when I flew off my broom. I'm not sure which part of my body would hit the ground, but I know it would hurt."

"You hopped right back on your broom. Madison and Skylar figured out ways to get out of the governors' antics. Dillon, I'm impressed. Your skills have immensely improved since yesterday."

"And then there are the two elderly people trapped in young bodies," Connor smirked.

"It's your fault. After watching you somersault a zillion times in the air and the teacher having to intervene to save your life, I decided slow and easy was the ticket," Joel said.

"Ditto." Natalie didn't mention that she didn't like flying near the ceiling.

"Tomorrow is another day," Mr. Xanders said.

"I'm pumped," Connor said, "bring it on."

Chapter 21

Foul in Another Way

"You know, at some point, we're going to need to focus on the Janus Club," Natalie said as they got out of the railroad cart and headed to the back of the bookstore.

"Not today," Connor replied. "Today is Friday, and it's all about winner takes all."

"Like you stand a chance," Madison scoffed.

"I'm going to make you eat your words."

"In your dreams."

"How about a bet?" Joel said.

"With you, Grandpa?" Connor laughed.

"Not with me, you dolt. It's a bet between you and Madison. You fear nothing when it comes to sports, and Madison has superior flying skills. It's a 50-50 which way it's going to go."

"You up to it, Madison?" Connor asked.

"Depends."

"Loser has to find the secret tunnel entrance of the Blemish," Connor said.

"No, Connor, you leave the Blemish out of this," Natalie snapped.

"Whoa, Natalie, I'm not saying we capture one of them."

"Just don't!"

"You sure know how to spoil the fun."

"Some things are off-limits, and that's one of them."

"I have a better idea," Joel said. "The loser has to sing karaoke in the courtyard, and the winner gets to select the songs."

"I can't sing," Madison whined.

"Are you confident you're going to win?" Joel asked.

"Absolutely."

"Then why worry about your singing abilities? Do we have a bet?"

"I guess so, even though I have a feeling this is going to backfire."

"I can sing. The dread is the selected songs to sing," Connor said.

"So, are you in, Connor?" Joel asked, and Connor nodded his head yes.

They flew from the bookstore to the Barracks, opened the door, greeted Hexel, and flew to the classroom. Their excited voices filled the room as they entered and took their seats. Mr. Xanders sat at his desk, waiting for them to settle down.

"I need your undivided attention up here so you understand the rules." Mr. Xanders stood up and moved to the front of his desk.

"Have they changed?" Connor asked.

Mr. Xanders ignored the question. "Here are the rules. The first glyph is Water, the second is Earth, the third is Fire, and the fourth is Air in that order, and for four laps. If you miss one symbol or if it's in the incorrect order, that lap doesn't count. The glyph will keep track of each participant's score. Each glyph has the ability to move up and down the column freely. When it's tapped, it disappears for five seconds. New to the game is collecting an element coin from each of the four fairy fountains in the courtyard. At random times, a coin will lift above the colored water for a few seconds before it drops and slowly dissolves. You must have completed collecting the glyphs in the correct order for four laps. You must collect a coin for each element before you can return. The mage with the lowest time with the four element coins wins."

"What's the prize?" Connor asked.

"A silver one-ounce coin." Mr. Xanders looked at the excited expressions and listened to the murmurs of approval.

"Is that silver coin good here and in the mageless world?" Madison asked.

"The silver coin is like any other silver coin. It's good here; it's good out there. Are we ready?" Mr. Xanders asked as he headed to the door.

"Bring it on," Connor yelled.

They flew to the courtyard and stressed, waiting for Mr. Xanders to amble over.

"Does he do that to annoy us, or is he afraid we'll laugh at his broom-flying skills?" Connor asked.

"A little of both," Joel replied.

"Why am I even asking you? Are you going to try today?"

"Nope, I will enjoy the show as my broom leisurely takes me around the arena."

"Wish me luck."

"I wish you luck staying on your broom," Joel said, laughing.

Mr. Xanders was still walking towards the group when he yelled, "Countdown begins now...3, 2, 1, go!"

Madison was first at the Water column, tapping the blue symbol. As she flew off, Skylar was right behind her, tapping the symbol. Skylar turned her head and laughed at Connor before zooming off for the Earth glyph. Connor impatiently hovered, waiting for the symbol to reappear as Dillon gained on him. As Dillon came behind him, Connor tapped the symbol and sped off, with Dillon waiting for the symbol to reappear. Joel and Natalie were far behind Dillon and taking their time getting to the Water glyph. Joel decided to fly high until he needed to tap a symbol. Natalie preferred the lower level. The first lap was complete.

The second lap started with Madison nosediving into the blue Water sprays of the Water fairy fountain. Drenched, she had her first coin. Madison flew to the side of the Water column and spotted the Water glyph at the top of the column. Almost there, the governor took over and put her in a spin. Within inches of the column, she squeezed her eyes shut and went with the spin. On the seventh spin, Madison regained control, but Skylar and Connor had already tapped the symbol and were on their way to the Earth column. Madison fumed as she reached the Water glyph, tapped it, and flew to catch up to them. Madison closed the gap when Skylar spotted a coin in the green water spray of the Earth fairy fountain. Skylar dove down to retrieve it. Connor and then Madison hit the Earth symbol. Madison was slightly behind Connor when he spotted a coin in the red water spray of the Fire Fairy fountain. Madison had no chance of getting it. She went ahead of Connor and tapped the Fire glyph. Glancing back, Madison saw Skylar gaining ground. Madison leaned into her broom and flew towards the Air element column. As she did, she heard a scream. Looking back, Skylar was nosediving toward the ground. Madison turned her attention back to the next symbol as Skylar pulled hard on the handle to bring her broom up. Madison, Connor, and Skylar completed the second round ahead of the others.

Madison was close to reaching the Water element glyph when it flew up into the clouds. Her intuition told her not to follow it, but she was determined to win. She went after it, with Connor and Skylar right behind her and Dillon catching up. Madison could see the faint blue glow in the clouds. She went straight for it, with the three gaining on her. As Madison reached for the symbol, the clouds turned black, and an inhuman scream reverberated throughout the Barracks. Lightning flashed in the upper sky.

Terrified, the mages abandoned the game and zoomed towards the ground. Halfway down, Madison's governor detached, extended his legs out, and floated above the broom. She leaned forward, trying to catch the governor.

Lightning struck Madison's broom. She slumped forward. The broom began to twirl as the governor fell onto it and reattached himself to the front of the broom. Taking control from Madison, the governor steadied the broom and glanced back at her. Unconscious, her head hung to the right side of the broom as her legs and arms straddled the handle. Raging lightning flashed around them as the governor let the broom drift down close to the ground. Inches from the ground, he brought the broom to Mr. Xanders, standing outside the classroom door.

"Joel, come help me get Madison inside!" Mr. Xanders yelled.

Joel came running from the back of the room and bent down to help move Madison. Mr. Xanders held her by the shoulders, and Joel had her feet. The governor hopped off the broom and wrapped himself around Madison's right wrist as they carried her to the windowless back wall. They lowered her to the cold floor. Joel went to the cabinets to see if he could find a blanket. Mr. Xanders checked her breathing and heartbeat. Both were strong, but she was unconscious.

Skylar ran into the classroom, followed by Connor and then by Dillon. They headed to the back of the room for safe shelter. Skylar spotted her sister on the floor.

Falling to her knees, Skylar brushed her sister's hair from her face and cried, "Madison, wake up."

"What happened?" Dillon asked.

"Lightning struck her broom," Mr. Xanders said. "When the clouds turned dark, I started yelling that the contest was over and to come inside. Joel landed and ran towards the classroom as I saw lightning hit Madison's broom. She started to free fall, but her governor kicked in and brought her here."

"I didn't hear you," Joel said. "The dark clouds brought me running for the classroom. Natalie and I weren't in it to win, so I was ready to come inside."

"Where's Natalie?" Mr. Xanders asked, now aware she was missing.

At that moment, another scream of horrendous emotional pain shook the Barracks.

"What's happening?" cried Skylar.

"I don't know," Mr. Xanders said, heading to the door to see if he could spot Natalie.

As he reached the door, it swung open. Angus Thornton burst into the room and pushed Mr. Xanders back inside.

"Chris, you don't want to see what's going on out there." He blocked the doorway.

"Natalie's missing. I need to find her." He tried to push Angus aside.

"Stop! You can't help her. I brought the summoning coin to call Draon. He's the only one who can stop this and save her." He tossed the coin toward the ceiling. Halfway down, the coin was suspended in the air.

"What do you mean?" they all cried as they watched the coin hanging midair.

"Natalie's suspended in the air in the courtyard. As far as I can tell, she's unconscious but alive."

"Why," Skylar cried, "all because of a stupid contest?"

"I don't know. It has something to do with Hexel."

"Did Hexel touch Natalie again? She won't survive a second contact with Hexel," Skylar asked in alarm.

"I don't have any answers. I'm hoping Draon knows what has Hexel so distraught," Angus Thornton said, still blocking the doorway.

"Let me run out to her and bring her inside," Connor implored, getting up and standing inches from the master wizard.

Angus Thornton blocked him. "Stay away from the door. Get back to the others."

"Can't you see, the longer she's out there, the more likely she isn't going to make it?"

"Connor, don't you think I or Mr. Xanders would be out there if we thought we could help her?"

"I don't know, but I can't sit here thinking she might be awake and wondering why we have abandoned her. I won't abandon Kira…Natalie!"

Before Angus Thornton could respond, Draon gave Thornton a light push and stepped inside the room.

"Draon, Natalie is out in that storm. She's suspended in the air over in the courtyard," Mr. Xanders exclaimed.

"I know," Draon said, turning around and walking out of the room.

"Let me go with you," Connor yelled.

"Stay where you are, Connor," Draon yelled. "You can't help her."

Draon placed a shield around himself and returned to Natalie's side. His shield still held around her, but he knew the lightning would not hit her. His shield protecting her was his way of feeling some control over the situation.

Draon walked through the lightning that never reached the ground and headed to the gatehouse. He pondered what could have happened that caused Hexel to be distressed. She dealt out justice, not punishment. None of it made sense, except that Hexel still had a connection with Natalie.

Before Draon reached the gatehouse, Hexel let out another anguished scream that reverberated throughout the Barracks. The heart-wrenching cry struck Draon's soul. It almost caused him to fall to his knees. So much pain and despair consumed him and smothered him.

"What happened to you, Hexel?" Draon whispered to himself.

Hexel came into view, floating from one side of the gatehouse to the other side. She moved anxiously as if she could not find peace. Draon recognized that feeling. He experienced the same thing when he discovered Nessa had died. The torture had almost sucked the life out of him.

Draon walked up to Hexel and whispered, "How can I ease your pain, Hexel?"

Draon stayed still as Hexel floated towards him and hovered in front of him. He struggled with how to ease the pain of someone who could not verbalize her feelings. For several minutes, he focused on a distraught Hexel floating before him. Then he remembered his wand. Pulling it from his cloak, he drew a big heart on the ground. He continued, making the middle of the heart look like a heart broken in two. Putting his wand back in his cloak, he had both hands free. He pressed his hands over his heart, and then he pointed to where her heart was and put his hands over his heart again. He watched as Hexel lowered her head and stilled before him.

Draon sighed with relief that he had reached her. Without warning, Hexel moved back, brought both hands high above her head, and clapped them together three times. The lightning disappeared. The air became electrified. Draon's hair stood straight up, as did the hair on his arms and legs. He stared at Hexel. He put his arms up and out with his hands open and shrugged his shoulders as if he were asking why. The answer came from a rattling of the Barracks' door.

Draon turned to face the door as it burst open. Stunned, his eyes grew wide as he backed up. He watched two porcelain-skinned beauties with long, flaming red hair and blue eyes wearing black leather pants, black leather jackets, and black boots enter the Barracks, spot Hexel, and head for her.

Draon stood speechless as he witnessed their loving embrace of Hexel, not caring that she smelled like a decaying body. He marveled that they whispered words of comfort and were able to hold her in a tight hug. Tears ran down his face as he realized Hexel had genuine comfort and contact. Time came to a standstill.

"Hexel, Natalie," Draon whispered.

He watched as the embrace ended, and the three turned to face him. Was he worthy? Standing before the three goddesses of justice, Draon was not so sure.

"Be still as our sister becomes one with us."

Draon did not move a muscle or say a word as he watched the two beauties speak an unfamiliar language while continuously circling their right index fingers above Hexel's head. His mind raced with thoughts of why her sisters had come, why Hexel was motionless, floating a foot above the ground, and why she was being transformed. His thoughts froze as he noticed a subtle change in Hexel. The change became more noticeable until Draon looked at a third porcelain-skinned beauty with long flaming red hair and bright blue eyes, dressed in black leather pants, jacket, and boots.

He stared in amazement. He could not tell them apart until one stepped forward, walked over, and took his hand. "You know me as Hexel, but I am Megaera."

"Megaera, I am happy you can communicate and touch, but I am puzzled."

"You are wondering what has caused this to happen."

"I know it has to do with a heartbreaking pain you have experienced, but I do not understand what caused the pain."

"I am lonely and isolated in the form of Hexel. My sisters could not find me hidden in this place where I cannot communicate or touch, which is another story. However, one mage made sure to acknowledge me every day she came to the Barracks." Megaera still held Draon's hand and stared deep into his eyes.

"Natalie."

"Yes. Natalie gave me a butterfly gemstone necklace as a gift. I treasure it as a connection to her, but someone has taken it."

"I'm so sorry, Hexel…Megaera. I will cast a spell to expose the thief and return the necklace to you."

"Before you do, know I will go with my sisters."

"I am truly sorry this happened to you."

"Thank you, Draon. I have looked, as have my sisters, at your heart, and you arc a good and wise man."

"I appreciate that compliment. It is rare to stand before the three Furies. Actually, it is nerve-wracking."

"I can imagine," Megaera said with a soft laugh, "but you do not need to worry. Also, even though the theft of the necklace has been heartbreaking, it has been a blessing. Losing the necklace has brought me my two sisters."

"Before we discover the thief and return your necklace, what about Natalie? She's over in the courtyard, hovering in the air."

"She is no longer in that state. When the lightning stopped, it released her from the trance."

"Are you going to say goodbye to her?"

"Yes, with the return of my butterfly necklace, I will speak privately with Natalie. She is unique beyond your understanding. As you probably guessed, it was through Natalie that the storm was created. That storm gave me the ability to connect to my sisters and call them to my side."

"I had wondered if Natalie had a role in your ability to reach out to your sisters."

"Energy was my first contact with Natalie at the gatehouse. It proved that, if needed, she could handle physical contact. When the Night Hollow needed destroying, my touch accessed her powers. With that touch, she became permanently connected to me. However, I promise never to abuse that connection."

"I trust you," Draon said as he pulled his wand from the inside pocket of his cloak while his ring activated. "Now, let's discover who has your necklace."

The tip of Draon's ring glowed green. Each of the four gemstones on the top of the ring glowed as Draon held his wand up in the air and said,

"Within this compound, a thief resides,
Within the dark, it cleverly hides.
Within these walls, discover its space,
Within your source, return to this place."

Instantly, a surprised Odious Rattus squirmed in Hexel's hands. It bit her. Shocked, Hexel dropped it to the ground. It bolted towards the elemental buildings. Draon raised his wand and yelled, *"Svelare!"*

A ruffled Gertrude Cunningham sat on the ground not too far from them. She dragged her ancient body off the ground and straightened up her dirty white gown and blue cloak. She turned and, taking her time, paused and sneered at one after the other. When her eyes rested on Draon, she raised her head in superiority and increased her smug look.

"It makes sense it would be you to find me, Draon. I knew that dimwit Thornton wouldn't have success at locating me," Gertrude gloated.

"No one inside the Barracks looked for you, Gertrude. You were safe until you stole from Hexel." Draon frowned, angered by her deceit.

The three sisters stood silently, listening to the conversation.

"Hexel," Gertrude scoffed, "needs nothing pretty. She wears black on black that has been decaying for years…just like her."

"It wasn't yours to take," Megaera said.

"It's none of your business, lady," Gertrude sneered.

"I am Hexel."

"Yes, and I am the tooth fairy," Gertrude snickered, putting her right hand in the pocket and grasping the butterfly necklace.

"Megaera and Hexel, please let me handle this." Draon walked towards Gertrude.

"Stop right there. I don't have my wand, but I still know powerful spells."

"Do you really believe you have a chance against the three Furies?" Draon continued towards Gertrude.

Gertrude's expression changed to surprise as she looked over at the three red-headed beauties watching her. She looked back at Draon, who was almost to her.

"That's rubbish! They look nothing like the descriptions in our books."

"The books describe the Furies exactly as you saw in Hexel. That was their form long ago. They serve justice now, and you will willingly go with them, or I will summon a Night Hollow to take you." Draon stood before Gertrude and watched as her smug expression disappeared. Fear showed in her eyes.

"I'll go with them. Maybe they can restore some of my former beauty." Gertrude walked around Draon and moved towards Megaera.

She hesitated before pulling the butterfly necklace out of her pocket. She held it up high and, one last time, watched the light sparkle in the aurora borealis gems. "It hid in my Odious Rattus pouch. I didn't smell like the other Odious Rattus."

"No, you didn't. You were foul in another way," Megaera said as she took back her butterfly necklace.

Megaera's sisters grabbed hold of Gertrude and headed over to the Barracks' door. Megaera didn't bother to watch Gertrude go. She changed her focus to saying goodbye to Natalie.

"I will be right back," Draon said before transforming into a crow and flying to Natalie.

Natalie sat on the courtyard ground and tried to clear her head, but it didn't help. She had another horrific headache. She was rubbing her forehead when Draon appeared.

"Where did you come from?" She didn't look up. She could see the feathered cloak.

"Hexel is getting ready to leave. She wants to say goodbye to you."

"What? Why would Hexel leave?" Natalie stood up with Draon's help.

"She is still Hexel, but you won't recognize her. Her sisters are here to take her home," Draon said as they walked towards the front of the Barracks.

Natalie started to cry. Tears streamed down her face to the point that she had to stop. She looked over at the uncomfortable expression on Draon's face and smiled. "Draon, I'm happy for Hexel. I've always felt she was lonely, but after the Night Hollow, it really bothered me."

"I am glad those are happy tears," Draon said with relief.

"You and my dad are two peas in a pod when it comes to seeing females cry."

"I'll be the first to admit, I'd rather fight a dozen livid Ruiri gnomes than see you cry."

"Thanks. Unfortunately, the crying didn't help with the massive headache."

"That will take time, as it is tied to Hexel. There's Hexel." Draon pointed to the red-headed beauty.

"No way!"

"She is one of the triplets. All equally beautiful. She is going with her sisters, but she wanted to speak with you before leaving. I am going to go back to the classroom and update everyone on what has happened."

Natalie half listened to the last of what Draon said. Between the headache and the stunning woman waiting to see her, she wasn't sure if this was real or if she was dreaming. Within inches of the woman, the woman reached out and grabbed her into a tight embrace. Natalie whispered, "Hexel?"

As Natalie and Hexel spoke, Draon headed to the classroom. It did not surprise him to see that most of them were pacing outside the door. He motioned for them to go inside, but Connor and Joel shook their heads no. He knew they wanted an update now.

"Thank you for not leaving and causing more problems. Everything is resolved. Natalie is speaking with Hexel," Draon said, with Joel interrupting him.

"Natalie's okay, and Hexel can speak?"

"Yes, and yes. Hexel is really Megaera. She has transformed and is leaving with her two sisters," Draon said as Skylar and Madison joined the group.

"Madison, why are you wearing a governor on your wrist?" Draon asked.

"Lightning struck my broom during the contest and knocked me unconscious. My governor took over and has decided he is my protector."

"And," Connor interrupted, "we have decided we all want one."

"I promised each of them a governor if they would stay in the classroom," Angus Thornton said.

"Angus is learning how to bribe teenagers," Mr. Xanders laughed.

"Can we see Natalie?" Connor asked.

"Yes, their conversation should be done. We may have time to say goodbye to Hexel," Draon said as they walked to the front entrance.

Draon's long legs were having a tough time keeping up with the group. He looked back and saw that Angus and Chris were not even trying to keep up with the five young mages. It was tempting to take the easy way and transform into a crow, but he appreciated their concern for Natalie, so he continued struggling to keep up with them.

"Natalie!" Connor yelled when he spotted her speaking with a red-haired woman.

"Hurry so you can say goodbye to Hexel!" Natalie shouted as Connor and Joel started to run.

"No way," Connor said, looking up into crystal-clear blue eyes.

"Yes, Connor, the one you wanted to gift a Christmas bath set," Hexel said, smiling.

"Oh, wow, how embarrassing," Connor mumbled.

"All in good fun." Hexel smiled before turning serious. "I've enjoyed protecting each one of you at the Barracks. Now, in my true form, I am joining my sisters, but not without sending the Barracks a new guardian."

As Hexel closed the Barracks door behind her, Natalie hesitated leaving and joining the other mages. She was happy for Hexel but also sad to see her go. It wouldn't be the same. She sighed and turned to walk back to the group. At the same time, a loud thump hit the door hard.

Silence followed. Then, several furious thumps shook the door. The mages stood wide-eyed, hearts pounding, worried about what lurked on the other side of the weakening door.

Backing up, they watched Draon go to the door, open it, and jump back.

Epilogue
Gertrude

"Can you reverse the years and make me beautiful again?" Gertrude asked as Alecto and Tisiphone walked on either side of the old, weathered woman in the musty tunnel, illuminated by the sconces of red, flickering dragon crystals.

"Your outside reflects your insides," Alecto said, keeping her eyes forward.

"My only goal was to protect the Barracks. It needed to remain the same."

"No, you only thought of yourself and your agenda," Alecto said, glancing over at her sister. Tisiphone's frown told her she struggled with delaying justice for this evil woman.

"That is not true!"

"You were ending the lives of all the mentors and familiars horribly and violently. That is evil."

"I am one of the original members. I deserve respect, and my views should be the deciding factor."

"You have not changed with the times. You want to live in the past. Your choice of action would have cost many lives so you could have your way. You planned murder by violence. Now, be quiet. You disgust us."

They were close now. They could see the back entrance to the bookstore in the distance. As they moved forward, Wilfred walked down the steps toward them.

Alecto and Tisiphone exchanged a glance. They slowed their walk so Wilfred could meet them in the tunnel.

"I see Wilfred. He so willingly introduced that riffraff to the Barracks. He and Jonathan are to blame for my actions." Gertrude sneered.

"You are the only person responsible for your actions. Now, stop and be quiet." Alecto watched as Wilfred approached. Again, she turned to her sister. Tisiphone shook her head no.

"Alecto and Tisiphone, why are you with Gertrude?"

"Her actions have caused us to intervene."

"Her actions deserve justice." Deep lines appeared on Wilfred's forehead as he frowned and glared at Gertrude.

"Don't pretend to be all big and bad, Wilfred. If you had any backbone, the Barracks would have remained the same, and I wouldn't have taken the steps I had to take to save the Barracks." Gertrude smugly raised her head and stared back at him.

"Alecto and Tisiphone, I would like to take Gertrude." Wilfred held his hand out for them to hand her over to him.

"We do not operate as judge and jury," Alecto said while grabbing Gertrude's arm. Tisiphone grabbed her other arm.

"Does she deny calling the Night Hollow? Does she deny sentencing the mentors and familiars to gruesome deaths?" Wilfred crossed his arms and waited for the answer.

"It's none of your business what actions I took to save the Barracks. My first and only thought was to keep our community as it has always been. Now go sort your books or whatever you do in your little shop." Disdain carried in Gertrude's voice.

"Did you call a Night Hollow?" Wilfred blocked the path. Alecto and Tisiphone did not move around him.

"You know the answer."

"I want to hear it from you."

"When did you get so high and mighty?" Gertrude laughed a forced, loud laugh.

"Answer the question, and I will decide the next step."

"Little man, you decide nothing. In case you haven't noticed, I'm with Alecto and Tisiphone."

"I am aware of who stands beside you. Answer the question."

"Of course, I called the Night Hollow. I'm the only one strong enough to make the tough calls."

"Are you strong enough to reap the consequences of your decision?"

"I made my choices for the good of the Barracks." As Gertrude snapped her reply, the back door to the bookstore opened. A tall man about Wilfred's size looked out.

"Is everyone all right?"

"Who is speaking?" Wilfred yelled out.

"Wilfred. Who are you?"

"Who am I, Gertrude?"

Gertrude's eyes went wide with horror. Her mouth dropped open as she gasped, and her right hand went up to her mouth.

"You summoned, and my brother responded. It cost him his life. You know the consequences of your decision to summon a Night Hollow."

"It wa-wasn't my fa-fault he fa-failed," Gertrude stammered.

"You summoned him. You knew the rule when you did. Either way, you lost because the Barracks' mages would have found the reason for the slaughter. Blinded by your self-importance and your agenda, you failed to think about what would have happened had you succeeded or failed. Now it is time to pay." Wilfred stepped within inches of Gertrude. His breath was heavy and smelled of blood.

266

Gertrude frantically looked from Alecto to Tisiphone and back to Alecto.

"Aren't you going to do anything to stop this?"

"You have confessed," Alecto said.

"It wasn't only the Night Hollow. If he takes me, you can't undo what will happen soon. You need to keep him away from me," Gertrude pleaded.

"Tisiphone?"

"Alecto, walk the real Wilfred back into the bookstore. He does not need to see this."

"No!" Gertrude screamed. Tisiphone tightened her grip as Alecto walked up to Wilfred. She waited until they stepped inside the bookstore.

"We serve justice, Gertrude. You have admitted to your crime. Your confession requires the contract to be completed, which means we release you to the Night Hollow."

Gertrude grabbed Tisiphone's hand, trying to rip it off her arm so she could run. Tisiphone held tight until the Night Hollow seized Gertrude's hands and pulled them behind her.

"Please wait until I am inside the bookstore." Tisiphone had already turned and headed for the bookstore.

"I will wait to carry out my revenge, but hurry." He tightened his grip as Gertrude frantically fought to get away.

As Tisiphone closed the bookstore door, she heard one terrified scream, followed by silence.

For more Shadowlink short stories - Facebook
Stefanie Schatzman, Author

www.ingramcontent.com/pod-product-compliance
Lightning Source LLC
Chambersburg PA
CBHW050720180626
46814CB00002B/522